STAY

WAGS SERIES

SARINA BOWEN USA TODAY BESTSELLING AUTHOR

NEW YORK TIMES BESTSELLING AUTHOR ELLE KENNEDY

ISBN13: 978-1-942444-90-9

Edited by Edie Danford
Cover photo by Joba Pro Photo, in cooperation with Dave Rogers and the Australian Firefighters Calendar. Thanks, guys!
Cover design by Sarah Hansen / Okay Creations
Formatted by Integrity Formatting

Praise for Sarina Bowen
and Elle Kennedy

"I read HIM in one sitting–it's so, so good! If I had to pick two authors who I'd have team up, it would be Bowen and Kennedy"

~ #1 *New York Times* Bestselling Author
Colleen Hoover

"HIM is my favorite read of 2015! Hot, sexy, romantic, funny, and full of heart. I LOVED Jamie and Wes!"

~ *New York Times* Bestselling Author
Lauren Blakely

"The way that Sarina Bowen and Elle Kennedy spun the tale of these two men falling and staying in love was absolutely timeless and beautifully real."

~ #1 New York Times Best Selling Author
Audrey Carlan

"Be still, my beating heart . . . It doesn't happen every day that two authors you love decide to write a book together. This sexy, fun, enchanting story was all I hoped it would be, and so much more."

~ Natasha is a Book Junkie

"Scorching enough to melt the ice on the rink."

~ RT Book Reviews

"Sarina and Elle are my new favorite Author Power Couple. Taking two fabulous NA authors and combining forces to give us the best M/M book out there is nothing short of pure awesomness."

~ Three Girls and a Book Obsession

More from Sarina Bowen and Elle Kennedy

Him
Him
Us

WAGs
Good Boy

More hockey romance from Sarina Bowen

The Ivy Years
The Year We Fell Down
The Year We Hid Away
The Understatement of the Year
The Fifteenth Minute

The Brooklyn Bruisers
Rookie Move
Hard Hitter
Pipe Dreams

More hockey romance from Elle Kennedy

Off-Campus
The Deal
The Mistake
The Score
The Goal

DEDICATION

*For Natasha, Nicole, Keyanna
and virtual assistants everywhere!
You guys make the world turn.*

IT'S ALL IN THE GRIP

Hailey

It's a busy day in the offices of Fetch, Inc., but I finally manage to duck out of the office for an espresso around two. And when I return, carrying my cup toward my private office, I spot Tad the Techie knocking on my door.

"I'm right here," I call out.

The tall, baseball-cap-wearing tech whirls around. Every time I see him he's wearing that Toronto hockey hat. I wholly approve, since I'm the team's number one fan.

"There you are," he says, looking a little startled. His eyes come to rest on my espresso cup. "I was just going to ask if you wanted to take a coffee break before I have to leave."

"Oh, sorry!" I scan my overworked brain, trying to recall a meeting I might have scheduled with him. I come up blank. "Got my cup already. Is there anything you needed to tell me about the servers?"

He blinks. "Servers are fine."

"Phew." I open my office door and walk past him. "So, I'll, uh. See you next week?" He's a contractor and not our employee, so I only see Tad on a semi-regular basis. Nice guy, though.

"Sure thing! Have a good one."

STAY

I don't even make it to my desk before I'm interrupted by another voice, this one belonging to my friend and employee, Jenny Dawes. "Hailey!" she cries from the doorway. "There's two new action items in your queue."

That was fast. My coffee jaunt took less than ten minutes. "Can I assume they're interesting if you're here to tell me about them?"

"Check your screen!" she says with obvious glee.

I nudge my computer mouse to bring the monitor to life. There are two new items in my queue, and they're *both* interesting. In fact, one of them gives me an inappropriate thrill.

That's exactly how glamorous my life is these days—a potential complaint is the highlight of my day.

Since I'm the co-owner of Fetch, Toronto's premier virtual assistant company, only the most critical client requests cross my desk. These fall into two categories: clients who are naturally problematic, and clients who spend a lot of money on our services. The two newest action items contain one of each.

"Well?" Jenny prods. The smile on her face is downright giddy.

I sip my coffee. "I haven't clicked on either of them yet. Come over here if you're so curious."

She very wisely closes my office door. Gossip isn't the sort of thing we want my co-owner Jackson to overhear. Working with my ex-husband is already complicated enough—I don't need Jackson thinking that I'm a bit too focused on one of our clients.

Jenny practically skips around my desk so she can see the screen. "Who are we going to open first? Mr. Dick or the one from your future husband?"

"You're hysterical." I take another sip and stall for a moment. It's really not okay that I have an active fantasy life involving one particular client. And it's worse that I'm so transparent. "I'm opening Mr. Dick first. His came through two minutes earlier than the other one. Company policy."

Jenny sighs. "It's high time we got someone to remove that

stick from your ass. And then spank you with it. I wonder if your favorite client is naughty in bed?"

My traitorous brain has all kinds of dreamy questions about that client.

Focus, Hailey! Thou shalt not perv on clients.

As a point of discipline, I click on the other request first—the one from a client who's given himself the unfortunate username of MrEightInches.

His username isn't even the reason we call him Mr. Dick. This dude earned his nickname by managing to include his crotch in every photo he sends over. A month ago, our employees began flagging his requests as not-safe-for-work, which is why they now come directly to me or Jackson. Or Jenny if the two of us are unavailable. We don't want to make any of our Fetchers uncomfortable.

Jenny and I think Mr. Dick is most likely harmless and definitely hilarious. So we often snicker together over his rather blatant attempts at getting our attention. Today's request is titled: *guitar tuner battery.*

Sounds boring enough. But we know better.

When the photograph he's sent resolves on the screen, Jenny snorts loudly in my ear. "Wow. This one might make the top ten list. It's all in the grip, right?"

Sure enough, the photo is a prizewinner. The guitar tuning device has a rounded . . . head. There is really no other word for it. Mr. Dick has positioned his hand in his lap, palm up, his fingers gripping the tuner suggestively.

As if that isn't enough, his actual, er, *member* is clad only in a thin pair of nylon track pants. As always, it looks really happy to see us.

"Good articulation of the glans today," Jenny observes. "Our man is an excellent photographer. He really uses the sheen of that fabric to maximum effect."

"He's a savant, truly," I agree. "Can you read the product number off that battery?"

"Oh, the *battery.*" Jenny sighs. "Right. Zoom in."

I center the photo on his other thigh, where a disc-shaped

battery is positioned, the numbers glinting. CR2032.

With a few taps on my keyboard I learn that CR2032 is a common lithium ion battery model used in watches, calculators, and other small electronics.

"Got it," Jenny says, making a note about the battery in her phone. "Forward this request to my queue. I'll run over to Bloor Street. Either the camera shop or that bigger jewelry store will have what he needs."

With one more click, I do just that. Mr. Dick will get his batteries delivered to the front desk of his apartment building, probably within the hour. He'll pay for the purchase, plus a twenty-five percent surcharge, as well as thirty-five dollars an hour for our time. All for something he could have done himself.

Rich people. They love good service, and they're willing to pay for it.

"Now hurry up and see what the future Mr. Hailey needs. I'm dying here," Jenny complains.

"Simmer down. I really hope it's not another dog-walking issue," I say, clicking back to the dashboard to find the request from Sniper87. "The last one was a disaster. I still feel bad about it."

Indeed, the subject of his request is: *Strike 2! Third time's a charm?*

"Uh-oh." Jenny bites her lip. "What happened now?" She leans in and we read the message together.

> *Hey HTE! Thanks for sending my mom her birthday gift. You said you knew your chocolates, and it's not like I didn't believe you. But Mom just won't shut up about the "single origin cocoa truffles" or whatever they were. My place as Favorite Child is secure for another year.*

"Aw!" Jenny sighs. "You made his mom happy. When she becomes your mother-in-law, it will be that much easier."

I don't dignify her joke with a response, because I've heard it from her before. And I have a bad feeling about the rest of this message.

> Now I hate to be a PITA, but unfortunately the new dog-walker was actually worse than the one who let Rufus eat my leather suitcase. That security camera you found for me shows the dog-walker spending a lot of time snooping around my apartment. Here's a sample of his activities.

"Whoa!" Jenny squeals. "Are we going to see his apartment?"

"Jen!" I yelp. "We sent a *stalker* to his place, and you're curious about his bachelor pad?"

Any other day, I'd be dying to see it, though. In fact, I've tried to picture it many times. When he got divorced last summer, Sniper87 used Fetch to quickly purchase an apartment's worth of furniture. Over the course of two months, I'd lovingly chosen each piece myself.

And here's the coincidence that set my curiosity aflame: as I scoured Toronto for "a big-ass sofa with a footstool thing" (his words) and "a TV so large I'll be able to see the nose hairs of the sports commentators for the games I'm watching," the gossip blogs were busy clucking over the breakup of Toronto veteran player Matt Eriksson's marriage.

That's when I'd taken a closer look at Sniper87's username. A "sniper" is what you call a skilled forward shooter in hockey. And my favorite player was born in 1987.

Still. It *might* be a coincidence.

One of the things that sets Fetch apart from our competitors is that we offer our clients the option to remain anonymous to the Fetchers who serve them. We had celebrities in mind when we offered that choice. Sniper87 has the privacy box ticked on his account. Hence the mystery. But every day my curiosity burns brighter.

My hand shakes on the mouse as I click the video link. The screen now shows a soundless, low-resolution video clip. In the background, someone moves through a spacious, open-plan apartment.

And there's the sectional I'd chosen and the throw pillows! They're centered in a beautiful, sweeping room.

"Omigod, he has a terrace!" Jenny gasps. "And that kitchen! Wow. He could put you right up on that island countertop and do you."

"Jenny! Focus." The guy on the screen is walking slowly around the room, like a police inspector on a case. The jerk slowly greets every object in his path, handling and studying each of Sniper's possessions. And as he fondles a book, a photo frame, and a stack of envelopes he's found on a table, a black dog trails behind him, leash in his mouth, looking forlorn.

"Aw!" I cry. "Poor doggy has his legs crossed, and this asswipe is reading our client's mail." My stomach clenches. "This is all my fault."

And then it actually gets worse. I drop my head into my hands as the creep pulls out his phone and begins taking pictures of Sniper87's apartment.

"This is *not* your fault," Jenny argues, patting my back. "You found him a dog-walking service. It just wasn't a *good* one. It happens. Now . . ." She takes my computer mouse and clicks back to an earlier frame in the video. "Watch this bit again. I think that's a signed jersey hanging on the wall."

I raise my head. "Really?" My heart spasms.

"Really." She points. "There. The glare on the frame makes it a little hard to see. But that's a sleeve right there. It's . . . a Rangers jersey?"

If anyone could spot that detail—even in black and white—it's Jenny. She has eyes like a hawk's. "Wow. Yeah! But that doesn't prove our theory about him. He might just be a hockey fan. And why would a player hang a signed jersey on his wall?"

"Players are fans, too. That's probably a Gretzky jersey. Your man Eriksson would have been a kid when Gretzky was at the height of his fame."

"You have an answer for everything," I grumble.

Jenny sniffs. "It would be awfully easy to shut me up, you know. Open his freaking customer file and look already. You're just torturing both of us."

"All clients who check the privacy box are entitled to remain that way."

She rolls her eyes. "Bet you're sorry you thought of that privacy option when you started the company."

"It has crossed my mind."

"Look. It's honorable that you don't allow all three dozen Fetchers to know certain clients' names. But you're the *owner*, and he's trusted you with his name, his address, his Amex black card and his underwear size. The terms of service state that you and Jackson have access to this information. So put yourself out of your misery and look at his file."

"Another day, maybe," I say to change the subject. "Right now I need to fix this problem."

Jenny actually lets out a little growl. "I swear sometimes that you've been snatched by aliens. The Hailey I know isn't a skitternatter."

"A what?"

"A *coward*." I flinch, but she keeps talking. "The Hailey I met a few years ago is a fearless entrepreneur and a go-getter. What happened, honey?"

My divorce, that's what.

She's not finished with me, either. "You could *meet* the man of your dreams, you know. Just call him up and thank him for being such a great client. Introduce yourself and make sure he knows how much you value his big"—she winks—"*business.*"

"I'm not doing that," I sputter.

"Why not? You need to get out there again and start meeting men. Techie Tad wants to date you, too. But do you give him the time of day? No."

"No, he doesn't." That's a ridiculous idea.

Jenny gives me a giant eye roll. "I just watched him invite you out for coffee.

You blew him off."

"He didn't mean it like that."

STAY

She puts a hand on my shoulder. "Hailey, he did."

"No way," I insist.

"He wears a Toronto cap every time he knows he'll see you, and I know for a fact he's not a Toronto fan! I heard him tell Dion that he was a Bruins fan."

"Oh."

"Now she gets it."

"I'm kind of slow sometimes." Techie Tad is a Bruins fan? Even if I *were* interested in him, it would never work, not with our split loyalties. When it comes to my team, I'm ride or die.

"But you're only slow about a few things," she says. "Though I can't harass you about it anymore right now because I'm off to buy batteries for a man obsessed with his penis. Later."

"TTFN."

She leaves, and I turn back to Sniper87's message. From my terminal, a few keystrokes would reveal his identity. And I'm tempted. But there are two problems with learning the truth.

In the first place, if Sniper87 really *isn't* Matthew Eriksson, the hottest, most rugged forward on Toronto's well-endowed team, I'll be crushed. The fact that I spend part of each day assisting someone who *might* be my long-time celebrity crush is easily the most romantic thing in my life right now.

If it isn't him, I really don't want to know.

And secondly, if I look up his account, that makes *me* a creepy stalker, just like the intrusive dog-walker in the video. At the moment I'm just *guessing* at my client's identity. It's a game I invented to amuse myself. But if I actually verified that Sniper87 is truly Matt Eriksson, that crosses a line that shouldn't be crossed. He's using Fetch because it promises anonymity. And keeping that promise is a bedrock principle of our business.

Enough with the speculation, anyway. There's a problem that needs solving. I open up a chat window in our Fetch app.

HTE: Hey, Sniper. I'm SO SORRY about the dog-walker! I will let the service know right away that their employee behaved inappropriately. And obviously Fetch won't ever hire them again. Watching that video made me ill, and I feel terrible about this.

We only hire services that have four stars or higher, blah blah blah, but it's really no excuse.

Immediately, telltale dots appear below my message, indicating that he's typing a reply. And just as immediately I feel an inappropriate tingle in my nether regions.

Since I've done so much work for this client, we chat pretty often. And I enjoy it much more than I should.

Sniper87: Hey, deep breaths! I know Fetch is awesome. Specifically you! That's why you hear from me so often. And this shit happens to me sometimes.

I already wrote Wag Walkers a scathing note, firing them. And it's not your fault, H! I trust you completely. But what are we going to do now? I'm on the road and Rufus needs a walk tonight and tomorrow morning.

HTE: I'm looking for another service as we speak.

Sniper87: Is there any way you could walk him yourself? I know it's against company policy to enter clients' homes (learned that when I wanted you guys to put together my kids' beds) but I'm in a bind here. Heck, you don't even need to go inside. Open the door with my security code and whistle. Rufus will bring his leash if you use the word "walk."

I hesitate. And then I hesitate some more.

He's right about the policy. Our employees do three things: 1) make reservations and other online plans 2) purchase and deliver goods, and 3) hire neighborhood services. That's what

STAY

our workers' comp insurance covers. So we *always* hire out other tasks. No exceptions.

Yet I'd sent a creeper to this man's home. If photos of his apartment end up on the internet, I will die of shame.

> _HTE_: All right. How about if I send a trusted employee to walk Rufus. Someone who loves animals.

> _Sniper87_: You are the best ever. Thank you, H.

His words give me a warm, gooey feeling inside. But if Jackson finds out what I'm going to do, he'll freak.

This will be a stealth mission. Not even Jenny can know.

MY GENTLE SOUL

Matt

Our game against Chicago is brutal. We lose 4-3. And by the time I trudge back into the locker room to shower and change, every muscle in my body has rigor mortis.

The past eighteen months have been humbling. My wife left, and I turned the big 3-0. Thirty isn't old, unless you play professional hockey. Sure, I've got maybe five years left, but I'm starting to understand that each one is going to feel harder than the last.

And I fucking hate that.

It's made worse by the fact that I'm surrounded by young, strapping, nowhere-close-to-arthritic men. Like twenty-three-year-old Ryan Wesley, who saunters toward his locker with an honest-to-God spring to his step. You'd think he'd just spent three hours lounging on a beach chair instead of skating like a madman and scoring two goals.

Will O'Connor, our new forward, is in his mid-twenties, but he acts even younger. Bare-chested, with his hockey pants undone and a towel draped around his neck, O'Connor does a weird dance shuffle move across the room before coming to a stop in front of me and Blake Riley, who also scored a goal tonight. Unfortunately, Blake and Wesley's efforts didn't pay off for us.

"Yo, Riley," O'Connor drawls, running a hand through his wavy hair. The kid has pretty-boy hair. And a pretty-boy face. He's . . . well, a pretty boy. With plenty of arrogance to go with it.

"Yo, O'Connor," Blake mimics.

"Lemming and I are heading up to the rooftop bar—supposedly it's the shit. You in?"

Blake shakes his head. "Nah. I got a date."

O'Connor's eyebrows shoot up. So do mine, because last I heard, Blake was still living in bliss with Jess Canning, Wesley's sister-in-law. I swing my head toward Blake, which earns me a loud guffaw.

"Chillax, Matty-Cake," Blake says. "It's a Skype date with J-Babe."

I relax. But only slightly, because the sonuvabitch knows how much I hate his stupid nicknames. "Tell her hi for me," I reply.

"Will do." Blake grins broadly. "Well, if I remember. I might not, you know, cuz Skype sex with Jessie always puts me in a love coma right afterward."

O'Connor rolls his eyes. Hard.

A few lockers down, Wes groans. "Dude, that's my sister you're talking about," he calls out. "You're not allowed to say the words 'Skype sex' and 'Jess' in the same sentence."

Blake snorts. "Yeah? But it's totally okey-dokey for you to look at dirty pictures of J-Bomb when you're sitting beside me on the plane?"

"Those weren't dirty pictures!" Wes protests. Cheeks red, he glances around at our snickering teammates. "He sent me pics of his new suit! He was fully clothed."

With a loud sigh, O'Connor turns toward me. "What about you, Eriksson? Rooftop bar?"

"Pass," I grunt. One, it's the middle of fucking November—who wants to be up on a roof? And two, I'm dead-ass tired.

"Pussy," O'Connor accuses. Then he chortles. "Or, actually,

pussy is what you're gonna miss out on."

I smirk at him. "Little boy, I was getting pussy while you were still in grade school. I got drafted at eighteen, remember? And we all know the bunnies love the young ones."

"Yeah, 'cause it makes it easier to scam a ring out of the poor sucker," O'Connor shoots back. "Which is what happened to you, old man."

Not quite. My ex-wife isn't even a hockey fan. To this day, Kara changes the channel when a game is on. And during the entirety of our six-year marriage, she never failed to remind me that I was a dumb jock who obviously married up.

There was plenty about the world of hockey that she didn't like, and she held me responsible for all the female attention I received. Like it was *my* fault that the groupies would swarm me and the boys after a game, or come on to me every time I stepped outside the house.

The attention is nice, but I never cheated on my wife. Nope, I kept my pants zipped from the second I said "I do" straight through to the ugly morning I signed those divorce papers and bleakly watched the ink dry.

"Whatever," I tell O'Connor, because he really doesn't want to hear the real reasons for my divorce. "This old man is going back to his hotel room and crashing. Have fun freezing your balls off on the roof."

The youngster winks. "Don't you worry. I'll find a sweet Chicago bunny to keep my balls warm."

"Enjoy," I grumble. It's hard to believe I was like that once—brash, overconfident, and sex-obsessed. These days, the only thing I'm obsessed with is figuring out how to spend more time with my kids.

I trudge out of the locker room with Blake and Wes, who are both engrossed with their phones. Outside, the bus waits to take us back to the hotel. I climb in next to Riley and close my eyes for the short drive. Yeah, I feel old, all right. Just turned thirty and I feel like I've already got one foot in the grave. Ah, fuck, okay. I'm being melodramatic. But I'm just . . . tired.

The green light letting me into my hotel room is the

cheeriest thing I've seen all day. I tug off my suit the minute my door closes. I need sleep.

But first I need to check on Rufus.

The security app on my iPad opens to show me a view of my apartment. The place still feels a little sterile to me, even though Hottie at Fetch has made it her personal cause to feather my nest.

She's done a great job, too. The furniture and dishes are attractive but unassuming. All I sent her was a floor plan and a cry for help, and she went to town. I didn't even know what I needed to buy, but she just handled it, including the stuff I probably would have overlooked. Like hand towels and a soap dish for each bathroom.

She even found this picture-frame thing for the kids' art that hangs on the wall. All I have to do is slip each new crayon drawing behind the glass, framing it like magic. Since I don't see my girls as often as I'd like, it's nice to have their artwork nearby to make me think of them.

Yeah. If my place looks lonely, it's not the apartment's fault.

Then, two weeks ago, I'd had to fire up the Fetch app and ask Hottie to find me a dog bed and dishes. My ex-wife decided without warning that Rufus was too much for her to handle. I got a text message asking me to choose between taking him in or sending him to an animal shelter.

The *shelter*. Who does that? But I really shouldn't be surprised. Since Kara kicked me to the curb, why should my dog fare any better?

My security cam comes into focus and I spot my furry pal immediately. He's napping happily on the sofa, his chin on his paws.

"Hey, buddy," I say, even though he can't hear me. Then I drag my finger across the timeline at the bottom of the app, rewinding the day, while I squint at the thumbnail images that pop up. Rufus with a chew toy on the rug. Rufus napping. Rufus eating dinner and . . .

There. Another person in my apartment. I go back even further so I can see how this encounter began, then play it forward at regular speed. The door opens and a young woman steps inside. I catch only a quick glimpse of her slender frame before she drops to her knees in front of Rufus, who has slid cautiously off the sofa. He gives her a cursory sniff, and she bends kindly toward him, offering her hands and words I wish I could hear.

Rufus's tail begins to wag like crazy, and I don't blame the guy. This chick is cute, in a punk-rock kind of way. She's got long black hair with messy bangs, huge eyes, and tons of silver on her ears—how many ear piercings does she have? I squint, but the image isn't sharp enough to tell me. She asks Rufus a question, and it must contain the word "walk" because he spasms with happiness before running off to find his leash, skidding on the wood floors with excitement.

A moment later they're out the door together. No stalking, thank goodness.

I glance at the clock so I can figure out if the new walker took my boy out for a proper ramble. There's nothing to see on the screen except my empty apartment, so I open up the Fetch website, because I have a theory.

There on the login screen is a photo I see each time I visit the site. It's an appealing woman in an office somewhere. She has her black hair swept up in a messy bun, exposing the soft skin of her neck, and a pencil in her teeth. Every time I use Fetch, which is pretty much every day, I admire her. It could easily be a stock photo. But it *might* be Hottie, the woman who handles most of my requests.

Okay, her name's not really Hottie. But I don't know what HTE stands for. In my head, I think of her as Hottie. And— this is pathetic—she's the only woman I speak to on a daily basis. We've never even met.

Except I'm pretty sure she was in my apartment today. The woman I saw on my security cam looks a lot like the one I've been ogling on the login screen.

A *lot* like her.

The security app shows no activity for a long time. I brush my teeth and get ready for bed. I check the scores of the other hockey games played tonight to see how the competition is shaping up.

Finally there's movement on camera again. The door opens and Hottie steps inside with Rufus. His wagging tail smacks her in the thigh. She's wearing slim jeans that make her legs look a mile long.

Then she bends over and gives Rufus a kiss on the nose.

Lucky beast.

Despite the fact that I'm exhausted, I find myself clicking on the chat icon in the Fetch app instead of shutting it off. Chances are, Hottie's asleep, but I still type in a quick note.

> *Sniper87:* Looks like Rufus had fun with his new dog-walker. Success?

To my surprise, little dots appear on the screen, indicating that someone's typing a response. A second later, her message pops up.

> *HTE:* You tell me. Only the client can determine if something was a success.

> *Sniper87:* Seems so. You're good to walk him tomorrow morning, too, right?

There's a short delay.

> *HTE:* I'll send the same employee, if you're happy with her.

I study the screen for a moment. I don't know why, but I'm convinced that Hottie walked Rufus today. I want her to admit it, but, again, not sure why I care so much. We've been chatting for almost a year, but it's not like we're online dating or some shit.

This is a business relationship. Except . . . it's not. This woman decorated my apartment. She knows the brand of boxers I wear. It feels pretty fucking personal by now. She knows I'm divorced. That I wish I saw my girls more. In fact, it was her idea to buy the twins the same exact beds they have in their bedroom at my former house. *It will feel more like home when they're with you*, Hottie had suggested.

> *Sniper87*: I'm very happy with this employee.

That was an understatement, so I add a little more.

> *Sniper87*: I'm grateful to her. Plus, she's cute.

I press Send on a whim, and I'm not surprised when there's another delay.

> *HTE*: Are you hitting on my employee right now??

I have to resist the urge to actually type: *No, I'm hitting on you.*

Truthfully, I'm shocked the thought even entered my head. Since the divorce, I've barely thought about women. Okay, not entirely true. I'm a man—I've jerked off a bunch, watched some porn. But I haven't made any attempts to hook up with a real-life chick. I turn down women left and right when I'm at the bar with my teammates. I'm in a weird place. I feel like I'm too old for one-night stands, but too jaded for anything more serious. That leaves only one other option: celibacy.

> *Sniper87*: Just pointing out how cute my new dog-walker is, that's all.

> *HTE*: I'll be sure to pass that along (sarcasm).

> *Sniper87*: She a hockey fan?

> *HTE*: Why do you ask?

> *Sniper87*: Just curious.

> *HTE*: I think she might be. Are YOU a hockey fan?

I snort to myself.

> *Sniper87*: I prefer chess. Hockey's all right. A bit too violent for my gentle soul.

> *HTE*: Uh-huh. I'm sure.

I narrow my eyes. Okay, I feel like she's goading *me* now.

STAY

Actually, she must be, because this woman must know exactly who I am. When I first started using Fetch, there were several different sets of initials popping up to fulfill my requests. But lately it's always HTE, and her signature says "co-owner, manager." Sure, I asked to remain anonymous, but I figured that only made me anonymous to the Fetchers. As the owner, HTE must have access to all the client profiles. Which means she is well aware that I'm Matt Eriksson, Toronto forward.

> *Sniper87: JK. Hockey's the best. What are you doing up so late?*

A long, long pause. I can almost hear the grudging note in her reply.

> *HTE: I stayed up to watch the Chicago game, and now I'm too keyed up to sleep.*

A huge grin splits my face. Fuck, why am I having so much fun right now? And my exhaustion seems to have dissipated like a puff of smoke. Chatting with Hottie always lightens my mood.

> *Sniper87: Hope the loss didn't devastate you too badly.*

> *HTE: It did, actually. I'm inconsolable.*

My fingers itch to reply: *I'd be happy to come over and console you* . . . I would, too. My libido has suddenly woken up and shaken itself off. My dick's actually getting hard—and we're not even talking about anything sexual.

> *Sniper87: Make sure you send the same dog-walker tomorrow morning at ten. There might be something for her on the kitchen counter.*

> *HTE: What the heck does that mean?*

> *Sniper87: Don't worry about it.*

Though . . . crap. Now I have to find a way to leave my little gift at the apartment when I'm still in Chicago. I search my brain until an idea forms. Katie Hewitt, I think in triumph. My teammate's wife has a spare key to my new place, and she'd totally be able to make this happen for me. Katie is a superwoman.

> _HTE_: What do you mean, there'll be something on the kitchen counter??

Still grinning, I ignore the question and type three short words.

> _Sniper87_: Good night, HTE.

> _HTE_: Answer the question, Sniper!

> _HTE_: We here at Fetch don't like surprises.

> _HTE_: Sniper? You there?

> _HTE_: Sniper??

SHOULDER FETISH

Hailey

toss and turn all night after that chat with Sniper. When my alarm goes off at six thirty the next morning, I groan loudly at the ceiling.

He called me cute. He said it more than once!

Maybe I'm the most pathetic girl in the world, but I read over that chat conversation about a hundred times before I shut off the light and tried to sleep.

I shouldn't have flirted with him. But, hell, it was fun.

When I eventually haul my tired butt into the office, the morning creeps by. I meet with our programmer to discuss some new functionality for the mobile app, but I'm watching the clock the whole time.

I'm desperate to walk a dog. That's what my life has come to. A *nice* dog. But still.

As ten o'clock approaches, I wrap up the meeting and shoo the programmer out of my office. I don't want to be late to walk Rufus. And, damn it, there's a flagged request waiting in the queue for me—a gig for Mr. Dick.

I text Jenny, who appears in my office a moment later. "What's he done this time?" she asks eagerly

"Didn't open it yet, because I know you enjoy being in on

it."

"You're the best kind of friend," Jenny says, dancing around my desk to stand behind me. "Want to go out for drinks tomorrow night? I can't do tonight because I have roller-derby practice."

"Sure." Jenny likes to drag me out to bars in the hopes that we'll meet some decent men. It never works out the way she plans, but it's more fun than sitting around in my apartment like a loser. "Pick a place with a TV, though? We're playing Buffalo at home. And I think we can win this one. I'm looking forward to it."

My friend groans. "*Not* a sports bar. I want glamour, not beer funk and peanut shells."

"But plenty of men will be there," I point out.

Her frown is contemplative. "I'll meditate on it."

"You do that." I click on Mr. Dick's request. It reads: *MrEightInches requires: one silk Kimono.*

"Oh God!" Jenny snorts. "This could be a good one."

And Mr. Dick does not disappoint. He requires a kimono in men's size medium. *At least forty-eight inches long,* he's supplied. *100% silk. Color unimportant.*

Naturally there's a photo. He's cropped off his face, which is a shame because Jenny and I have been curious about him for ages. But a man's body is shown—naked except for a stretchy pair of bright blue briefs, barely covering his erection, which lays angled in the briefs, straining the fabric.

Jenny giggles, but I'm in a bit of a hurry.

In the shot, a tape measure dangles from his shoulder, hanging down his body. The tape passes his unit, ending at about his knee. I zoom in on the end to see that it's fifty inches at that length.

"Do you think you can find a kimono?" I ask. "Use my computer if you want. There's something I need to run out and do." A glance at the clock tells me it's almost time to walk Rufus.

"Wait. Zoom in! We can finally verify whether MrEightInches is telling the truth! The angle of the tape isn't quite right, though. So we'll have to do a little trigonometry to discern whether his hypotenuse is eight inches. We can use the Pythagorean theorem . . ."

"Gotta run," I say, getting out of the chair. "I'll text you in twenty, okay? If the kimono proves hard to find, we'll brainstorm."

Jenny slides into the desk chair I've vacated, but her eyes are following me as I grab my jacket and shove my arms inside. "You're acting a little weird right now."

"Just late. Bye!" I escape, leaving Jenny to wonder, and hopefully to buy a kimono for a rich guy with a long dong.

Is my business fun, or what?

Sniper's apartment is just a couple blocks from my office, so it only takes me a few minutes at a slow jog. I wore very sensible shoes today for my romp with Rufus. The building is the kind with a shiny-buttoned doorman waiting to usher me inside.

"I'm here to walk Rufus in 303," I tell him.

"He'll be happy to see you. It's been several hours since I let him relieve himself on my cigarette break. Go right on up."

The elevator delivers me to a corridor carpeted to muffle footsteps. Sniper's door is opened by a keypad. The code is 1967. That's the year Toronto last won the Stanley Cup.

But, hey. This is Ontario. Half the security codes and ATM-machine PINS might be 1967. We love our hockey.

"Woof!" says Rufus, leaping from the couch. It's a happy sound, and it's accompanied by a full-body tail-wagging. I drop down and show him the love. He gyrates and sniffs and bounds around. *See what a good boy I am?* his body language demands. *I've been home alone for hours and I didn't eat Daddy's furniture.*

"You are a very good boy," I agree. "The best. Why don't you find your leash so we can go for a walk?"

He gallops off, and I stand, turning toward the immaculate kitchen at the far end of the room. The island countertop is completely bare except for two things. A fruit bowl I picked out to match my client's dishes.

STAY

And a white card, tented on its edges.

I cross the room because I can't see what's written there. As I approach the card, I find there are two words inked onto it.

When I yank the card off the shiny surface to study the lettering, there's something underneath. Two tickets. To tomorrow night's home game.

In row D.

I let out a little whoop of joy a split second before remembering that there's a security camera in here.

Rufus barks in agreement with me. Sheepish now, I zip the card and those tickets very carefully into my jacket pocket.

I take Rufus out to the park, running all the way there. And then I text Jenny. *Change of plans. Come to the game with me tomorrow night. Just scored a pair of excellent seats.*

Reeeeeeally, comes her instant response. *And how did that happen?*

It's top secret, I try. But who am I kidding? She'll have me spilling the whole story the instant I get back to the office.

Really, who could keep it in?

I'm weirdly nervous the next night. As if I were actually about to meet Matt Eriksson. Which I'm not. I'll probably never meet him. But I take a little extra time in the ladies' room anyway, applying lipstick as if for a date.

Back at my desk, I send Jenny a text. *Leaving now. Meet you at the main doors in 20!* Then I tuck my keys and phone into my bag, preparing to depart the office.

But there's one more big decision to make. Jersey or no jersey? That is the question. And I've been waffling on this point all day.

On the one hand, a good fan always wears her jersey to the game. And, fine, I'm a little superstitious. The one time I forgot my jersey, my boys lost.

Yet my jersey says ERIKSSON across the back. And just on the outside chance he knows which seats he gave me and looks to see if I've used them, I'd rather not out myself as a superfan. Even if my tongue hangs out every time I see his face on TV, I need to at least keep the appearance of professionalism so long as we're working together.

What to do?

I'll miss the puck drop if I worry much longer. So I shove the jersey into my oversized bag and leave my office, flicking the lock shut before I pull the door closed.

Outside, in the bullpen area where the other Fetchers sit, I take a quick glance around. Dion is quarterbacking the night shift, and he looks up to give me a salute, which I return. That's good news for me. Dion is a solid employee who rarely contacts me with problems.

Fetch is open 24/7 in order to serve our rich customer base at any hour. We charge more for services after eight p.m. and before eight a.m., too. It makes good business sense. There are five Fetchers on duty tonight, including Dion.

Since it's an even-numbered day, I'm on call tonight. There's a small risk I'll be yanked back to the office to solve a problem during the game.

But everything looks quiet in the bullpen, so I make my way toward the door. Just before I exit, I notice the strip of light under Jackson's door. Since I'm the one on call, I'm a little surprised that he's still here at seven thirty. A problem, maybe?

It's just four feet or so down the hallway to his door. I lift a hand to knock, but then stop short when I hear voices.

"The property looks great," Jackson's voice says. "It's a first-class place. Melinda went with me, and she loves that neighborhood. It's beautiful over there."

STAY

My heart plummets. Melinda, huh? I'd heard whispers that Jackson was dating someone. It was bound to happen eventually. But they're looking at real estate together? Already?

The freak-out I'm having almost prevents me from hearing more. But then I hear my ex's father speak, and it starts to dawn on me that I've misinterpreted something.

" . . . Great foot traffic," Mr. Emery is saying. "The income level in that neighborhood is even higher than here in Yorkville. You're gonna make a mint."

"But we're not ready to expand the business," Jackson hedges. "The timing just isn't right."

"And whose fault is that, son?"

In the brief silence that follows, I feel a chill on my back. Jackson's father is the most argumentative person alive. And Jackson isn't very good at telling him where to shove it.

"Dad . . ."

"Buy her *out*, Jack. Do it *now*. You can't grow your business if Hailey is still riding your coattails."

The chill I'd been feeling becomes an arctic gust.

"Now that's unfair," Jackson says softly, while I quietly die on the other side of the door. It's good of him to come to my defense, but the fact that they're having this conversation at all makes me want to howl. "Fetch is as much Hailey's business as it is mine."

"Which is why she might jump at the chance to cash out," his father presses. "The way you two have things set up, the girl has to be cash poor. What if I lent you a half million to send her on her way? You could have Fetch offices in four cities by a year from now!"

It's awful how easy it is to picture myself pushed aside. Mr. Emery never wanted Jackson and me to start this business, but the minute we became successful he'd tried to muscle in as an investor. We always turn down his offers.

At least, we always have until now. But now that we're divorced, maybe I don't know Jackson's mind so well anymore.

There is movement behind the door, and the fear of getting caught unsticks me. I take two quiet steps backward, spin around, and exit as fast as I can.

Dashing out of the office, I hurry down the set of exterior stairs, not even pausing to admire the brickwork and the antique iron sconces. I love this office, hidden just out of view of Yorkville's multimillion-dollar real estate. And I love this little company I built with my ex-husband.

They can't buy me out. I won't let them.

As I stomp down Scollard Street toward the subway station, my heart is full of angry thoughts. *Screw you, Mr. Emery.* I *never* rode Jackson's coattails. Damn that man! He never liked me.

When I say he never liked me, I mean *never*. Even when I was seven years old and climbing trees with Jackson in the backyard, he used to curl his lip at me. He let me know at an early age that I wasn't good enough for his only son, that the tomboy daughter of a middle-class single mother would never belong in his millionaire household.

Many times during the past year and a half I've reminded myself that the only silver lining to getting divorced at twenty-seven is not having Herbert Emery as a father-in-law anymore.

My rage carries me into the subway station. But by the time I'm swiping my Metropass at the turnstyle, my anger is already giving way to the heavy drag of sadness.

I am, after all, the only person I know who co-owns a business with her ex-husband. It's weird. I'll admit it. And it's not like we're silent partners, either. I see him every day at work. Or almost every day. We don't share a home anymore, but it wouldn't be fair to say that I've moved on.

Will I ever?

When I was nineteen, I literally married the boy next door. By then, Jackson and I had already known each other all our lives. We grew up in the suburbs of Toronto, both in tense homes. His was tense because his father was super successful and overbearing. Mine was tense because my mother was verbally abusive and occasionally violent.

Jackson and I found refuge in our friendship from an early age, retreating to the treehouse in his backyard when things got too crazy at home.

STAY

Sometime during high school, our relationship changed from sleepovers in the treehouse to sleeping together in the treehouse. We headed off to the same college a year later. And when I was nineteen, we eloped during a spring-break trip to Vegas. That was ten years ago.

Five years ago Jackson and I came up with the idea for Fetch while watching a reality TV show. At first, it was just our weird little brainstorm. But when Jackson's company relocated to Vancouver, he was out of work. So our idea became a plan. I quit my banking job to help him start the business. Three years ago we turned our first profit, and we've been growing ever since.

And eighteen months ago . . . Jackson and I were having coffee together at his desk when he very gently brought up the idea of divorce. "We're great friends. We run a kickass business together. But I don't think we've ever set the standard for world's most romantic couple," he'd pointed out.

Even though my gut said he was right, my heart broke right then and there, crumbling and landing among the crumbs of the oatmeal cookie I'd just eaten.

I was crushed. I still am, if I'm honest. The rejection still stings so sharply that I've done nothing but work like a dog for the past year and a half.

Jackson moved out, leaving me our apartment and all its furnishings. He'd meant it as a kindness—so I wouldn't have to search for an apartment or buy new things. But now I live in a museum of our old life. I still eat my morning cereal out of bowls we chose together at the Eaton Centre. After a shower, I dry off with towels that I bought because he liked that particular shade of blue.

Maybe we hadn't had the most passionate relationship on the planet. But passion isn't everything. We're so well suited in many other ways. And losing someone you've known your whole life leaves a big hole.

Now his father wants to push me even further away.

As the train pulls into the station at the hockey stadium, I actually consider Mr. Emery's idea. If I sold my stake in the company, I'd have enough money to move somewhere else, to get a fresh start. I could travel like I've always wanted to, and then find a new job.

It's not like it never occurs to me to put a little distance between Jackson and me. But, damn it! That business is half mine, and it's a *success*. My mom spent my whole childhood trying to convince me that I'd never succeed at anything. And now I have.

Even if the success is only half mine.

I hadn't known Jackson was so hot to expand into other neighborhoods. We'd mentioned expanding "someday" before.

Maybe he's been waiting all these months for me to realize I need to move on? Now there's an unsettling idea. But I can almost see it. He's a kind man—his father's opposite. It would be just like him to wait me out. To let me realize for myself that it was time to go.

We were always good to each other. The only couple I knew who never fought. And he wanted a divorce. Because that makes so much sense. Whenever anyone asks me about it, I always say we're *amicably* divorced, and how great it is. Though only the first half of that is true.

Luckily, there's hockey to ease my pain.

I emerge into the excitement of game night. Red jerseys swarm toward the turnstiles as I circle this happy chaos in search of Jenny.

"Over here!"

Turning, I realize she's been hard to spot because her jersey matches too well with the photos on the wall behind her. She wears a replica jersey for the team captain and a giant smile.

"Come on!" she squeaks. "Puck drops in fifteen minutes. And we have to buy food." She hefts a sign under her arm as I approach.

"Wait." I eye the poster board. "What does that say?" Jenny is a little, um, freer spirited than I am, and for all I know the sign offers a blowjob for every goal scored.

She angles the cardboard and lifts her arm so I can see the message she's written there. C'MON BOYS! THIS IS OUR

STAY

YEAR! Thank God. Now we probably won't end up on ESPN's psycho-fan-of-the-night segment.

"Let's get pulled-pork sandwiches and beer. My treat."

"You don't have to pay," I protest.

"I know. But this way if the future Mr. Hailey gives us seats again sometime, you'll have to invite me because I bought you dinner."

"You've got this all planned out, huh?"

"You bet I do." She gives me a slightly evil grin, and my appreciation for her quadruples right on the spot. Jenny was one of our first hires at Fetch, right before we officially opened our doors. She's one of our managers, and definitely my best friend. I'm technically her boss, but we just pretend I'm not a lot of the time.

I own a business with my ex. I party with my employee. Maybe my life is a little claustrophobic. Sue me.

After we buy some food we make our way down to the best seats in the world. "Wow," I gasp as we get our first view of the warmup skate.

"Wow," Jenny echoes, her eyes widening as our idols whip past on their blades. We're so close to the action we can hear the scrape of steel against ice. "This is as close as I've come to having a religious experience."

"You said that when we saw U2 last year."

"But Bono wasn't stretching his powerful thighs ten feet in front of me." Jenny sighs happily as big forward Blake Riley glides past the glass with a smile. Then he blows a kiss right at us. No—right *near* us.

"Love you, baby!" someone calls from two feet behind me.

Turning around is merely instinctual. A pretty blonde waves Riley off, and I glance at the man sitting beside her.

Then, ever so casually, I turn back around, my heart thumping. "Jenny!" I squeak as soon as we're standing for the national anthem. I risk a whisper into her ear because another occupant of the row right behind us is singing "O Canada" at a volume unmatched by most humans' lung capacity. "We're sitting in front of the players' families. Including one half of

Wesmie."

Jenny's eyes widen, and I see her sneak a glance back at Jamie Canning, who's famous for marrying star player Ryan Wesley. "These are incredible seats," she hisses. "You'd better keep walking that dog, missy. I want to come back next week."

That's when I spot Matt Eriksson, and my pulse jumps several notches. He skates out with Wesley and Blake, and the three of them get into position for the face-off. His attention is focused entirely on the puck, a serious expression on his rugged face.

I'm tense as the puck drops, and I don't even know why. Then they're off like a shot as Wesley wins the puck and passes to Eriksson. A little shriek of excitement escapes me as I lean forward in my seat.

I am a Toronto girl in her element tonight. Hear me roar. "KILL THEM, MATTY!" I holler.

"Ow!" Jenny complains, covering an ear. "Pace yourself. U2 wasn't this loud."

"Sorry."

"BUT HOCKEY FANS DON'T HOLD BACK!" the woman behind us roars. "GET 'EM BLAKEY! CARVE HIS TURKEY!"

"YEAH!" I belt out. "DROP 'IM LIKE A DRESS ON PROM NIGHT!"

"Wow," Jenny says, eyes wide. "I knew you were a fan, but I didn't know—"

The sentence goes unfinished because Toronto charges the net. Wesley passes to Eriksson, who shoots and it's . . . My blood stops circulating.

Denied. The Dallas goalie makes a highlight-reel save off the tip of his glove, and a defenseman flicks it away.

"GOOD TRY!" Jenny screams, getting into the fray.

For the next twenty action-packed minutes, we forget everything except the game. The first period is fast and furious. Our boys don't manage to score, but they're giving Buffalo a very hard time.

"We have seventeen shots on goal," Jenny grumbles,

draining her beer after the buzzer. "Their goalie must have been to church this morning or something."

"Doesn't matter," I growl, my voice hoarse. "We're winning tonight. I can just feel it."

We hit the ladies' room and then buy two more beers. The kiss cam does its thing, and I don't watch the jumbotron. Tonight I'm not the girl who got divorced at twenty-seven. Tonight I'm a party girl with coveted seats to the best game on earth.

And for once the universe is with me. We score three times in the second period and twice in the third. Matt Eriksson gets a goal and an assist. I scream my head off for him both times. Buffalo can't keep up, and the score is 5-2 when there are only three minutes left on the clock.

I'm tired and sweaty as my heroes line up for one more face-off. They know they're going to bring this victory home, and the whole stadium is excited. "Wow." I sigh, fanning my flushed face. "This is very invigorating. It's been over a year since I . . ."

"Had sex?" Jenny finishes.

" . . . saw a hockey game in person," I correct, even though that other thing is also true.

"Whoa!" Jenny says, drawing my attention back to the ice. Naturally my gaze gravitates to my favorite player. "Eriksson's going to get a penalty for tripping."

Sure enough, the announcer calls for a two-minute bench minor. And suddenly my celebrity crush is skating right toward me, his handsome face creased with displeasure. I've never been so close to him before. The way his broad shoulders move with each stride makes me strangely hungry.

Is it weird to have a shoulder fetish? *Get a grip*, I tell myself as he sits down. *You're only ogling his padding, anyway.* But that just makes me more curious to see what's under it.

That's when he turns his head and looks right at me.

"Omigod," Jenny squeaks.

My thoughts exactly. I'm sort of frozen now. Like one of Mr. Freeze's victims in those comic books Jackson collects. I can feel myself staring, and it's possible my jaw is hanging open a little. But those gray eyes! So sexy. This man's press photos don't lie.

There's a scramble at my left as Jenny does something. I don't look. Still frozen.

But then—I swear to God—a flicker of a smile crosses his sensual mouth before he turns back to watch the action on the ice. And the spell breaks. I turn to Jenny, opening my mouth to say something. She's holding her sign. No—she's holding a *different* sign. "Omigod. What did you do?"

"It's just a funny little joke," she says, trying to tuck it back down below her chair.

"Jenny!" I gasp, grabbing her wrist and taking a second look.

HOTTIE IS SINGLE! the sign shouts.

"What . . . Oh. God. You didn't!" My whole body flashes with the heat of embarrassment.

She grabs both my wrists with a ninja move. "Breathe, okay? He said you were cute. He calls you Hottie, for heaven's sake. I just gave him a little push."

"He's a client!"

"I don't care! This is your *life*, Hailey. The only one you get. The old Hailey was the most confident woman I knew. She was always hustling to get what she wanted. Bring her back, okay? Stop moping around like a kicked puppy and have a fling with the man. I'm begging, here. Even if he gives you a raging case of the flutterstutters, it's still worth it."

"The . . . what?" Jenny likes to invent words, but I'm too shaken up to understand them tonight.

"The nerves. The butterflies. You practically had an aneurysm when he looked at you."

"I didn't," I lie. "Not until I saw your stupid sign."

Jenny only grins. And then the buzzer sounds, and fifteen thousand fans stand up to cheer.

Well. Even if I die of embarrassment the next time Sniper87's name appears on my computer screen, at least we beat Buffalo.

BREAKFAST EMERGENCY

Matt

ottie is single.

H I'm still chuckling to myself the morning after the game. The sign had been funny, but the bright red cheeks of the woman sitting next to the sign-holder? Priceless.

And even while tomato-faced, Hottie had looked gorgeous, even prettier in the flesh than on that security footage. Her eyes are dark blue, the color of the ocean after a storm. They were really nice to look at—well, for the three or so seconds I looked into them. I still can't believe she even showed up to the game, but with seats like those, she'd have been a fool not to.

Maybe I should ask her to dinner.

I ponder this new idea as I brush my teeth in the master bath. I rinse, spit, and then study my reflection in the mirror. I haven't shaved in a few days, so I'm rocking dirty-blond scruff. My eyes look a bit bloodshot. And my hair, which I usually keep buzzed, has grown out and is now sticking up in all directions. Everything about my appearance tells me I'm not ready to ask Hottie, let alone any woman, on a damn date.

Divorce fucking blows.

I've spent the past eighteen months feeling angry at Kara

for leaving me. Even though we'd hit a rough patch, I would have *never* done that to her. But there are times when . . . I . . . fuck, I might be . . . relieved.

Shame has me turning away from the mirror. I hate it when thoughts like that creep into my head. I'm not relieved that my marriage blew up in smoke. I'm saddened.

And relieved.

No, I'm devastated.

But also relieved.

A silent groan lodges in my throat. I march into the bedroom and grab some clean clothes from the dresser. Fine. I have to concede to my traitorous subconscious—that last year with Kara had been pretty fucking awful.

Just the last year? my asshole brain mocks.

All right, maybe it was more than a year. Maybe I'd felt us growing apart long before that. Truthfully, the strain started after the twins were born. Other than some possessiveness and unwarranted jealousy on Kara's part, and lots of traveling and some laziness on mine, our first two years of marriage were a blast. It wasn't until the girls came along that Kara decided every single thing I did was absolutely wrong and that shit needed to be done *her* way—no highway option.

Don't get me wrong, I'm not blaming my kids for the tension in the marriage. I love my girls. I wouldn't give 'em up for the world.

Buzzzzz.

I brighten as the landline on my nightstand gives a loud buzz. Speaking of my girls . . .

I grab the phone and press the button to contact the doorman. "Tommy, my man," I say cheerfully. "Please tell me there are two lovely ladies on their way up."

"Three," he corrects, and I hear the smile in his voice. "They just got on the elevator."

"Thanks." I hang up and tug my sweatpants into place, then throw a Toronto hoodie over my head and hurry toward the front door. The floor-to-ceiling windows that span the massive main room sparkle in the early morning sunshine. It's a gorgeous day, blue skies and yellow sunshine on my rug. In the warmth of my apartment, I can pretend that it's a summer day and not freeze-your-balls-off cold out there.

I'm wired with anticipation as I wait for the knock. I have the girls until tomorrow morning, at which point their mom will pick them up so they can spend the day with their grandparents in Markham, a nice suburb northwest of here.

I'd been brutally disappointed when I found out I wouldn't have them for the whole day tomorrow. I wanted to point out that they see Kara's parents every Friday for lunch, a tradition that started when they were still in diapers, but arguing with my ex is about as effective as conversing with a wall. She always wins arguments. Always.

"DADDY!!" two voices shriek the second I open the door.

In a nanosecond, I'm bending down to scoop both girls into my arms. Two pairs of little hands wrap around my neck. Two sets of beautiful, heart-shaped faces peer up at me in delight. And two mouths release squeals of laughter when I smack kisses all over their chubby cheeks.

"Oh, I missed you guys!" Emotion is thick in my throat as I hug my four-year-old daughters tight to my chest.

"Missed you too, Daddy!" June yells.

"Me too!" Libby pipes up.

"Yeah? How's my Junebug doing?" I ruffle June's dark hair before doing the same to her twin. "And my Libby-Lu?"

"Mommy got us new hats!"

"With pom-poms!"

I gasp. "No way! Why aren't you wearing them?"

"Mommy says it's not cold 'nuff yet," June informs me.

I stifle an irritated curse. Of course. Kara is an expert in all things. I guess that includes determining the precise point of Toronto's seasonal change in which our children are allowed to wear their hats. To distract myself from my annoyance, I swing the girls in my arms again, eliciting more happy squeals.

"Would you put them down, please?" a sharp voice asks from the door. "They haven't had their breakfast yet and all that spinning around will make them nauseous."

STAY

The curse that's jammed in my throat is now a string of expletives that are dying to fly out. Instead, I take a breath and then gently set my daughters on their feet.

"RUFUS!" June shouts when she catches sight of the dog, who's just rounded the corner to see what all the commotion in the front hall is about. His delayed entrance only highlights what a shit guard dog he'd make. Lazy bastard.

As the twins scamper off to pet their dog, I turn to my ex-wife and force myself to make eye contact. And there she stands, her glossy brown hair streaming down her shoulders in bouncy curls, her lithe body decked out in jeans and a leather jacket, a bright wool scarf setting off the color in her cheeks. Divorce obviously agrees with her. Or maybe it's her new boyfriend, the dentist. Good old Dentist Dan, the man who gets to spend more time with my kids than I do.

But who's bitter?

This is the woman who decided I wasn't good enough to remain a full-fledged member of the family. That my children would be better off seeing Daddy once every couple of weeks. She cast me aside like she does with her designer clothes when she determines that they're out of style.

Anger curls in my gut. But that's not how I want this day to go, and it's not the tone I want to strike with Her Highness. So I force myself to say something nice.

"How's it going, Kara? You look good." I'm not lying, either. My ex is still as beautiful as the day I married her.

"I'd say the same for you, but . . ." Her nose turns up slightly. "Did your razor break?"

I manage a wry grin. "Nah. I'm trying out the rugged look." I gesture to my beard growth. "What? I'm not pulling it off?"

A reluctant smile tugs at her lips. "Sorry, Matty, but no, you're not."

Her use of my nickname causes me to soften a bit. I never know which Kara I'm going to encounter when she shows up—the laughing, easygoing girl I met at twenty-two, or the sharp-tongued, rigid woman who divorced me at twenty-nine.

It still confuses me sometimes, how much she changed. I

mean, certain aspects of her personality, which I didn't always like, were constant throughout our marriage—her pessimism, her candidness, her impatience. But in those early days, she was fun. She took risks, she laughed, she knew how to relax. Somehow those moments of relaxation became less and less frequent, and she became more and more unyielding.

She blames it on me, of course. Says the hockey lifestyle broke us, that I broke us. "I'm tired of being disappointed," she'd whispered after one of our fights only months before the divorce. I'd missed her parents' anniversary dinner the night before because the team's flight was delayed in Michigan thanks to a snowstorm. Fuck, it wasn't like I'd set out to miss an important event, but for Kara, it was just another neon sign that screamed, *"My husband neglects me!"*

Matthew Eriksson, folks. Chronic disappointer of wives.

"Anyway," my ex is saying, "I'm sure you already took care of it, but I wanted to remind you that the girls are off gluten, so no waffles for breakfast this morning."

"Wait, what?" I blink in bewilderment. I always make waffles for the girls. That's our thing.

Kara huffs impatiently. "No gluten, Matt. Scramble some eggs instead. I also sent you options for lunch and dinner."

What the fuck is she talking about? "What the fuck are you talking about?" I ask aloud. Then I cringe and glance toward the living room, but the girls are too busy fawning over Rufus to notice that Daddy said a bad word.

"You didn't check your email," Kara says flatly.

"I had a game last night," I answer through clenched teeth. I'm already heading for the kitchen counter, where I left my cell phone. I hurriedly open my email app and click on Kara's name.

"And you didn't check it this morning?" Kara's tone is laden with disapproval.

I ignore her and scan the message. For fuck's sake. It's essay-length. And yup, she did include potential meal plans for me to implement during this way-too-short visit with my kids. She refers to them as "suggestions," but we both know better.

STAY

"What do we have against gluten?" I ask tightly.

Her lips pinch together in a frown. "I told you last week—Elizabeth has been having some stomach sensitivity lately. I've monitored her food intake and I believe the gluten is wreaking havoc on her system."

Or she just had one fucking stomach ache—probably because she snuck in some cookies when Dictator Mommy wasn't looking—and it has nothing to do with fucking gluten.

"We spoke about this," Kara says irritably. "And you agreed that we needed to change the girls' diet."

I don't remember agreeing to that at all, but truth is, I probably did. Our weekly phone calls consist of Kara droning on for about an hour, while I say things like "uh-huh" and "sure" and "sounds good."

"Fine," I mutter. "Libby can't handle gluten. Gluten is evil. Gluten will be banished from this household."

"Are you mocking me?"

"Not at all."

Kara's dour expression tells me she knows I'm lying. Then she pastes a smile on her face and calls out to the twins. "C'mere, angels! Say goodbye to Mommy!"

June and Libby rush over to hug and kiss their mom. Kara squeezes both of them tight before saying, "Be good for Daddy, okay? Call me if you have any questions. I've got dinner plans tonight, but I'll have my phone on."

"Big date with Dentist Dan, huh? Don't forget to floss beforehand."

She gives me a dirty look over our daughters' heads. "I am having dinner with Daniel, yes. But I repeat, my phone will be on."

My daughters are four years old, and great at telling me exactly what they need. But Kara doesn't think I can make it twenty-four hours without consulting her on their care? Anger rushes through me once again, and it takes a superhuman effort not to say something snarky.

Honestly, I've had divorced teammates before, and I'd never understood how they could still carry a grudge against their exes. But now the joke's on me. Right now I'm more ready to throw off the gloves with Kara than our team enforcer is when someone fouls our goalie.

Fortunately, a moment later she's gone, and it's like a weight has been lifted off my chest. Kara is a difficult woman. She loves our children dearly, I know that, but she acts like she's their only parent. I have no say in anything when it comes to the girls. None.

Elizabeth has been having some stomach sensitivity lately.

Elizabeth. Libby's full name brings on one last ripple of anger. I didn't even have a say in naming my kids, for fuck's sake. Kara informed me after the delivery that the girls would be named after her great-grandmothers—June and Elizabeth. I didn't get a veto.

And, Christ. What am I going to do about breakfast? I promised the twins waffles when we spoke on the phone. Waffles are our ritual, damn it. They already don't get to see me as often as any of us would like.

Drawing a deep breath, I grab my phone again and pull up the Fetch app. In the subject line, I type: *SOS! BREAKFAST EMERGENCY! MAYDAY!*

Hopefully that sounds dire enough to trigger an insta-response. The message itself is less crazy.

> *Sniper87: Hey HTE! I've got my kids this morning and I've just been informed that gluten is the devil. I require gluten-free waffle mix—ASAP. Please help.*

I don't expect her to answer the SOS herself. I mean, I'm sure she's got better things to do than field the pettiest client emergencies. But surprisingly, it's Hottie's name that shows up in the response box.

> *HTE: Oh boy! Does someone have celiac disease?*

> *Sniper87: I doubt it. But my ex-wife lives to make things complicated.*

> *HTE: Gotcha. Will send someone with gluten-free*

STAY

waffle mix ASAP.

Sniper87: For reals? You can keep me out of the penalty box?

HTE: Get out that waffle iron, Sniper.

"Daddy!" June appears at my side, tugging on my pant leg. "I'm hungry!"

"Me too!" Libby chimes in, and suddenly I've got two pairs of gray eyes peering up at me in accusation.

"Working on it," I assure them. "How about some OJ for now?"

"Fruit punch," June orders.

"And ice cream!" Libby shoots me an angelic smile and adds, "I missed you, Daddy."

I narrow my eyes at her. "Stop trying to manipulate your old man, Elizabeth. You're not having ice cream for breakfast."

"What's *manipoolate*?" June asks.

"It means your sister is trying to trick me into giving her a tummy ache." I head for the fridge and peek inside. "You're in luck. We've got fruit punch." I always put this stuff on my grocery order because it's Junebug's favorite juice.

Also? It's organic. Take that, Kara! I give her the mental finger as I pull out the carton and then grab two small plastic cups from the cupboard. Rufus, my jerk of a dog, decides to pick that moment to dart into the kitchen and run between my legs, causing me to lose my balance. I end up spilling fruit punch all over my light-gray hoodie. Awesome.

"BWAHAHAHAHA!!" The twins break out in laughter, pointing their chubby fingers at me. "Daddy! You're all purple!" June exclaims in delight.

"Don't laugh at your father, you little monsters." Groaning, I strip off the soaking wet, purple-stained hoodie and toss it on the back of one of the counter stools. I'm pretty sure some of the juice seeped through the fabric, because my chest feels wet. I glance down. Yup, there are purple splotches on my left pec. Double awesome.

I grab a dishrag and quickly wipe up the liquid that spilled on the floor and counter. Then I pour two glasses, plant the girls' butts on two stools, and watch as they happily sip their juice.

Man, it's easy to please my children. Give them some fruit punch and they're smiling like it's Christmas morning. Though once their little tummies start growling and they realize their waffles still aren't ready, I doubt they'll be smiling anymore.

I get out the waffle iron, and a skillet to fry up some breakfast sausage. Hopefully Hottie comes through for me on short notice. I swear, the woman is a saint for all the miracles she busts out.

And she doesn't disappoint—less than fifteen minutes after I sent my SOS, the lobby buzzes to inform me I have a delivery from Fetch.

"Hey, Tommy?" I ask my doorman. "Is there any chance that the delivery was brought by the same woman who walked my dog?"

"Yeah, it's her."

"Do me a favor? Ask her name for me."

I wait while Tommy confers with her, and I feel goose bumps rise up on my neck.

"Her name is Hailey Taylor Emery," Tommy says a moment later.

Hailey Taylor Emery? As in, H . . . T . . . E? Hottie is downstairs in my lobby?

"Send her up," I blurt into the receiver.

"Actually, she's requested that the desk clerk take it up to—"

"No," I interrupt. "Tell her I won't accept the package unless she delivers it herself." Jesus, what is wrong with me? Why am I badgering this poor woman to come upstairs to see me?

There's a short delay before Tommy speaks again.

"She'll be right up."

JUST PLAY IT COOL

Hailey

"Miss Emery?"

"Yes?" I don't understand this holdup. Especially since I'd been headed for the exit faster than you can say my-friend-embarrassed-the-crap-out-of-me-last-night. But I turn around again at the doorman's prompt.

His eyes gleam with amusement. "Mr. Eriksson requests that you drop off the package yourself. He won't accept delivery, otherwise."

I groan aloud. Why now? The November wind whipped my hair into the shape of a large shrubbery on the way over here.

The doorman holds out the bag and I take it. As I stomp toward the gleaming bank of elevators I hear him say, "She'll be right up."

You know how an elevator tugs on your belly when the car begins to rise? Today the tug is followed by a wave of full-on panic. My palms start to sweat, and the plastic bag from Whole Foods grows slick in my hand.

I'm about to come face-to-face with Matt Eriksson, the man I've secretly crushed on since I watched his first NHL game in college.

The ding of the elevator arriving on his floor sends a spark of nerves shooting throughout my body. I step out and walk a few paces to his door. I hear voices inside—the high pitch of a little girl's giggle, and then Rufus's friendly *woof.*

Okay, Hailey. Just play it cool.

I raise my hand to knock, but the door jerks open and I miss. My arm falls clumsily down to my side as a little girl throws the door wide open. "Hi! Did you bring waffles? Daddy always orders stuff."

"That is *not* true!" a male voice argues, and the rough timbre of it sends tingles down my spine. "Who makes the best sausage in the world?"

"Mommy says sausage has too much sodium," another little voice says from inside. "What's sodium?"

"It's . . . Libby? Did you open the door?"

I'm just standing there like a mannequin, trying to make sense of the chaos. And then the doorway is filled by another body.

A *big* body. Specifically a broad, bare chest with rippling muscles all over it. I mean, they are actively rippling. It's fascinating. I didn't know anyone had pecs that well defined in real life. And abs like my great-grandma's antique washboard. Holy shit.

Now the abs are shaking a little bit.

"Hottie?" someone says with a chuckle.

"Mmm?" I finally wrest my gaze away from that glorious tummy and look up. But then I'm blindsided by those cool, searching eyes. Mr. Freeze gets me again, and I'm solidified into a statue of a delivery girl.

"Did I get it right? Does HTE stand for hottie?"

The weird question penetrates my stupor, but only halfway. "N-no," I stammer. "Hailey Taylor Emery," I rattle off like an automaton.

"Nice to meet you, Hailey Taylor Emery." He thrusts out a hand to shake, and I manage to grasp it. But the dry warmth of his hand against mine is kind of mind blowing. Matt Eriksson is holding my hand. He made thirty-two goals last year with this hand. And it's attached to the body that stars in all my dirtiest fantasies.

And now I realize I'm clutching his hand awkwardly. So I drop it they way you'd let go of an electric fence you'd accidentally grabbed—suddenly and with great force.

That's when Rufus spots me. First there's a great *woof* of joy, then the scrambling of toenails on polished wood. He takes out the four-year-old in his way like an eager bowling ball knocking aside a pin. He pushes into the hallway, his whole body shaking with excitement.

My brain is still sludgy with lust, so I don't immediately give Rufus the love he demands. The dog is forced to take matters into his own paws. He rears up, setting his paws on my hips. His considerable bulk catches me off balance. Or maybe I'm still reeling from the proximity to Matt Eriksson. But I lose my balance and go down in a heap on the plush carpeting of the hallway.

"Oof," I manage before Rufus licks my face.

"Jesus," Matt breathes. "*Off*, Ruf. Let the poor girl alone." He shoves the dog aside. "Are you okay?"

I make a garbled noise of assent. Something like "yrrm," because now he's looming over me, godlike, and that fine chest is all I can see. He has a dusting of dark hair that thickens to a happy trail as it enters his low-slung sweatpants.

And I'm staring again.

I slam my eyes shut and roll to the side, scrambling to my feet while my cheeks burn with discomfort. Rufus has run off again, most likely in search of his leash.

"Daddy?" says the little girl who'd opened the door. "Are we having waffles now? I'm *hungry*." She tugs on his hand.

"Here," I say, grabbing the bag with the waffle mix off the floor where it's fallen, thrusting it toward him. I've got to get out of here and regroup for a minute or maybe a year. And after that I'll probably look for another job somewhere else. A good distance from Matt Eriksson, probably. Like, Tahiti would almost be far enough away.

He slips the bag over his wrist. Then he leans down and scoops his preschool-aged daughter onto his hip. She slides her arms around his neck and lays one soft cheek on his bare shoulder.

Pop, pop! That sound you're hearing is both my ovaries exploding.

"Thank you," he rumbles. "Sorry it's such chaos here." Then he smiles and my IQ drops another five points. "What did you think of the game last night?"

"It was awesome," I say truthfully. It's my first successful sentence since I stepped onto his floor. "Great offensive communication during the second period. Really generated some nice chances."

When his eyes widen with amusement, I realize that my inner hockey wonk has found a brand-new way to embarrass me. "Anyway. I'll run along unless there's anything you need." *Like my naked body in your bed, for example.* Something about standing near this man makes me think very un-Hailey-like thoughts.

"There's another overnighter coming up," he says, his big hand patting his daughter's back. "I'll send Rufus to the doggy ranch for the long road trips. But if you could walk him Sunday evening and Monday late morning, that would be great."

"Okay." I'd do anything he asked of me. Sad but true. "Sunday I should be available . . ." I try to gather a couple of brain cells together, but his scruffy jaw makes it difficult. My hand itches to reach out and touch those bristly hairs and test their texture under my fingers. " . . . around sex thirty or seven."

His eyes crinkle at the corners, so, in my brain, I rewind what I've just said.

"*Six* thirty or seven," I correct. Abort, abort! I need to get the hell out of here. This man has hungry children to feed, and I'm practically drooling on his doormat. I'm worse than Rufus. "Gotta go. Nice chat," I stammer, backing away.

"Later, Hailey," he calls as I turn to leap for the elevator button.

"G-bye!" I manage before I hear the beautiful sound of an apartment door finally closing. I'm sweaty and almost panting from the difficulty of keeping it together in front of the world's hottest hockey player. As I step into the elevator, my phone buzzes with a text.

I'm afraid to look, but when I do, it's only Jenny.

WELL? she demands.
Did you bring the man his gluten free waffles? Did you invite yourself in for breakfast and a quickie?

You're hilarious, I reply.
Could you please Google job openings in Tahiti?

The next two days pass slowly. I spend them trying not to relive my mortifying encounter with the hunky God of Hockey. So much for playing it cool. Clearly my divorce messed with my head and did a number on my confidence—the old Hailey had no trouble flirting with cute men, although any flirting I'd ever done was harmless since I was married for half my life.

Jenny's advice that I should get out there again and start dating isn't wrong. But I need to start small, with a guy who doesn't turn me into a babbling idiot.

Putting our awkward encounter aside isn't going to be easy because I have to return to the scene of the crime. When I go to walk Rufus on Sunday night, I feel a little sweaty just stepping off the elevator on the third floor.

Of course, there's nobody home except one dog. And he still loves me. I scratch his ears and try not to think of anything I said the other day when I stood in the hallway losing my mind.

Ugh.

We have a nice time together before I take him home again. One more walk is probably all I have, too. Matt had said something about sending him to the doggy ranch when the team goes on road trips.

When Monday comes, I have to face up to the *other* awkwardness in my life. I've been avoiding Jackson at work, but my luck runs out eventually.

STAY

"Got a minute?" he calls as I'm darting for the door midmorning.

Crap.

"Sure," I say, although it really isn't true. I'm supposed to walk Rufus, but since I don't want Jackson to know that, I follow him into his office and sit across from him.

"How've you been?" he asks, a smile on his narrow face. I can't help comparing him to my hockey idol, and it really isn't a fair fight. Jackson is a little geeky, but he's a great guy. I feel guilty noticing how scrawny his neck looks poking from above the tidy collar of his dress shirt.

"I'm well," I lie. "You?"

He smiles again, and I glimpse a little flash of why I'll always love him. Kindness radiates from him like sunshine at high noon. "Can't complain. How's the mobile app upgrade coming along?"

"Not bad at all. Should have it ready for beta before Christmas. Giving our subcontractor an ultimatum finally did the trick."

Jackson winces. "I'm glad they didn't walk."

"I knew they wouldn't." This is why I deal with the programmers. Jax is smart as hell, but he can't play hardball. I fill him in on our progress, and he asks a few questions that I'll need to follow up on.

"Thanks for handling all this," he says, adjusting the position of his pencil so that it aligns perfectly with the blotter on his desktop. "We'll need a few favorite customers to beta this version. Do you have anyone in mind?"

He's right, and I haven't gotten around to figuring that part out yet. Probably because I only have one specific client in mind at all times. "Good point. I'll get right on that." It's a struggle not to check my watch. But I can't tell Jackson where I'm off to, because it violates company policy.

Next, he shows me some photographs he's taken of holiday promotional items. "I think I've got the giftwrap concept right," he says, pointing at a lovely photo of a box wrapped in white paper with silver stripes. "We'll let the clients choose the color of the ribbon that's appropriate to the holiday they're celebrating. I ordered blue, red, and silver."

"That's beautiful," I tell him. "So I'll add those ribbon colors to the giftwrap menu." I grab my phone out of my pocket and tap a note to myself. Jackson is the artistic half of this endeavor. While I run the technical aspects of the business, he's the one who designs our website, our branding, and all our communications with clients.

He's also the one who put my picture on the web portal. We took that shot five years ago when we couldn't even afford a photographer to help us. It was his idea to put that red pencil in my teeth, the one that matches the text in our logo.

"Anything else?" I ask, hoping he'll say no.

My ex tips his head to the side, looking thoughtful. "My dad had me look at a piece of real estate in the Bridle Path neighborhood. With expansion in mind."

Just like that, my stomach tightens.

"But I'm not sure we're ready for that, right?" Jackson asks. "Not before our new app launches."

"Right . . ." I say slowly, trying to read between the lines. "But, uh, I know you want to expand."

He frowns just slightly. "Expansion is a pretty crucial way to grow the bottom line. But we need to be fully prepared to take that on. Right now we're finally in a place where we can almost take a breath. Expansion will put us right back in scramble mode."

"Hmm," I say, trying to guess at the subtext of this conversation. "If you need scramble, I can scramble." *I will show no weakness!* If he wants me to leave the company, he's going to have to come out and say it.

"I'm going to mull it over," he says instead.

"Okay," I answer, springing out of my chair. "Is there anything else?"

Slowly, he shakes his head.

"Later!" I say with false cheer, then sprint for the exit. And even though I know Jackson's not chasing me down the street, I keep it at a jog all the way to Matt's apartment building. (Is it weird that in my head we're on a first-name basis?)

Rufus is as happy to see me this morning as he was last night. I take him to the nearby park where there's a dog run and let him off the leash. He knows me well enough now that he'll come when I call, so I'm not worried that I'll end up chasing him around the place when it's time to go.

Plus I bought him a gourmet doggy treat on my way into the office this morning, just in case this is our last time together.

While he sniffs butts and socializes in the dog enclosure, I spend time solving a couple of problems in the office by texting instructions to Dion. Before long my hands are freezing and I've lost track of time. "Come on, Ruf!" I call. "Time to go! Want a cookie?"

He comes running when he sees the treat, and I clip on his collar while he's bolting it down. We walk back to Yorkville Avenue at a nice clip, and I'm humming to myself when I beep into Matt's apartment.

"Sit," I tell Rufus when we get inside. "Good boy." I drop down to my knees, and he wags his tail when we make eye contact. "Yes, you're a very handsome boy." I give him a kiss on the nose. I unclip him, and he wags some more, probably wondering whether I have any more of those treats. My hands undoubtedly smell like doggy biscuit. "Sorry, pal. I gave up all the goods already."

"Did you, now?" a low voice asks, and I nearly leap out of my skin.

My heart spasms with surprise as I whip around to see Matt Eriksson standing in front of his kitchen island grinning at me.

POKER NIGHT

Matt

Hottie nearly topples over with surprise, and I feel bad for startling her. She seems to have a poor sense of balance for some reason. But even wobbly, she's the best sight I've seen in days. She's wearing skinny jeans and a blue winter coat the same shade as her eyes. The tip of her nose is red from the cold, and I have the dumbest urge to plant a kiss on it. She's got a really cute nose, and the tiny jewel in it is strangely hot. I've never really been attracted to punky chicks, but I'm definitely attracted to this one.

Rufus recovers first. He bounds over to say hello, but then runs right back to Hottie. That traitor. He's already one up on me. He's been on the receiving end of a couple of Hottie's kisses.

I've got nothing. It's the first time I've ever been jealous of my dog.

"You're home early," Hottie says, rising carefully to her feet.

"True story," I agree. "Our charity luncheon was cancelled, and we flew home two hours ahead of schedule."

"Right. Well . . ." She makes a break for the door.

"Whoa. Not so fast," I complain. "I just put a pot of coffee on. Will you have a cup with me?"

STAY

Her eyes look a little wild, and I try not to smile. My hottie is a hockey fan, apparently. It's obvious that I weird her out. This happens sometimes. A perfectly functional human being can get a little loopy when it comes to hockey players. I know this firsthand because I misspelled my own name once when asking Wayne Gretzky to sign that jersey hanging on my wall.

"I would love some coffee," she says in an almost normal voice.

"Awesome. How do you take it?"

"Black," she says, and her shoulders relax by a degree or two. "Thanks."

"Have a seat," I prompt, gesturing toward the sofa. "Take off your coat."

I turn my back and fix us a couple of mugs of joe. When I carry them over to the sofa, I find Rufus on his back, his head in Hottie's lap, having his belly scratched.

She looks up when I set the mugs on the table. "Thank you so much."

"Actually . . ." I take a sip of my coffee. "That's exactly what I wanted to say to you. You've been a real help to me, Hailey. I've had a really shitty year, to put it bluntly."

She winces. "You mean your divorce?"

"Yeah. Wasn't my idea. But I moved out when she asked me to, because I didn't want my girls to be uprooted from their home. Furnishing an apartment wasn't something I ever planned to do, you know? I was so pissed off. But then you did everything, and I didn't have to spend any energy on the details, and I really appreciate it." I glance around at the tasteful things Hottie chose. "Place looks great."

Her smile is my reward for opening up like that. It really lights up her face, and it makes those blue eyes come alive. "You're welcome. And I totally get it."

"You do?"

She nods, and the wattage of her smile cools by a few degrees. "I'm recently divorced, too. It happened right around the same time as yours—about a year and a half now. Also not my idea."

"*Oh*," I say, and a tightness grips my chest. I try to imagine someone telling Hottie to move out, and I feel a surge of anger on her behalf. "I'm sorry, Hottie. I mean Hailey." *Shit.*

She laughs, luckily. "It's really just fortunate that my initials aren't U.G.H."

Now I'm laughing, too. "Or I.C.K."

She giggles. "We do have an employee whose initials are D.T.H. We call him the Dark Lord."

Still chuckling, I lift my mug and take another sip. As I swallow, I notice Hailey's gaze is fixed on my throat. Then she notices me noticing and her cheeks take on a pinkish hue. Yeah, I definitely make her nervous.

"So, um. Your daughters are super cute," she says after a beat of awkward silence. "You and your ex have joint custody, I assume?"

"Barely. I don't get to see them as often as I'd like," I admit. "The team's travel schedule is a bitch, you know?"

She nods in sympathy. "That must be rough."

"Yeah. It is." I set my cup on the table and lean back against the couch cushions. Rufus is lying between us, and I absently reach out to stroke his belly. Except Hailey's still petting him, too, so my fingers unintentionally brush hers as I go in for the pet.

Her breath hitches. Then she snatches her hand away as if Rufus's belly—or maybe my hand—is covered in fleas. Or maybe she did it because of the little jolt of static electricity that went through our fingers when they collided.

She's blushing wildly now, and I watch in amusement as she wraps both hands tightly around her mug.

"They must miss you," she says, awkward again. "Your girls, I mean."

My heart clenches painfully as I remember the shiny tears in Junebug's eyes when Kara came to pick up the girls the other morning. June's always been more sensitive than Libby. She cries the drop of a hat. Libby's more reserved. Well, for a four-year-old. She still has her wailing tantrum moments, but for the most part, she's better at hiding her emotions than her sister.

"I miss them, too," I say gruffly. Then I swallow the lump in my throat and promptly change the subject. "What about you? You and your ex-hubby got any kids?"

Hailey shakes her head. "We were too busy building our business. We planned on having kids eventually, but the timing was never right."

"Your business?" I echo. "You mean Fetch?"

"Yes. Jackson and I co-own the company."

My eyebrows shoot up. "You work with your ex-husband?" Man, that's about as rough as me not seeing my girls on a regular basis. I'd never be able to handle seeing Kara at some office every day.

"We're actually good friends," Hailey confesses. Her blue eyes soften, and I catch a flicker of sorrow there. "We've been friends since we were six."

"Oh. Wow. You've known him that long?"

She nods. "We were neighbors. Grew up together, dated as teenagers, got married during college." A pause. "Got divorced at twenty-seven."

"I'm sorry." I almost feel bad about asking her to stay for coffee. I'd wanted to thank her and get to know her a bit, but somehow I took us down this serious, way too intimate path. So I change the subject again. "You're twenty-eight, huh? You look all of fifteen." I cringe. "No, scratch that. You look eighteen, as in *legal*. Otherwise I can't keep calling you Hottie in my head."

Hailey laughs, and it's a sweet, melodic sound that makes my ears happy. "I'm twenty-nine, actually. And yeah, yeah, I look young. It's a curse."

I snicker.

"Seriously," she insists. "I still get carded at the theater when I buy tickets for rated-R movies."

"Take it as a compliment," I advise. "You'll be walking on air when you're, like, sixty and everyone mistakes you for thirty."

"True."

A lull falls over the room. Rufus is snoring quietly between us. Hailey is sipping the last of her coffee, which alerts me to her impending departure. I know she'll probably shoot out of here like a bat out of hell the moment her coffee's done. If I'm going to ask her out, then I need to do it now—

Ask her out?

Shit, where did that come from? Do I want to ask her out?

I work the idea over in my head for a few seconds. Yeah, I think I do. I haven't been on a date since the divorce, though. Dressing up and going to dinner and spending an evening with a woman without the expectation of sex? I haven't done that in a long, long time.

Unfortunately, I take so long thinking about it that I miss my window. Hailey has set her mug on the table and is rising to her feet.

"I should go," she says, and I hear both reluctance and eagerness in her tone, as if she's simultaneously dying to stay and dying to flee.

I guess she picks the latter, because she starts edging toward the hall. "Hold on, I'll walk you out," I tell her.

"Anyway, I assume you want me to keep walking Rufus, so just let me know your schedule for the week and I'll pencil it in on my calendar." She's babbling again, while averting her eyes. "We'll confirm everything through the Fetch app and I can send you updates, and thank you for the coffee and the conversation. This was really nice. Enjoy the rest of your day, Math—I mean *Matt!* We'll talk soon. Bye!"

She's out the door before I can blink, leaving me to wonder—did she just call me *Math?*

Since I don't have a game tonight and the girls are with their mom, I'm quick to say yes when Blake Riley calls and invites me over to his place for poker night.

"Who else will be there?" I ask, balancing the phone between my ear and shoulder as I hurriedly shove my sweatpants down my hips and replace them with faded jeans.

STAY

"Wesmie, Hewitt, and Lemming," Blake answers. "I was hoping Luko, too, but his in-laws are in town. Shame, because that's free money, y'know?"

I do know. Our team captain's poker face is like a window without curtains—you can see right fucking through it.

"I'll be there in thirty," I say. "Want me to bring anything?"

"Just your fine ass—" Blake suddenly yelps. "What the what, J-Babe! Cheezus! That *hurt!*"

I hear a muffled female voice in the background. It's Jess, Blake's live-in girlfriend. "Her *fine ass?*" she asks. "Who are you talking to!"

There's a howl of laughter in my ear. "Eriksson!" Blake shouts between laughs. "I was referring to Eriksson's fine ass!"

"My ass *is* fine," I agree. "Tell Jess I'd be happy to show it to her when I get there."

"Sure, I'll tell her," Blake answers cheerfully. "After I chop your balls off and feed them to a sheep."

A sheep?

Before I can question that, my teammate says, "See you in a New York minute!" and then hangs up.

Blake is really fucking weird. I don't understand half the shit he says. Granted, I don't think anyone does, his girlfriend included.

I pull a hoodie over my T-shirt, then leave the bedroom in search of my coat. This apartment doesn't have a coat closet by the front door, so I always toss the damn thing somewhere and then can't remember where. I find it on one of the kitchen stools, shrug it on, and tug a toque over my head on my way out the door.

Blake lives near the lake, and it's too far to walk, especially now that the weather has turned on us. I grew up in Tampa, so the Toronto winters took a while getting used to. I'm still not a fan. The chill in a hockey arena, I fuel off of. Canadian winters? Suck balls. So I ride the elevator down to the underground and get into my Porsche Cayenne, clicking on the seat warmer.

When I walk into Blake's apartment a half hour later, the rest of the crew is already there. Wes and Jamie live in the same building, just a short elevator ride away. Lemming and Hewitt live nearby, too.

"Yo! Matty-Cake!" Blake shouts from his seat by the green felt-covered poker table. "You ready for an ass-whupping?"

I grin at him. He's wearing a visor and has a toothpick sticking out the corner of his mouth, like some old-timey card sharp. "Maybe I should've stayed home," I remark dryly.

Jamie Canning, who'd let me in, offers a wry smile in return. "Was thinking the same thing the second I saw that visor."

Blake proves to have superhuman hearing. "What's wrong with my visor?" He looks genuinely insulted. "Don't you know that saying? A visor makes ya wiser."

"That's not a saying." Wes sighs from the kitchen counter. He's in the process of pulling two beers from the stainless steel fridge. "Eriksson, beer?"

"Yes, please." I grab the bottle he hands me and join the others at the table.

Ben Hewitt and Chad Lemming, a left winger and d-man, respectively, greet me with nods and grunts. Blake is busy shuffling a deck of cards, while Wes starts doling out colored chips.

"Where's Jess?" I ask our host.

"Downstairs at Wesmie's. She's studying for a nursing test and claims she needs complete silence." Blake shakes his head. "I don't get it. She can study in the bedroom, right? It's not like I'm loud. You guys think I'm loud?"

"Dude, loud is an understatement," Wes informs him. "You're . . ." He stops, searching for the right word.

"Decibel-ly challenged," Lemming says helpfully.

Wes purses his lips. "Still doesn't accurately describe it."

"Wall-rattling," Jamie offers.

"Better."

"Quiet-deficient," Hewitt suggests.

"Fuck you all very much," Blake grumbles.

"Hey, at least you're not as loud as your mom," I say in an attempt to reassure him.

Jamie blanches. "I'm pretty sure one of my eardrums is

STAY

permanently shattered thanks to Blake's mom."

"EAT THEIR BABIES, BLAKEY!" Wes yells in a perfect imitation of Mrs. Riley, and everyone bursts out laughing, including Blake.

"C'mon," Hewitt says, reaching for his pile of chips. "Let's do this shit. Katie wants me home by ten."

Lemming makes a *whip* sound.

"If you're implying I'm pussy-whipped, then yes, I certainly am." Hewitt shrugs. "And I'm damn happy to be. My wife is awesome."

"She is," I have to agree. Katie Hewitt is brash, fiery, and a ton of fun. I always wanted Kara and me to double date with the Hewitts, but she found Katie to be too "in your face"—her words, not mine.

"Of course she is," Lemming says kindly, before breaking out in a grin. "But you know what else is awesome? The single life. That bar OC and I went to in Chicago was like an all-you-can-eat chick buffet. No lie."

"OC?" Jamie echoes as Blake deals out the cards.

"Will O'Connor," Lemming explains. "We're trying out some new nicknames for each other. I wanted to call him Willie but he punched me when I suggested it."

"What's his nickname for you?" I ask, trying not to roll my eyes. Ever since Lemming broke up with his girlfriend, he's been spending a lot of time with O'Connor, who gives new meaning to the word *manwhore*.

"Madagascar," Lemming replies before glancing down at his cards.

"I don't get it," Wes says.

I don't, either. I check my cards—queen and seven, off-suit. Blake deals the flop and my spirits rise. I'm looking at a queen, seven, and ten. Nice.

"You know, because my last name is Lemming? Madagascar has a huge lemming population."

Jamie snorts loudly. "False. Those are *lemurs*, dude."

"What the fuck's a lemur? You just made up that word."

Jamie, Wes, and I bust out laughing. "It's not made up!"

Wes sputters. "That's a real animal."

Lemming puts his cards facedown on the table and narrows his eyes at Wes. "What's it look like? What animal family does it belong to?"

That stumps Wes for a moment. "It's, like, a rodent?"

Hewitt wrinkles his forehead. "Nah, man, it's a primate, I think."

Jamie nods. "I think it's a primate."

Lemming looks around the table, his expression suspicious. "You fuckers are messing with me."

That sparks another round of raucous laughter, until Blake clears his throat and taps his visor in an exaggerated motion. "Boys. Please. We're pokering."

"Yeah," Lemming mutters. "We're pokering, so shut the fuck up."

"I raise five," Blake announces.

"Call." Hewitt.

"Fold." Wes.

"I see your five and raise you ten." Jamie.

"Big spender!" Blake crows. "Now we're talking!"

I call and so does Lemming, and then Blake deals the turn—another ten. Not great, but I'm still looking at queens and sevens. There's another round of betting. Lemming and Blake fold this time, leaving me, Hewitt, and Jamie to battle it out. Blake flips the river and *hot damn*. Another queen. Full-fucking-house, baby.

I go all in during the last betting round, prompting Hewitt to gape at me. "Seriously? On the first hand?"

"He's bluffing," Jamie decides, intently studying my face.

I smirk. "Am I?"

"He totally is," Blake agrees, but the three hundred bucks' worth of chips in the middle of the table is apparently too pricey for both Jamie and Hewitt. They fold. I gleefully rake in my winnings.

As several more hands are dealt, we shoot the shit about nothing in particular. Our upcoming schedule. The juniors team that Jamie coaches. The new Escalade that Hewitt bought for his wife. Eventually the conversation turns back to Lemming's escapades with "OC." Or, more specifically, the fourgy they indulged in after that Chicago bar visit.

"Wait—so you were doing one chick and O'Connor was doing the other, and it was just in the same room?" Wes asks curiously. "Or were you guys all, you know, up in each other's bizness?"

Lemming snickers. "No offense, Wesmie, but I'm not into dicks. So, no, there was no dude touching involved. But the girls were happy to touch each other . . ." He glances over at me, waggling his eyebrows. "You should've come, E. It was good times."

Honestly, it sounds terrible, but I don't say that out loud. Lemming's allowed to have his fun. He's six years younger than me and still enamored with the pro-hockey lifestyle that I took full advantage of before I met Kara.

These days, I'm not looking to tag-team two chicks with one of my teammates. I'd rather watch Disney movies with my kids and catch some sports highlights before bed. And maybe enjoy a nice dinner with a particular hottie . . .

"Matty-Cake?" Blake prompts.

I realize they're all waiting for me to play. I check my cards—seven, nine. Then the table—king, queen, king, ten, ten. There's about five hundred bucks in the pot.

"I'm out," I announce, slamming my cards down.

"Anyway," Lemming says, eyeing me again. "I don't get you, dude. You're single now. Take advantage of it."

I shrug. "I'm over the whole hook-up scene. Been there, done that."

Hewitt speaks up in a careful tone. "What about more than hooking up?"

I bat my eyelashes at him. "Aw, Ben-Ben, are you saying you want to 'more than hook up' with me? You're in love with me—I knew it."

He flips up his middle finger. "No, jackass, I'm talking about dating. As in, you dating someone."

Blake nods earnestly. "Yeah, Luko and I were talking about

it the other day—"

Um, what? Why are my teammates discussing my love life?

"—and he was saying how Estrella's sister is a F-O-X-X fox."

"Fox only has one X," Jamie pipes up.

"Not when you look like Estrella's sister," Blake declares. "She definitely deserves two X's. Or three—yeah, that makes more sense. Triple X. So, F-O-X-X-X."

I roll my eyes. "Have you even met Estrella's sister?"

"No," Blake says glibly. "But I trust Luko's eyes."

"Uh-huh. Well, I think I'm going to pass," I say in a gracious tone. "I can't date my captain's sister-in-law—what if I break her heart? He'll string me up by my balls." I hesitate. "Besides, I, uh . . ." I stop abruptly. What the hell is the matter with me? Was I really about to tell them about Hailey? This is poker night, not an episode of *Sex and the City*.

But Blake is quick to pounce. "Besides what?" he demands.

I cave. "There's someone I might be interested in."

"The plot thickens!" he shouts, maniacally rubbing his hands together. "Who is she?"

"My dog-walker," I blurt out.

Everyone laughs. "Seriously?" Jamie says.

"Yes and no. She walks Rufus as a favor to me because I'm a good customer of this cool business she owns called Fetch."

"Oh yeah!" Lemming says, shuffling the cards. "OC uses Fetch to buy groceries and pick up his shirts. He showed me the app. There's a babe on the home screen."

My jaw ticks with irritation. I've always thought of that photo of Hottie as mine, even if that's ridiculous. "That's the place."

"How does it work?" Wes asks, draining his beer.

"You pay them by the hour," I tell him. "And they take a surcharge on the things they purchase for you. But it's totally worth it. If you're flying home to an empty fridge and the cleaner's is closing in an hour, they'll take care of it."

"Boom!" Blake agrees.

"They'll find you anything," I add. "If you need a gift for

your mom's birthday or reservations to a restaurant, you just put your instructions into the app and it gets done. They furnished my entire apartment. I didn't set foot in a store."

"Huh." Wes nudges Jamie with his elbow. "It's like they know me. I'm gonna try this out."

Jamie shrugs. But I've probably just improved Hottie's bottom line. If the whole team starts using Fetch, that's got to be good for business.

"Can they find me a date to the opera?" Lemming asks, stacking up his remaining chips. "Our favorite benefit is in ten days."

Everyone groans. Players are required to attend eight or ten events a year, but they aren't all created equally. The opera benefit is everyone's least favorite. The team owner is about ninety years old, and he loves the shit out of the opera. Without fail, the performance is three hours long. Minimum. Even good food and booze afterward aren't enough to keep us cheerful.

"Here's an idea," Blake says, dealing the cards. "This round isn't for cash. The winner gets to call in sick on opera night, and the rest of us have to vouch for his twenty-four-hour stomach virus."

Wes picks up his cards. "I love this plan."

Me, I'm just happy that the conversation has shifted away from Hailey. My teammates seem to have forgotten about my little confession, and that's a good thing, because I still don't know how I feel about dating again. My marriage imploded due to my career, and it's not like I've changed careers. Any new relationship I get into is pretty much doomed.

"You probably like the opera," Lemming jokes.

"Because I'm queer?" Wes snorts. "Think again."

"J-Bomb?" Blake asks. "How do you feel about opera?" He tips his beer bottle up toward his mouth.

"Well, Blake. I'm bisexual so I only like it half as much as Wes."

"Naw, honey," Wes argues. "That means you'd like it *twice* as much."

Blake laughs so hard that beer comes out of his nose, and then we're all dying.

I have a great hand of cards, but it really doesn't matter. "You know we're all going to this damn opera, anyway," I grumble. "It's the annual ass-kissing fest at the owner's favorite event."

"Not for me!" Jamie says with a grin, pushing his chips into the center of the table.

"Oh, you're totally going," Wes grumbles.

"My kids have a game that night."

"Hang on." His husband looks up. "Do you even know what night it is?"

"Nope. But I'm *very* busy."

God bless poker night. The bickering and the smack talk keep my mind off the more difficult stuff. I accept another beer and relax with my boys.

Sniper87: Mayday! My tux is holy.

HTE: Your tux is a churchgoer?

Sniper87: Christ. I meant holey. Full of holes.

Sniper87: Grrr. I need it for the world's most boring benefit next week.

HTE: Okay. Rent or buy? You probably wear it pretty often?

Sniper87: Buy, I guess. I wear it about 8 times a year. Can you do your thing and make one appear?

HTE: I will absolutely help you. But this isn't like the waffle mix. You have to try it on. And if you're going to wear it frequently, it can't be just a quick cuff adjustment like they do for weddings. You'll need a fitting.

Sniper87: Grumble grumble.

STAY

HTE: Don't shoot the messenger. I can find you a shop with good inventory in tuxes and make you a fitting appointment. How does that sound?

Sniper87: Fine. Checking my calendar.

HTE: Take your time. Just sitting here eating bonbons.

Sniper87: Really?

HTE: No. Hurry up. It's crazy here today. Moon must be full.

HTE: *Drums fingers on desk.* *Waits for Sniper.* *Wonders how he can skate so fast but take 80 years to look at a calendar.*

Sniper87: Are you impatient with all your clients? I could try on suits tomorrow after morning skate. So 12:30 is safe. Or Friday same time.

HTE: When is the benefit? I'll need to make sure they know we're in a hurry.

Sniper87: Next Friday. Unfortunately.

HTE: Who's a grumpy boy today? I'll go find you a penguin suit. But not a Penguins jersey.

Sniper87: I should hope not.

HTE: You're right. Bunch of losers. Who wants the Stanley Cup, anyway? Back in a jif, Snipes.

HTE: Klingerman's, tomorrow at 12:30. Attaching the Yonge Street address. I sent along your measurements so they can pull some things off the rack for you to try. They're asking if you need anything else fitted while you're there. OK for suits?

Sniper87: I hate trying shit on. I wish it could just appear in my closet.

HTE: And I want a blue pony. Do you need anything else while you're standing in front of the tailor in your boxers?

Sniper87: I'm a boxer briefs guy. You should know. You bought them.

HTE: *beats head on keyboard*

Sniper87: I could use another suit. My pinstripe is looking seedy and I haven't shopped since Kara made me go two years ago.

HTE: I'll tell them. Have fun tomorrow.

Sniper87: I have one more request.

HTE: Hit me.

Sniper87: I want your help picking shit out. Clothes are not my forte.

HTE: The men's shop is pretty good at it. Just saying.

Sniper87: You won't come?

HTE: I will if you want me to. Seems like overkill, though.

Sniper87: Please?

HTE: THERE'S THE MAGIC WORD. :) See you tomorrow.

LOSING IQ POINTS

Hailey

I used to think of myself as an intelligent, high-functioning human. And when I'm texting with Matt, we have fun and I manage to complete my sentences and avoid drooling on myself.

Yet I spend the first fifteen minutes at the men's store tripping over my own feet and babbling like a maniac. This man turns me into the village idiot every time I see him.

The problem is that he's standing in front of the aging tailor in his undies. He's wearing a pair of skin-tight boxer briefs in bright orange, and I can see the outline of his perfect ass in all its glory. And his bare legs, the powerful hamstrings tensed for battle.

When I glance into the sizeable triple-panel mirror in front of him, it's even worse. Powerful thighs and abs that ripple beneath his undershirt. I manage not to check out his package, though it takes some serious effort, and I'm prattling on about the weather to the tailor like an over-caffeinated monkey.

At last the tailor has all the measurements he needs. Matt is handed a tux shirt, and I expect him to step into a dressing room somewhere to try everything on, but we're already *in* the enormous dressing room. So he slips his powerful arms into the shirt right in front of me.

I lose another five IQ points.

The tailor starts firing questions at Matt. Shawl cowl jacket or peaked lapels? Satin or grosgrain?

"Hottie?" he cries, a scowl on his face.

That snaps me out of my stupor. I waltz over to the rack and begin to flip through the choices. "I think the shawl collars look a little stuffy. You'll be more comfortable in a peak." I push the shawl collar choices aside and study the remaining three jackets. "This velvet is pretty cool, but it's not versatile enough for you." It too gets a nudge to the side. "That leaves this." I hold up a very traditional black tux jacket. "Or the midnight blue. I think the midnight blue is really hot, but if you want to be strictly traditional, go for black."

He hesitates. "I like the blue. You're sure that's not too weird?"

"Let me see . . ." I whip out my phone and pull up Pinterest. "Here's Matt Bomer wearing one. Jake Gyllenhaal. And, wow, Ryan Gosling." I let out a sigh, because the pictures are so beautiful and my hormone levels are already off the charts.

"Hand it over," Matt grumbles, still grumpy.

He looks amazing, of course. The tailor brings the matching trousers and fusses over the fit, pinning the trouser cuffs and making notes on his clipboard. Meanwhile, I try not to swallow my tongue. The man in front of me outshines Ryan Gosling any day of the week, with his bottomless gray eyes and sleek Nordic features. The rugged jaw looks a little tight today, but for some weird reason it only adds to his appeal.

I've got it bad.

Matt checks his reflection in the mirror. "Sold," he says. "Let's move on to the suits." But of course the tailor needs to do some pinning while Matt glowers.

And then—before I'm ready—he's stripping off the suit, his broad shoulders emerging from the sleeves. His hand falls to his waist, where he unbuttons the trousers, just like he's done every night in my dreams for a week.

Swear to God it's two hundred degrees in this room. Is twenty-nine too young to have hot flashes?

I flip through the suit jackets on the other rack to distract myself. "I'm not sure about this style," I say to the tailor, holding out a jacket. "Most of what you've got here is cut too straight for him. He needs more of a taper from those strapping shoulders to that . . ." I stop myself before the word *delicious* pops out. " . . . narrow waist."

Heat climbs up my neck, and I can feel Matt's smile even without looking at it.

"Strapping, huh?" he mutters under his breath.

"Miss makes a good point," the tailor says. "One moment." He disappears, and then we're alone.

And he's in his underwear again.

"Sorry I'm such a grouch," he says quietly, those gray eyes studying me.

"You're not so bad."

He gives me a grateful smile. "The boondoggles aren't the best part of my job. When I was twenty I didn't mind it. The parties were a real eye-opener. All that money in one room, you know?" He reaches out to fiddle with the tailor's measuring tape where it dangles over a mannequin's shoulder. "But it gets old."

"I'll bet. And you said this was your least favorite event of the year. Not an opera fan, huh?"

"Not in the slightest. And it was supposed to be my night with the girls. So now I have to beg the ex to trade me. That should be fun."

"Sorry."

He shakes his head as if to push out the thought. "I like the blue tux, Hottie. It's a nice change. When I discovered all those moth holes in the black one, it seemed like fate."

"Why?"

His grin is wry. "I got married in that tux. Kara chose it. So as much as I dislike shopping, it's probably time for a change."

"Yeah. I'm still living with stuff I picked out with my ex. Seems stupid to throw away all the nice things we got for our

STAY

wedding and start over with Walmart replacements. But I have to look at it every day."

"Have you started dating again?" he asks suddenly.

The question takes me completely by surprise. "No, actually. This is going to sound really weird . . ."

He gives me a shy smile. "Maybe you're just not ready?"

"It's more like . . . I don't even know how it works. I've never been on a date."

His eyebrows lift. "You mean, not for years?"

"No. Not ever. Jackson and I were pals forever. Then we were a couple. One day in high school he kissed me instead of hugging me goodbye. And that was that. It was more than a decade ago. I've never been asked out. I've never gone to dinner and a movie with someone I haven't known my whole life. Small talk and protocol and first kisses? I've only seen it in movies."

I should probably shut up now, because I sound like a freak even to my own ears, and Matt is staring at me the way you'd look at an alien being. He grins suddenly. "And I thought I'd been off the market a long time."

"I'm just here to make you feel better," I tell him. And now I'm self-conscious again.

The tailor returns with several suit jackets, and I convince Matt that the gray one is the best choice. "The cut looks great, and . . ." It's really hard to give this man fashion advice without panting on him.

"And? Finish the sentence. Because Kara told me I should never wear gray."

"Really?" I smooth down the lapels because my hands itch to touch him. "Was she the jealous type?" I lift my eyes to his, and I'm clobbered by the reality of how close our bodies are.

"Sometimes. Why?"

"Because gray really makes your eyes pop. You look great in this color."

"Thank you, Hottie," he whispers. "It's been a long time since anyone said something like that to me."

"Well." I get trapped for a second in his steady gaze.

"Someone should."

The tailor clears his throat, and I take a quick step backward.

And since Matt has made his choices, there's no more reason for me to stay. I make my excuses and get the heck out of there.

DIAL DOWN THE CRAZY

Hailey

"A twist!" Jenny crows the next morning, peering over my shoulder at the screen.

"The plot thickens," I agree in a serious tone.

We stare at the photo for three more seconds, then turn to each other and burst out laughing. Between hysterical giggles, I manage to get the gist of Mr. Dick's latest order. He's in the market for double-sided tape so he can ensure that his neon-green Speedo doesn't ride up. Though maybe we should be calling him Mr. Butt now, because the attached pic features a back view of him in said neon-green Speedo—and yes, it's totally riding up. His buttocks are round, taut, and tanned. They're kind of appealing, actually.

"Man, I could bounce quarters off that ass." The deep voice causes both Jenny and me to jump in surprise. I swivel my head to find Matt Eriksson standing right behind us.

"Math!" I blurt out. "I mean Matt!"

Jenny snickers.

"You always call me Math when you're nervous," he remarks as he steps closer. "What's up with that?"

"I'm not nervous," I grumble. "I'm startled. You startled me!"

STAY

"Sorry about that. You guys don't have a receptionist, so I just wandered down the hall until I saw a door with your name on it."

Oh crap. He was just wandering around? What if someone saw him and realized he was a client? Why is he just showing up at my office?

"You shouldn't be here," I say uneasily. "You wanted your client profile to be anonymous."

Matt waves a hand. "Ah, I don't care about that. So what if the world knows I use Fetch? It's a wicked service."

He moves even closer, leaning in to get a better look at the computer screen. Since I'm still sitting at my chair, I'm trapped between the desk and his shoulder. His very broad shoulder, which nudges mine as he bends that big, sexy body of his. He smells fantastic, and I have to hold my breath so I don't inhale his citrusy scent and get a contact high.

"So what are we looking at?" he asks curiously. "Butt porn? Your job is more fun than I thought."

"No." I immediately click the mouse to close the screen. "Sorry," I say when I notice him raising a brow at me. "It's a client request. Confidentiality and all that."

He relaxes at the word *client*. Hmmm. Was he a bit jealous at the thought of me browsing butt porn? Nah. Of course he wasn't. He probably thinks I'm a weirdo.

"I got you a coffee," Matt says as he straightens. He holds out a paper cup from Starbucks. "Black, just the way you like it."

Jenny's eyebrows shoot up. I can almost hear her thoughts—*Just the way you like it? Tell me everything!*

I avoid her intensely curious gaze and accept the cup. "Thanks," I say, smiling at Matt.

"Anyway, I came by to . . ." With an awkward look, he trails off, then glances at Jenny.

She doesn't get the hint. Or maybe she does and she's choosing to ignore it. Rolling my eyes, I rise from my chair and gesture to the door. "We need a minute," I tell Jenny.

"I've got a minute," she chirps.

In a firm voice, I repeat my earlier statement. "Client confidentiality."

"Oh, fine." Clearly disappointed, she huffs out the door, closing it behind her.

Matt props a hip against my desk. "This actually isn't a business call," he admits.

"Even so," I answer wryly, "Jenny's not great at picking up social cues."

He smiles, and the sight warms my heart. This man is so frickin' attractive. Like melt-your-brain, dampen-your-panties attractive. And when he smiles, it totally short-circuits my system. My legs feel more than a little wobbly as I sit back down. I don't think I can support my own weight in the face of this guy's potent sex appeal.

"So what's up?" I ask.

Matt is still leaning against the desk. His leg is about five inches from my knee. I wonder what he'd do if I reached out and stroked his thigh. Not that I'm going to. That would take me out of weirdo fangirl territory and skyrocket me into psycho land.

"I was thinking about what you said yesterday at the store," he starts.

I furrow my brow. I said lots of things at the store. Most of them probably gibberish, because seeing Matt Eriksson in his underwear had turned me into a blubbering fool.

"About how you've never really dated?" he prompts.

I feel my cheeks heat up. "Oh. That."

"I don't know, it seems kind of unfair that you've never been on a real date." He pauses. "I thought I'd change that."

My heart jumps into my throat. Oh my God. Is he asking me out? Matt Eriksson is asking me out? On a date? Matt Eriksson wants me to go on a date with him? Matt Eriksson wants to go on a date with *me*? Matt Eriksson wants—

Dial down the crazy!

I take a deep breath and force myself out of my mental tailspin.

"And I have a fascinating first date in mind," he finishes,

and then flashes me another one of those heart-stopping smiles.

"Yeah?" My pulse is racing. I should say no, right? *Crazy fangirl* isn't exactly a good date candidate for this man. He needs a woman who doesn't call him "Math" and stammer every time he's around.

"*Rigoletto*," he says solemnly.

I wipe my clammy hands on my jeans. "Oh, I love Italian food. I've never heard of that restaurant, though."

He chuckles. Low, deep, and tinged with humor. "It's an opera," he corrects.

I falter. "Oh. That sounds . . ."

"Awful?" he supplies. His lips twitch until finally another laugh slips out. "Yeah, opera is not my first date of choice, either. But I can take you out for tapas first. It's a mandatory team event, and I figured if you went with me, we could have some fun with it. We get to fancy ourselves up—I'm gonna wear that new tux you helped me pick out. We can console each other during the opera part, and then there's a kickass spread afterward." He waggles his eyebrows enticingly, adding, "Plus an open bar . . ."

"You want me to go to a team event with you . . . as your date," I say slowly.

"Yes." He rubs the side of his neck, looking awkward again. "Would you like to go?"

Yes yes yes yes yes yes yes!

"Yeah, sure," I say casually. Except I sound so casual that it borders on indifference, and his slight frown tells me he's not thrilled by the flippant response. "It sounds fun," I assure him, injecting a dose of eagerness to my voice.

A smile curves his lips. "Awesome. It's next Friday—pick you up at seven?"

"Sounds good." That gives me a week to dig up an opera-worthy dress. I have a feeling that my simple, mostly discount dresses are not going to cut it. Jenny to the rescue!

"Nice. I'm actually looking forward to this now." There's something very genuine about the way he's looking at me, with warmth and anticipation.

"Because you roped a poor sucker into suffering with you?" I joke, mostly because I'm unnerved by the intensity of his gaze.

Matt's ice-gray eyes stay locked on mine. "No, because I get to spend some real time with you."

Oh my. I can't turn away from those eyes. I feel like something is happening right now. Something weirdly intimate and scarily intense, and yet all we're doing is looking at each other. But there's this strange electricity in the air. And Matt's gaze has dropped to my mouth. His intent focus has me biting my lower lip, and a spark of heat flares in his eyes.

"Hottie." He slowly pushes forward.

One big hand grasps mine, tugging me out of my chair and to my feet. And . . . Oh God, I think he's going to kiss me. His lips are parted, and his tongue comes out briefly to moisten them. I don't know if I'm ready for this. I haven't kissed anyone since Jackson—

"Hailey," a voice says from the doorway. "Needed to talk to you about—oh. Hello."

Speak of the devil.

Jackson saunters into my office without knocking, holding a file folder in one hand and a coffee mug in the other. Matt smoothly takes a step back at my ex-husband's appearance.

"Jackson!" I squeak.

His brow furrows. "Sorry, didn't mean to interrupt. I didn't know there was anyone else in here." Jackson studies Matt, and I can see him trying to figure out where he knows him from. Jackson and I watched lots of Toronto games together, both on television and in person, so he's familiar with many of the players. After a few seconds, it clicks. "Wait—are you Matt Eriksson?"

Jackson's long delay allows me to gather my composure, and my tone sounds steady and professional as I make the introductions. "Jax, Matt's one of our clients. Matt, this is Jackson Emery, the co-owner of Fetch."

Even if I hadn't already told Matt that I work with my ex,

the last name would have given it away. I still haven't gotten around to dropping "Emery" and going back to just "Taylor." I should probably do that, I know, but the idea of filing the name change paperwork feels so . . . final. Like it'll make the divorce . . . real.

It is real.

Fuck. Yes. I know it's real. I'm just a sappy fool, I guess.

"It's nice to meet you," Matt says politely. He extends a hand, and Jackson shakes it.

"Nice to meet you, too." Jackson smiles. "It's kind of cool that our client roster has a professional hockey player on it."

"And Hailey's opera date," Matt says, winking at me.

Jackson frowns.

I gulp. Oh my God. Why did Matt say that?

"You're going to the opera together?" Jackson's gaze slowly shifts from me to Matt and then back to me. "Since when do you enjoy the opera, Hails?"

"I don't," I stammer. "But . . ."

"I twisted her arm," Matt finishes for me.

"I see." Jackson pauses. When he speaks again, there's a bite to his tone. "Melinda is actually a big fan of the opera. I should take her one of these days."

My entire body clenches. Painfully. Did he seriously just bring up the woman he's seeing? Something burns like acid in my throat. Anger. Or maybe a sense of betrayal? Not jealousy, though. I'm *not* jealous that Jackson is dating someone.

But that doesn't mean I want to hear about her.

"Anyway." Matt sounds wary now as he looks from me to Jackson. "I'll call you later to go over the details," he tells me.

I manage a nod. "Okay."

"Later, Hottie."

Jackson frowns again.

To my disbelief, Matt smacks my butt lightly before strolling out the door.

I gape after him, unsure whether to be pissed or amused. I think he might have been trying to make Jackson jealous on purpose by calling me Hottie and touching my butt, but . . .

why? Maybe he saw the way I flinched when Jackson mentioned Melinda?

When I turn back, I find Jackson's eyes burning with annoyance.

"What was that?" he demands.

"I should be asking you the same thing," I shoot back.

His jaw falls open. "Are you kidding me? What did *I* do?"

"We talked about this," I bite out. "We agreed not to discuss our love lives with each other, and you brought up how your new girlfriend is a *huge* fan of the opera."

"You brought up that you're going to the opera with Matt Eriksson!"

"*He* brought it up," I grumble.

"Well, either way, it was brought up." Jackson glowers at me. "Since when are you dating Matt Eriksson?"

"I'm not."

His jaw tightens. "So I just imagined this entire fucking conversation?"

I flinch at his sharp words, because Jackson typically doesn't curse. "I mean, we haven't gone out yet," I amend awkwardly. "The opera will be our first date. He came by today to ask me."

"And you said yes."

"Should I have said no?"

"Yes!" His face turns red. "He's a client, Hails! You can't fraternize with clients. It's against the rules."

"The rules we laid out are for our employees, Jax. We're the co-owners of this company."

"Exactly," he snaps. "You're the co-owner. Which means you need to lead by example. We can't have our staff thinking it's okay to date clients!"

"Nobody even knows Matt is a client. Only we have that information," I answer tightly. "And me dating him doesn't affect the business." I'm not about to tell him which rules I'm breaking to walk Rufus, though. Crap.

"What if it goes south and you break up, and then we lose him as a client?" Jackson challenges. "Did you ever think of that?"

STAY

"Matt and I are adults. Even if it doesn't work out, we won't lose a client." God, I don't think we will. "If you really think it's a big deal, I can stop handling his requests."

Jackson runs an agitated hand through his hair. "I don't know. This just seems unprofessional, Hails."

Indignation sticks in my throat. "Really? And you gushing about your girlfriend in front of a client is professional?"

"I wasn't gushing," he says coolly. "You're saying you can flaunt your hockey player in my face, but I can't mention the woman I'm seeing?"

Another arrow of pain pierces my heart.

We stare at each other for a moment.

I let out a heavy breath.

So does he.

"Jackson . . ." Misery hangs onto those two syllables. "What's going on here?"

"I don't know." He sounds equally bleak.

After a long beat, we sit side by side on the edge of my desk, both of us staring straight ahead. God, how did this happen? Where did this distance come from? This is the boy I grew up with. The boy I fell in love with and married. Jackson and I never raised our voices to each other—not even once—during our eight-year marriage. It's disheartening that we're doing it now.

So many questions bite at my tongue as I peer at his handsome profile. Does he want to buy me out of the business? Stop working together? Why is it so hard to think about him with another woman? And why am I secretly happy that it bugs him to think about me with another man?

How did we get here?

Jackson clears his throat. Then he finally speaks. "I knew it was going to be rough, but I didn't think it would be this rough," he admits.

I swallow again. "What?"

"Dating other people. I mean, we're divorced, but I still care about you, Hails."

"I care about you, too."

"I . . ." He stops awkwardly. "I'm sorry I mentioned Melinda out of the blue like that. I was caught off guard, and it was just a knee-jerk thing."

"I know. It's okay. I probably overreacted a little."

After a moment of hesitation, he puts his arm around me. I lean my head on his shoulder, and it's such a familiar pose that my throat tightens.

His voice is thick with emotion. "I just don't want to see you get hurt."

I wrinkle my forehead. "Why would I get hurt?"

"Eriksson is a professional hockey player," Jackson points out. "Pro athletes have a certain type of reputation, you know? I don't want him to play games with you."

"He's not like that, Jax."

I can't explain why I'm so certain of that, but I am. I saw Matt with his daughters, how gentle and loving he was with them. I know he's home most nights when he doesn't have a game, because that's when he sends his Fetch requests, and he's always there to accept deliveries. A lot of the other guys on the Toronto team are all over the Internet, all the time. Like that O'Connor guy—the hockey forums constantly say how he was spotted at some nightclub on Richmond or canoodling with a model on some rooftop bar. Matt's name, on the other hand, barely ever shows up on those sites.

"Do you want me to stop handling his account?" I offer.

"No." Jackson sighs. "We're friends, aren't we, Hails?"

"Always," I whisper.

"That's never going to change," he vows, before planting a light kiss on the top of my head. "No matter what happens, we'll always be friends."

He rises to his feet, gathers up his file folder and mug, and walks out of my office.

No matter what happens? As in, he's going to try to push me out of the business? Is that what he meant?

I stare at the empty doorway, the answers eluding me. But there's a very bad feeling in the pit of my stomach.

LIKE THE PENALTY BOX, BUT PLUSHER

Matt

'm standing on the steps of the opera house, oddly nervous. This is a stupid first-date idea. I wanted to take Hottie out for a quiet dinner first, somewhere I could feed her and tell her all my best jokes. But that's not how tonight worked out. Instead I'm treating her to a night with my hyper teammates, at an opera where I'll have trouble sitting still.

Slick, Eriksson, I chide myself. *Well done.*

Hottie couldn't meet me for dinner tonight because she had an emergency meeting with her programmer. So that sucks. The evening's only saving grace is that my tux fits perfectly. It's yet another thing in my life that she's helped me with.

"What's this opera about, anyway?" Wes asks, nudging me with his elbow.

"Fuck if I know."

"I *wish* it were about fucking," Blake says slowly.

"Oh, come on, you guys!" Jess Canning yelps. "*Rigoletto* is Verdi's most famous creation. It's amazing, and I promise it's right up your alley." She's our resident artsy friend, so she should know.

"Well, don't hold out on us, J-Babe," Blake demands of his girlfriend. "What's the story? God knows we don't sprechen

STAY

Sie Deutsch!"

"It's in Italian, you goof. Here, I found a synopsis earlier..." She taps her phone. "The story opens with the Duke at a big party. He's trying to decide which women to seduce first. The song is 'Questa o quella,' which means 'this woman or that?'"

"Now we're talking," Blake says. "It's just like me in ye olden days. Before I found the perfect one." He puts one of his big mitts around Jess's waist. "When I picked up our tickets, I noticed this place has a kickass coat room. You know how we enjoy coat rooms..."

She gives him a silly smile, but Wes makes a growling sound. "TMI, okay? Now tell me about the damned opera."

Jess continues to explain the story. There's a curse on the Duke and his jester, and the jester's beautiful daughter. Instead of listening, I'm scanning the street, eyeing every taxi that pulls up, looking for Hailey. I can't find her anywhere.

"The song in Act Three is something you'll recognize," Jess promises. "'La donna e mobile.' It means, 'the woman is fickle.'"

"Sounds okay," Lemming says.

"Eh," I caution. "These things always sound better on paper. But it'll be three hours long, and they'll manage to suck the joy out of the story." I've been to quite a few of these opera nights already.

"Speaking of sucking and joy," Blake says with a grin. "Matty-Cake has two tickets in his hand. Something we should all know, my boy? Are you and the dog-walker an item now?"

I wish. And tonight probably won't improve my chances. Asking Hottie to this thing was a terrible idea. If she stands me up, it might even be for the best. "How about you don't make any *sucking* jokes for the rest of the night?"

"What fun is that? I arranged for us to sit in a box together. It's like the penalty box, but plusher."

"You . . . what?" Just as I'm worrying about this new development, another taxi pulls up. When the door opens, a pair of long legs appears from the darkness inside. Then Hottie unfolds those smokin' legs from the car and stands up on a pair of spike heels, her dark hair shining under the street lamps.

"Amirite, Matty-Cake?" Blake says, jabbing me in the ribs. He's still talking, but I've tuned him out.

"Everyone shut it," I hiss. "Here comes my date. Pretend you're normal."

"Good luck with that." Wes snickers.

"Mamma mia," Lemming mutters under his breath. "That can't be your date, Eriksson. She's too hot for you."

I want to tell him to keep his trap shut, but there isn't time. Hottie spots me and smiles. I watch her navigate the busy sidewalk, and I descend a couple of steps to greet her. "Hey, you made it." I take her hand, then lean in and give her a kiss on the cheek to show my appreciation. Her perfume invites me to linger, so I take a deep breath before I step back. "Thanks for coming."

She blinks at me for a long moment, then looks down at our clasped hands. "It's my pleasure." Her voice is soft and a little tentative, her blue eyes sparkling. I feel the warm buzz of arousal, and I wish I could just hail one of these cabs and ask the driver to take us back to my apartment.

But I can't, of course. And that's not what Hailey signed up for.

Right. Opera it is.

"I'll apologize in advance for my friends," I say, stalling.

"Why?" She smiles at me again, and it hits me full force. If this is how Hottie looks at me after she's gotten a little used to me, I may not survive it. "They didn't shower after practice?"

"It's not quite that bad," I manage, smiling back at her. We're both standing here grinning like a couple of idiots, but I can't stop. "They're just kind of rowdy. Not opera fans. Except for Jess." I tip my head toward Blake's girlfriend on the stairs.

Hottie glances at my fellow players and shrugs. "I'm from Toronto, Snipes. I'm not afraid of a few hockey players."

I chuckle. "Snipes?"

STAY

"If I have a nickname, you get one, too. It's only fair." She gives me an appraising look. "Nice tux. Some smart person must have helped you pick it out." She licks her lips and glances up at the theater.

I am in so much trouble.

Taking her arm, I lead her up the steps. "Guys, this is H . . ." I *almost* say Hottie. "Hailey Taylor Emery."

"Awesome!" Blake bellows with his usual deafening enthusiasm. "I love a chick with three names! Like, um . . ." He pauses. "James Earl Jones!"

"Not a chick." Jess sighs, shaking Hottie's hand. "Welcome to the asylum."

"Sarah Jessica Parker," Wes offers.

"Julia Louis-Dreyfus," Lemming adds.

I cut off this recitation of stupidity by introducing each of these chuckleheads, and then the lights flash outside the theater, prompting everyone to go inside.

"C'mon, guys!" Jess says, clapping her hands. "I don't want to miss the beginning!"

"I wouldn't mind," someone else mumbles.

We enter the theater and I give Hottie my arm as we climb a curving staircase. Someone shows us to a private box, where another usher waits to hang our coats in a little closet right outside.

"Fancy!" Jess says approvingly.

But I can't even hear her, because I've slipped Hailey's coat off her shoulders. And now I almost swallow my tongue. She's wearing a sparkling, backless dress. That's not even why I'm speechless. Hottie has an intricate tattoo of ivy vines all across her shapely back.

I let out a little moan of longing, and she turns her head with a questioning look. "Everything okay?"

"Yeah," I say, my voice a rasp. But no, it ain't okay. The opera just doubled in length if I have to sit beside her all night trying not to imagine the full picture of those tattoos across her naked body. "Where would you like to sit?" I ask, dragging my reluctant eyes off the swell of her ass.

"Anywhere."

The box has six armchairs upholstered in velvet. I steer Hailey toward the ones in the front. The others are for Blake, Jess, Wes, and . . .

"Made it!" Jamie says, appearing in the doorway in a tux.

"Baby!" Wes exclaims with no small amount of surprise.

"My second practice got cancelled. Ran home and changed."

"Aw. Now I *know* you love me." He pulls Jamie in for a kiss.

And then something beautiful happens. Someone on staff offers us glasses of champagne from a cart in the hallway. I hand one to Hailey.

"Classy," she says.

"We definitely didn't have drinks last year," Blake recalls. "It must be the box seats. Sit on my lap, Jessie. It's almost a party now."

She perches on his thigh and they clink their glasses together, then kiss.

I'm the last single man on the planet, apparently.

"This is so civilized," Jess remarks, slipping off Blake's lap and into her own chair.

"That's exactly what we don't like about it," Wes agrees.

Hailey smiles, and I relax by a degree or two. "Thank you for coming with me tonight," I tell her. "Maybe the opera wouldn't be your first pick, but I really enjoy your company."

She glances down for a second, as if she finds it difficult to accept this bit of praise. "It's nice to step outside my rut sometimes, Snipes." She lifts her elegant chin. "Have you seen *Rigoletto* before?"

"I have no idea," I say without any shame, and she laughs.

When the house lights fade to black a moment later, I smile into the pregnant stillness inside the theater. A couple of coughs and the rustle of clothing are all we hear for a moment.

"Freebird!" Blake whispers from behind me, and I hear Hailey's giggle even if I can't see it.

STAY

The orchestra starts up with a swell of brass and timpani. When the curtains part, it's on a bright stage where a big party is taking place, just as Jess described. I try to settle in and watch, but it's not easy. I'm too aware of Hottie beside me. I want to watch her instead of the opera.

I sip my champagne and look more closely at the costumes onstage. They aren't from the correct historical period. Someone decided to set this opera in . . . Las Vegas? Atlantic City? There are mobsters and women in fifties dresses.

As usual, my mind wanders to better topics. Hailey and then hockey. Pretty soon I realize I've spent a big chunk of time thinking through offensive strategies for our game against Vancouver. Any hope I had for following the opera is long gone.

Onstage, the rich guy from the opening party scene sits in a chair drinking champagne while two dozen others stand around him in a semicircle, singing.

I lean over to Hottie and whisper, "Do you have any idea what's happening right now?"

Slowly, she turns her head until her lips brush my ear. My senses all stand at attention and salute her as she whispers, "No fucking clue."

Her warm breath brushes my face as the music swells, and I'm hit with a wave of pure longing. It's not just for sex, either. I'd gladly take her home to bed with me. But I crave this, too—a joke in the dark. A private laugh with a partner in crime.

I turn my head until my nose subtly brushes past her soft cheek. "Actually, it's pretty obvious what's going on," I breathe into her ear.

"Is that so?"

"Yup. That rich guy—I think he's a mafia don—is telling his goons to whack someone."

She nods earnestly. "The man who stole his cocaine."

"Right," I whisper, my lips grazing the shell of her ear. She shivers. "But I think we're getting a car chase first. They'll find the drugs in the back of a souped-up minivan. Guarded by Sister Maria, my warty third-grade teacher."

Hailey turns her face into my shoulder, and I can feel her chuckle. On the stage, a woman in a blood-red dress suddenly appears. She opens her mouth and begins to sing in a sweet soprano.

"Oh shit," I whisper to Hailey. "You know who she is?"

"Of course I do," she hisses. "The estranged love child of Sister Maria and the don. She's come to warn of a curse she's put upon them. She never got a pony for her birthday, so she's casting a pox upon their houses."

"In her defense," I say solemnly, "the don totally promised to get her that pony."

"In *his* defense," Hailey counters, "the recession hit the mafia pretty hard."

"Truth."

We stare at each other, lips twitching wildly. Jesus. I can't remember the last time I had this much fun with a woman.

Her slim hand grasps my wrist. "Oh no." Her whisper is so soft, it's barely audible.

"What?"

"The curse is rumored to be expanding."

"Will everyone break out in weeping pustules?"

She shakes her head, and silky hair brushes against my jaw. "They'll all be attacked momentarily. By a giant squid."

That's what does me in. A bark of laughter very nearly escapes my chest, but I gulp it down just in time.

But my laughter sets Hailey off. She's so determined to hold it back that she swallows with an awkward cough in the back of her throat. Yet—as in the real Sister Maria's class—that only makes it funnier. I can feel her trembling beside me.

And wouldn't you know, my stomach starts shaking in sympathy. I bite down on my lip, but real laughter still threatens. I grin down at my tux pants and laugh silently.

Beside me, Hailey is fighting for control. She takes a deep, slow breath and lets it out. But she convulses again on the

STAY

exhale.

Trying to be helpful, I sit up straight and give her the side-eye, which she returns, grinning. Her lips twitch, and my gaze is drawn to the sweet curve of her mouth.

Her lips twitch again, her shoulders pulling together with the effort of not laughing. And of course, it's all my fault. Luckily there's a cure for this problem.

Without a second thought, I close the distance between us and kiss her.

The moment our lips touch, the silly mood evaporates. The brush of her soft lips against mine halts my laughter in its tracks. Hailey goes completely still against my body. The floral scent of her hair hits me like a warm mist. The kiss happens in slow motion, as we both push past our mutual surprise.

Meanwhile, my libido practically stands up and cheers. *Yaaaaas!* it shouts. *More of this!*

More indeed. One soft kiss is simply not enough. I lean in, tilting my head, perfecting our connection. Hailey exhales, her warm breath caressing my skin. She tastes of champagne and lipstick, my two favorite flavors. I touch my tongue to her lower lip, asking for more. My chair creaks as I lean closer to her, but I barely register the sound as she opens for me.

I taste her, then break out in goose bumps everywhere. It's been so long since I felt like this—eager and desired. When two soft hands land on my chest, my body lights up like a flare.

Below us, the orchestra kicks in to a faster rhythm and the chorus raises its voice in song. I kiss her again and again. We don't stop until the audience breaks into sudden applause, startling us apart.

"BRAVO!" yells Blake. "And of course I mean you two. Who could watch the opera with all that nekkin' right in front of me?"

Hailey's eyes are a little wide, and a flush has crept across the exposed skin of her long neck. I wink at her to let her know she can feel free to ignore my teammate. She seems to pull herself together, joining in the applause for the performance we've just ignored.

My tux pants are now uncomfortably tight, and the night stretches before me like a long walk through the desert without a drink of water. I have to survive more opera after the intermission, and then a cocktail party with the team owner and his stuffy philanthropist friends.

If I'm lucky I can get a few more of those kisses in the taxi home. I take Hottie's hand in mine and give it a squeeze.

Did I mention I've got it bad?

NO WONDER I'M DIVORCED

Hailey

The day after the opera, Matt flies off to the West Coast with his team on a seven-day road trip. And Rufus is staying at the doggy ranch, so I won't see either of them or set foot in Matt's apartment for at least a week.

Jenny almost murders me when I tell her how I feel about his departure. "I'm a little relieved," I admit as we wait for our drinks at the coffee shop.

"That makes no sense," she sputters. "Why would you be relieved?" Her eyes narrow. "Unless you had sex all night long and need a break. It's been a while for you, right? Your stamina might need work."

My face, neck, and lots of other parts flush when she says this. "There was no sex." *But there would have been if I were braver.*

My friend chews her lip. "Did you chicken out?"

"Well . . ." It really depends on your viewpoint. "He was a gentleman. The car brought us first to my place, even though it's pretty far out of the way. He kissed me goodnight, and then the car took him home."

"Oh. My. God." Jenny swallows roughly. "You didn't invite him in? The man rode with you all the way out to Yonge and Eglinton and you said, 'Thanks for the opera, see you later?'"

STAY

Even the grumpy barista is eyeing me over the milk fluffer, a disbelieving expression on his pimply face. "It was our first date," I protest. "I wasn't going to invite him in."

Jenny yanks our two cups off the counter and marches toward the door. I pause to tip the barista and then follow her out.

She's waiting outside with a stern expression on her pretty face. "Let me get this straight. Your lifelong crush wanted to peel you out of my sparkly dress and do the horizontal pachanga, but you sent him home?"

Pretty much.

I remove my coffee cup from Jenny's hand and take a scorching sip just to avoid answering her. After the curtain fell on the opera, Matt led me downstairs for food, more wine, and small talk with Blake, Jess, and Wesmie. Then the elderly team owner approached, and Matt made a point of complimenting his choice of operas.

The moment the man moved away from us, Matt breathed a sigh of relief. "I have fulfilled my duties this evening. Shall we go?"

So we got in the car together, where Matt kissed the daylights out of me all the way home.

The memory of his hot, eager mouth on my neck gives me an inappropriate flutter down below. In fact, the ride home was basically the hottest sexual experience of my life, and that's without anyone rounding any bases at all.

He didn't pressure me, though. When I shakily thanked him for a lovely evening, his smile was warm and happy. "See you soon, Hottie. Plan on it."

The problem? Those words are as terrifying to me as they are thrilling. Matt makes me crazy, and not just in a good way. When I'm around him, I feel giddy and weak-kneed, but also nervous and uncertain. I don't have experience with men. I have experience with *man*, as in, one man. Jackson. I'm not sure if the nerves I feel with Matt are normal, or a sign that maybe he's a bit too much for me.

"So now what happens?" Jenny demands. "Are you getting

another at-bat?"

"Maybe?" I guess. "If he's the type to be pissed off that I didn't put out after a long evening of opera, then I haven't missed a thing."

She makes a choking sound. "Not true. You missed a trip to pound town with the hottest body on the best hockey team in the world."

Right. Except for that.

When Jenny and I arrive at the office five minutes later, it's already chaos, even at nine in the morning. The holidays are approaching, so Fetch is seeing an uptick in shopping business. I welcome the distraction, and lose myself in the work.

The next few days are filled with petty emergencies and meetings with our principal developer. Techie Tad swings by to help with the integration of our new app. He's wearing his Toronto cap and asks me out to coffee again, but before he can even get the sentence out, Jackson yells for me from the other room.

"Sorry," I say, squeezing Tad's elbow as I run past. "We'll grab one sooner or later." Though I still don't know if I'm flattered or insulted by his fake Toronto loyalties. On one hand, it's sweet. On the other hand, I don't want anyone forsaking their team to win my favor.

I spend an afternoon finalizing our holiday promotions with Jackson, and then coding them into our website in my office. It's not the most stimulating part of my week, and my mind keeps wandering back to the opera and the first time Matt kissed me. The soft huff of his breath against my lips, followed by the brush of his lips over mine . . .

By my calculations, my last first kiss was over a decade ago. Maybe that's why Matt's kiss lit me up so much?

And—this is terrible—I don't actually *remember* my first teenage kiss from Jackson. I can't tell you where we were or whether or not I liked it.

No wonder I'm divorced.

Matt's kiss, on the other hand, keeps sneaking up on me at odd moments. As I wait for a file to load, I recall the sensation of his big hand cupping my thigh. And as Dion tries to explain to me why we can't order the imported tea that a new customer demands, I have a sudden, urgent memory of Matt's tongue in my ear on the taxi ride home.

"Are you okay, Hailey?" Dion asks.

My attention snaps back to the man in my doorway. "Fine!" I say quickly. "So, uh, there'll be a delay?" I try to remember what we were discussing.

"Yeah. He's not happy, but I told him he could talk to you if he had questions."

"Right! Well done. Anything else?"

Dion gives me a patient smile. "The unlabeled boxes are piling up in the hallway again. Have a look when you get a second."

"I'll do that," I promise.

He walks away, and I sit back in my chair, trying to pull myself together. The evening I spent with Matt was a kind of emotional earthquake, and the aftershocks keep rattling me.

Maybe I'm ready to concede that Jenny is right—I should start putting myself out there again. But Matt isn't a great reintroduction to dating. He's too intimidating. Too amazing. Too . . . everything.

Just as I form this thought, my computer monitor dings, and his login name appears on my screen.

> *Sniper87*: Hi there. Today's request is for a dinner date next Tuesday at 7pm. Oh, and reservations. Wherever my date wishes to go.

For a moment my heart soars. A dinner date. Wherever I want to go! With the most potent man on the planet. *Alone.* Just the two of us.

A wave of lust rolls through me. Unfortunately, it's quickly followed by a wave of panic.

A private dinner date? I'll probably turn into a babbling lunatic with the conversational skills of a frightened chimpanzee. The man has no idea how many hours of worry and preparation went into that night at the opera. And, thanks to the performance onstage, I didn't even have to speak for much of it.

If I'm honest, the conversation parts of that evening were the best parts. Somehow I'd finally relaxed and enjoyed Matt's company. Right around the time we began inventing opera plotlines, I forgot he was Matt Eriksson, Toronto forward, and began to see him as Matt, the funny guy I enjoy talking to.

But was my competent performance a fluke? Lightning rarely strikes twice in the same spot. And even if I manage not to babble or embarrass myself, let's be honest. The man has more testosterone than I'm used to dealing with. He'll expect sex—the kind of passionate, dirty sex that famous athletes are used to.

With me—the woman who isn't even sure she likes sex.

Don't get me wrong—the idea of Matt Eriksson naked and moaning is very appealing. But the deed itself has always been a big letdown. So even if I screw up my courage and go through with the whole adventure, the result will be a soul-crushing disappointment, right?

Right. I'll let him down easy.

HTE: Hi Snipes.

Sniper87: Just the girl I was looking for! Sitting here in the hotel all by my lonesome. Thinking about a date I had recently. On the way home . . .

HTE: I have to stop you right there, sir. The Fetch chat is stored in your client file and can be read by anyone who assists you.

Sniper87: Hmm. But a certain HoTtiE always assists me. That can't be random luck.

Oh, heck. He has me there.

HTE: It's not random, but it is luck. Certain accounts are always routed first to an owner, who looks after that customer personally.

Sniper87: Ah, so that's how it works. For your big customers?

HTE: Big ones and troublesome ones.

Sniper87: Well I know which kind I am. :-) Why don't you find out.

HTE: !!!

Sniper87: :-)

HTE: Not joking here. If I take an unplanned day off, or you sent in a request in the middle of the night, you'll be hitting on the guy we call the Dark Lord, maybe.

Sniper87: So you're saying we can't have really fun conversations over the Fetch chat.

HTE: Precisely. Sir.

Sniper87: I do like it when you call me sir. Gives me ideas.

HTE: Snipes!

Sniper87: Sorry, sorry.

Sniper87: I'll be good. If you insist.

HTE: I really do.

Sniper87: Five days is a long time not to chat. But I'll live. Later, HTE.

HTE: Later.

Whew. And now I've bought myself a little more time to think about whether we'll go out on a second date. I won't hear from him for a few days, and I'd be able to clear my head.

Ding!

I check the monitor again, and Sniper87 appears. Instead of writing a personal message, he's filled out the standard request form.

Request type: Pickup and delivery

From: Frankie's Florists on Yorkville Ave

When: After 2pm today.

Destination: Fetch offices, 99 ½ Scollard Street, for Ms. Hailey Taylor Emery

Notes: Please route this request to any staff member other than the elusive HTE. Gracias.

He's sent me flowers?

Wow.

That starts up a fresh aftershock. In my mind's eye, I see his sexy smile loom closer, and then he captures my mouth as I gasp . . .

Gah!

With a single click of the mouse I route the request to Jenny. Then I get up to go check out the pile of boxes that Dion warned me about. I'm not so addled that I've forgotten there's real work to be done. As I pass the bullpen, I hear Jenny let out a little squeal, but I don't catch her eye because I don't feel like seeing her I-told-you-so face.

Sure enough, there are a bunch of boxes accumulating outside Jackson's office. I sink down on my knees to sort through them. We receive lots of parcels for our clients here in the Fetch offices, because only by taking delivery can we verify that our orders actually arrive.

Many of these items come properly tagged with the customer's name or—in the case of those clients who remain anonymous—a Fetch ID on them. (*FBO MrEightInches*, etc.) But quite often the shipping label only says *Fetch, Inc.* So Jackson and I open the unlabeled boxes ourselves in order to preserve our clients' privacy.

The first box I open is an imported Japanese volleyball. The invoice says that it cost us seventy bucks. I stand and lean into the bullpen. "Anyone missing a fancy volleyball?"

STAY

Dion turns his head and cries, "WILLLLLSON!" just like Tom Hanks in *Cast Away*, while everyone laughs.

Then another Fetcher claims it for a client. Mystery solved.

The next package is full of toner cartridges for our office printers. Yawn.

But the third package leaves me in a quandary. After I open it, it takes me a moment to identify the contents. My first guess is sporting equipment, because there are stretchy bands attached to loops. But this contraption is accompanied by a weirdly large feather. And a pair of . . . furry handcuffs? They're actually pink leopard fur. No self-respecting leopard would be caught dead in this color. But whatever.

I find the invoice and note that the stretchy thing is an item called "personal restraints." And underneath the bubble wrap is a flogger. Medium weight, apparently.

Oh.

Oh.

The delivery is fascinating, but also problematic. In the interest of customer privacy, I can't hold these items up and yodel for their owner. Instead, I carry the box into my office and place it on the desk while I pull up our Fetch database. I re-enter my password and start trying search terms. Personal restraints comes up empty. Handcuffs pulls up seventeen different requests, but all of them are fulfilled, and none of them recent. Feather is equally useless.

"Hailey?" Jackson says from the doorway. "Where's the file on . . ." His eyes fall on the box and its contents. "Um . . . ?"

A nervous giggle escapes me. "These aren't *mine*, Jax. They arrived in a shipment today, and I'm searching the database for a hit."

His eyes close for a beat and then open again. Then, wordlessly, he steps further into the room. He pushes all the sex toys back into the box and closes the flaps one at a time. Then he tucks the box against his hip and carries it out of my office.

I watch him go, while my brain struggles to understand. Those items can't be for . . .

No. Really?

Really?

I can't wrap my head around it. Mild-mannered, skinny Jackson and his new girlfriend have a brand new flogger? Mr. Missionary Position on Alternate Tuesdays wants to dominate his girlfriend?

Or . . . The opposite? An image of Jackson kneeling naked in submission flashes through my mind, and I shudder, and then giggle hysterically.

What is the world coming to? Jackson, who alphabetizes his hair-care products, is having a torrid affair, and I'm cowering after a few good kisses.

A couple of hours later, Jenny appears with a cut-crystal vase containing three dozen long-stemmed pink roses. "There's a note!" she sings, waltzing into my office and plunking the flowers in the center of the desk. They practically fill the room. I've been trying not to think about Matt, and this will make it a hell of a lot more difficult.

He probably knows that. The bastard.

"Open the fucking note. I'm dying here," Jenny pleads.

"I'm surprised you didn't read it already."

She looks guilty.

"Jenny! Pass it over."

The envelope lands in my hands and I untuck the flap, pulling out a tiny piece of paper.

> Hottie. I had so much fun with you the other night. And I'm pretty sure you had fun too. Don't worry so much, okay? I just want to spend time with you. Text me on your personal phone at this number. M.

STAY

"Does he have you figured out or what?" Jenny asks, smirking.

"I hate you."

"Sure you do. But don't hate me too much or I won't help you figure out what to wear next time."

Oh shit. "I only hate you a little."

Jenny grins. "I love you a whole lot. And if you turn this man down again, I will not be nice about it."

"Right." I take a deep breath. "I'll be brave. I really will."

"You'd better."

And . . . I'm not.

I do not text him on his personal number.

Instead, I take a snapshot of the flowers and write a safe-for-work note on his Fetch request indicating that the flowers reached their destination and that they were lovely.

That night at home, I don't text him because he's busy. From the safety of my sofa I watch him beat L.A. He is *magnificent*, with a goal and an assist. And when I shut off the TV, I'm in awe.

I don't text afterward, because he's a hockey star who is busy with his teammates.

And I don't text the next morning, because he's on a plane to Denver.

I tell myself that Matt doesn't really care if I text. He'll probably meet a dozen attractive, available women at every stop on his trip. Maybe one of them is better positioned to handle all the terrifying hotness of Matt Eriksson.

Maybe one of them is in his bed right now.

That idea makes me feel cold inside. But Matt is probably the kind of guy who can have a one-night stand and forget about it the next day.

And I'm not.

Matt takes me so far out of my comfort zone that our first date caused me a week of shallow breathing and a loss of focus. I've never been so shaken by anyone.

That can't be a good sign.

I coast along with this logic until the day arrives when I know he's returning to Toronto. It's not that I'm a stalker. I'm a rabid hockey fan, and I know the team has a home game the following night. Yet I'm practically buzzing from the knowledge that Matt Eriksson is headed into the Toronto metropolitan area.

God, I'm hopeless.

Sitting at my desk, I spend the whole morning wondering whether he's back yet and what I should do about it.

"Hailey?" Jackson startles me out of my reverie by poking his head into my office. "Do you happen to have the information we compiled last year on piano-tuning services?"

"Sure." I look up and meet his gaze for the first time since our awkward moment over the box of bondage equipment. He looks the same as he ever did, with a crisp, button-down shirt covering his slim frame, and tidy brown hair.

"Is it in here?" he prompts, waiting. And I realize I'm staring.

I tug on a file drawer and rifle through it, pulling out the information he's looking for. "Here you go."

He departs, and I watch him leave. This gentle man who divorced me has branched out to try new, exciting things. (Exciting to him, anyway.) And I'm just sitting here like a lump instead of sexing up my ideal man.

For the tenth time this week I tell myself to buck up. Only this time I dig out the florist's card with Matt's personal phone number on it. I wake up my phone and . . .

Ding! The Fetch queue on my computer screen announces a new priority request from Sniper87. Speak of the devil.

I click. I read.

> <u>Sniper87</u>: *From Whole Foods please bring two New York Strip steaks, and a double serving of whatever potato side dish they have. Hopefully it's that cheesy one. And salad greens for two. I also require a bottle of a meaty red wine. Cabernet, something the wine*

STAY

guy likes for around thirty smackers. Also a bottle of champagne, chilled. And two slices of whichever cheesecake looks good. But not the whole cake because I'll eat the leftovers. Delivery between six and seven, please.

I read the whole thing three times, cursing myself. But facts are facts.

Matt is having someone over for dinner. He's serving steak and champagne. Furthermore, he's basically asked me to plan his romantic evening at home for him. It couldn't be more obvious if he'd taken marker to cardboard, like Jenny's hockey sign, and written: THIS COULD HAVE BEEN YOU.

Unhappiness slices through me, and it's a long time before I remember to breathe. But right before I pass out, I take a gulping breath and remind myself that this was all avoidable.

Lesson learned. Message received.

I spend the rest of the day trying not to feel sorry for myself. At five I go into the bathroom and reapply my makeup. If I should happen to run into him in the lobby of his building, I don't want to look like a loser.

At five twenty I descend into the madness of Whole Foods at rush hour. I choose wonderful things for Sniper87—beautiful cuts of meat and a bottle of red that the wine guy swears will make even cynical angels weep.

It's all for the best. It really is.

At ten minutes to six I arrive at his building. My timing is calibrated to bring me to his door *before* he'd be home. I'd rather miss him than see him.

"Perishables? Those have to be brought upstairs," the concierge informs me when I try to hand over the bag. "I can't handle that for you."

I should have sent Jenny.

When the elevator brings me to the third floor, I've already thought up a solution. I'll leave the bag outside his door and then mark his order "delivered." He's a smart man. He'll find the food.

But when I reach the door, there's a piece of paper taped to its surface. *Hailey Taylor Emery*, it reads.

I grab the paper off the door and flip it over.

Hottie— Since you won't text me, and I can't ask you out on the Fetch website, will you please come inside and have dinner with me? —M.

The relief I feel is so swift and strong that I almost collapse on the rug like Rufus after a long walk.

I stand there on the carpet for a moment longer, trying to get a grip. But it's pretty much hopeless. Matt Eriksson is on the other side of that door, and he's waiting for me, even if I'm an idiot who can't write him a text.

I'm terrified, but I'm going in anyway. Raising my hand, I knock on the door.

HANGING UPSIDE DOWN FROM A CHANDELIER

Matt

I feel like a teenager on prom night as I get up to open the door. Not because I'm anxiously wondering whether I'll get laid—I got laid long before prom night—but because there's something nerve-wracking about this whole thing. I haven't seen or heard from Hailey since the night at the opera, and now I'm forcing her into a date I'm not sure she wants.

As I reach for the doorknob, it occurs to me that maybe she's not even at the door anymore. Maybe she knocked, left the food on the mat, and sprinted back to the elevator. I wouldn't blame her. I mean, what man asks a woman to pick up all the stuff for their dinner date and deliver it to him? Is that romantic as fuck, or a total dick move? Could go either way, I guess.

A breath of relief slides out when I find her on the other side of the door. She looks a bit shell-shocked as she holds up a large paper bag, all big eyes and slightly flushed.

"Hi," she says.

"Hi," I answer. A small smile springs up as I gesture to the bag. "Hope you got us the good stuff."

"Everything you requested."

We stand there for a second, eyeing each other. She must have come straight from the office, because, underneath her winter coat, she's dressed in a white button-up and simple gray pants, similar to what she wore the day I stopped by Fetch unannounced.

"Would you like to come in?" I tip my head toward the space behind me.

After a beat, she nods. "I really would."

In the front hall, she slips out of her coat and looks around for somewhere to put it.

"Let me take that," I say, my voice roughened by nerves. Her dark hair looks thick and glossy under the bright hall light, and I resist the urge to slide my fingers through it. She's damn pretty. Shorter and thinner than what I'm usually attracted to, she makes me feel like a giant. I find that I don't mind it, though.

"WOOF!" Rufus gallops into the room. He skids to a halt when he sees who it is. And five seconds later he's located his leash and dropped it at her feet.

"You just went for a walk!" I scold. "Leave Hailey alone. She's here for me this time. Tough luck, pal."

Rufus lets out a whine that makes both of us laugh.

My dog has broken the tension. I lead Hailey into the kitchen and unpack the groceries. "You didn't text," I say bluntly.

"I know."

"Why's that?"

She shifts her feet and says, "Because."

I fight another smile. She shouldn't be reminding me of my kids, but Junebug does the same thing sometimes—sticks out her chin and says "because." Hailey didn't do the chin jut, but still. "Because what?" I prompt.

But I know the answer, even as she goes quiet to contemplate her response. The opera date—or rather, the ride home—freaked Hailey out. Truth is, it freaked me out a little, too. I was hard as a rock that night, dick straining to burst out of my pants. It's been a long time since I wanted someone that bad. But holy smokes, the dress she had on, and that fucking tattoo—I wanted to run my tongue all over it. I wanted to devour her that night.

I probably came on too strong.

So I voice that thought. "I came on too strong on our date last week," I say with a sigh.

Hailey fixes those blue eyes on me. "No," she assures me. "You didn't. I had a really great time. And I, uh . . . enjoyed making out with you . . ." She trails off, and I have to swallow a laugh.

She looks so embarrassed, and it's cute as hell. "I enjoyed making out with you, too," I say solemnly.

"Oh. Um. Good to hear."

Yeah, I still make her nervous. I wish I knew how to fix that, but I'm not a Hailey expert yet. I'm still just getting to know her and what makes her tick. Kara used to accuse me of being clueless about women. She expected me to know what she was thinking and feeling at all times, and when I fucked up, it was because I wasn't trying hard enough. According to her, anyway. But I'm not a mind reader. I can't even begin to guess what goes through a woman's mind at any given time.

Hailey's easier to read than Kara, though. Right now, she's squirming and blushing, and I feel oddly proud that I'm picking up on that. I step closer and place a hand on her arm. "We probably moved too fast that night," I admit. "So how about we slow it down? Let's just have some dinner and go from there?"

She hesitates. Then nods again. "Sounds like a plan."

It's a plan that actually works.

Twenty minutes later, I've grilled up our steaks to perfection, Hailey's tossed a salad, and we're moving to the dining room table that Hailey or someone else at Fetch picked out for me. The steak is fantastic and the wine is perfect, and even though it was my black Amex that paid for the spread, I praise Hailey for her choices until she finally rolls her eyes and tells me to quit complimenting her.

Throughout dinner, I see her truly relax. I tell her about our recent string of road trips, and her eyes light up as I offer "behind the scenes" intel about my teammates and the games we've played. When I mention that Blake's knee took a ding during the last game, she gasps.

"No! Will he be okay to play tomorrow night?" Hailey sets down her wine glass and vehemently shakes her head. "I *knew* he looked wobbly skating off to the bench after that hit!"

I grin. "You watched the game?"

"Of course," she says haughtily. "The only way I'd miss a game is if I were lying in a full body cast in a hospital bed and couldn't reach the remote. And even then I'd bribe the nurses to put it on TV for me."

My grin falters slightly. I love that she's a rabid hockey fan, but at the same time, I can't help but wonder if that's the only reason she's here. Does she just want to bang Matthew Eriksson, pro hockey player? God knows I've encountered those women before. One of my ex-wife's biggest draws was that she didn't give a shit that I played hockey.

But I don't get the sense that Hottie is only here to bag an athlete. In the first place, she'd scurried off like a frightened rabbit after making out with me. I would've been more than happy to drop trou for her the night of the opera. *Ungh.* Just thinking about her tongue in my mouth makes my dick twitch happily.

Then again, this could be part of her game—the fidgeting and stuttering and nerves. Groupies have been known to get creative to stand out from the crowd.

No.

My gut tells me Hailey isn't a groupie. A fan, yes, but not one who wants to sleep with me just so she can tell everyone she did.

"Matt?"

I glance across the table to find her watching me as she raises her fork to her mouth. "Yeah?" I ask absently, because now I'm watching her chew and it's distracting. Her lips do this hot quivering thing that fascinates me.

"You just spaced out mid-conversation." She lifts an

eyebrow, and I like the challenge in her expression. "Am I boring you?"

"No, of course not." *You're making me hot.* Feisty Hailey is even more fun than shy Hailey.

She sets down her fork and dabs a finger on the corner of her mouth to wipe away a tiny dot of steak sauce. Then she licks the tip of that finger, and yeah, I don't think she's purposely trying to be sexy, but damn if a growl doesn't leave my lips.

"What was that?"

The words pop out before I can stop them. "I like watching you eat."

Jesus. That sounded like a cheesy come-on from a porno.

"Thanks?" Her cheeks turn brighter than tomatoes, but her voice is dry as she adds, "Yeah, I'm a great eater. Self-taught, too."

I snicker, and force myself to stop thinking dirty thoughts. This is only our second date, and I already freaked her out during the first one by mauling her at the opera. I really need to play it cool here, especially if I want a third date.

Do I, though? Want a third date?

I think so. Yeah, I do. But three dates is . . . a lot. By the third date with my ex-wife, we were already spending the night together and talking about our future. Granted, we were young and impatient and a bit stupid. We probably should've taken our time with the relationship instead of plowing forward at Mach speed.

With Hailey, rushing feels like the wrong move. But dating her could be the wrong move, too. As my ex can attest to, I suck at relationships. My job definitely isn't conducive to them—the lifestyle, the long absences, killed my marriage. I don't know what Hottie is looking for with me, but if it's something long term, I'm not sure I'm capable of that. But I can't come out and ask her what she wants, not on the second date. That would totally be rushing things.

STAY

Let me help you clean up." Hailey picks up her empty plate.

I quickly rise from my chair and swipe the plate from her hand. "I'll take care of it. Why don't you pour us some more wine?"

"Are you sure?"

I'm not sure about anything right now. "Positive. Go sit down in the living room. I'll be right there."

I cart our plates to the kitchen and do a half-ass job of rinsing them off before leaving them in the sink. From the corner of my eye, I watch as Hailey carries the wine bottle and our glasses to the huge leather sectional. She refills our glasses, then takes a dainty sip that makes me smile.

Yeah, I like her. I really do.

A moment later, I join her on the sofa. She's sitting at one end. I choose to sit in the middle instead of the other end, but I make sure to keep a foot of space between us. Playing it cool, remember?

"Should we put something on?" I ask, gesturing to the remote.

"Sure." Her eyes dart toward me and then back down at her wine glass. "You, uh, pick, though."

"Okay," I say slowly. It seems that the nervous Hailey is back. And all I did was sit down on the couch next to her.

Hmm.

"I have Netflix," I tell her. "But I don't make much use of it. I'm either on the road, or else I have the girls, and all they want to watch is shit with singing princesses."

Hailey's smile is sweet, but she doesn't look me in the eye.

Pointing the remote at the TV, I turn it on. A hockey game is the first thing to appear on the screen. That's no surprise because this is Canada and I watch the sports channels when I'm alone. "We could watch Montreal get their asses kicked by Detroit."

Hottie perks up. "Now there's an excellent idea."

She relaxes as we watch our rivals let in a couple of goals. But when I stretch my arm over the back of the couch, she freezes. Then she freezes again when the tips of my fingers brush her shoulder. Her shirt has sleeves, so I'm not touching bare skin, but the way she reacts, you'd think I was running an ice cube all over her naked body.

I gently move my fingers away. Hottie is attracted to me. I already know that. But she's a little afraid of me, too. We had a lot of fun during dinner, but physical stuff makes her jittery.

And now she's sitting a few inches away from me looking as tense as I've ever seen her.

I pull my phone out of my back pocket. "Hey, Hottie?"

"Mmm?" Her spine straightens like she's been called to the principal's office.

"Do you still have my phone number?"

"Yes."

"Good. Text me something so I have yours."

She rises from the sofa and fetches her purse. She's typing something as she settles back on the couch, and a second later my phone beeps.

I smile at what she wrote.

> **Hailey:** It's Hailey!

> **Matt:** Hi honey. Are you okay over there?

Her eyes lift to mine. She blushes, then starts tapping her phone.

> **Hailey:** I'm sorry. I'm terrible at this.

> **Matt:** At what?

> **Hailey:** Dating.

> **Matt:** Not true. We had a lot of fun during dinner.

> **Hailey:** Okay. We did. It's the after dinner part I suck at.

> **Matt:** You're bad at . . . sitting on the couch?

She looks up and gives me an eye roll. I grin back at her.

> **Hailey:** I'm bad at being so close to you. You're all big and intimidating and hot.

STAY

"You think I'm hot?" I say aloud, trying to keep a shit-eating grin off my face.

She blushes wildly but looks away, and I realize I've cut off the flow of words again.

Matt: I think you're incredibly hot.

Hailey: I'm not kidding. I'm so bad at this, Matt. I turn into a puddle of nerves when you're sitting next to me.

I take that as compliment, because it means I affect her as much as she affects me.

Matt: So you have a little phobia that makes you afraid to touch me. Do you know how they treat phobias, Hottie? With desensitization therapy.

She bursts out laughing on her end of the couch, so I run with it.

Matt: Seriously. We'll just ease you into it. What's your favorite sexual position?

"Seriously?" she yelps. "That's not a first-date conversation topic!"

Matt: Technically it's our second date. Just answer the question. This is an important step in your healing process.

With a snicker, Hailey bends over her phone. Two seconds later, another message pops up on mine.

Hailey: Wouldn't you like to know.

Matt: Um, yeah. That's why I asked.

Hailey: What's yours?

Matt: All of them. I studied the Kama Sutra in college.

She hoots with laughter. And, yeah, it's weird that we're texting on our date instead of talking to each other, which I can honestly say is a first for me. But it's working. Already her shoulders are losing some of their tension, and the blush on her cheeks is from laughter, not fear.

> **Hailey:** *All of them? Did you try the one where you're hanging upside down from a chandelier?*

> **Matt:** *Oh, you mean the Inverted Monkey? Of course. First thing I crossed off the list. But I'm not 19 anymore. That position requires some serious stretching. We could just keep it basic tonight. Lotus for a warmup, maybe. Then the Mating Mantis. A couple of headstands. Keep it simple.*

She snorts as soon as she reads it.

> **Hailey:** *This is how you convince me I'm not in over my head?*

> **Matt:** *Good point, honey. The truth is I'm a really simple guy. And I've been simply fantasizing about seeing that tattoo on your back again. I want to trace it with my tongue.*

After I hit send, I watch her face and see her breath stutter when she reads what I've written.

> **Matt:** *I want to figure out if it wraps around onto your breasts. I'd have to run my hands over your skin while I check. Then I'll need to inspect you everywhere for more tattoos, because I wouldn't want to miss any.*

She whimpers, and I harden just from the sound.

> **Matt:** *First, maybe I can convince you to kiss me again. I'm right here, honey. Come get me.*

I set my phone on silent and toss it on the coffee table. I look around for my wineglass, but I don't get the chance to reach for it. Because suddenly Hailey slides onto my lap, straddling me. There's a hot look in her blue eyes as she takes my face in two hands and pulls me into a kiss.

Not for nothing have I spent two decades of my life practicing my reaction time. Wrapping my arms around her, I pull her in, parting her lips with my tongue and tasting her. She melts down onto my chest with a sigh, and the kiss goes wild immediately. We battle for control, tongues tangling.

When Hottie makes up her mind about something, then watch out, world. My dirty mind wonders what she'd look like riding my dick, a determined gleam in her eyes . . .

"You made that sound," she informs me as we break apart, panting.

I blink. Swallow through my lust. "What sound?"

"The growly one." She bites her lip. I want to bite it, too, and it takes superhuman strength to keep my hands off her.

"Sorry." I swallow again. Then I think fuck it, and say, "I'm ridiculously attracted to you, Hottie. I figured I should be upfront about that."

"Shut up and kiss me again, Snipes."

I feel like a fucking god right now. So I drag out the anticipation by planting a hand on her shoulder and stroking gently. The other drifts up her slender neck before cupping her cheek. I sweep my thumb over the corner of her mouth, over the same spot where that bead of steak sauce had lingered before. I wonder if that tangy taste is still there. So I decide to find out.

Hailey makes a tiny sound of surprise as my lips brush that spot. My tongue comes out for a taste and *yeah*, it's tangy. Sweet, too, because now I'm nibbling on her bottom lip.

A breathy noise escapes her lips. "Matt . . ."

"Mmmm?"

"You're still not kissing me."

My tongue licks a sweet line across the seams of her lips. "Soon," I whisper.

"Now," she whispers back, and that one passion-laced syllable snaps the thread of my control.

My mouth is on hers in a nanosecond, tongue slipping out

to tangle with hers. It's the kind of mind-melting, toe-curling kiss that hardens my cock and numbs my senses. All I can feel is the heat of her mouth, the delicious taste of her, the bite of her fingernails as she digs them into my shoulder.

"Fuck," I groan. And then I plant my hands on her ass, pressing her lower body against mine.

She moans against my mouth. I eagerly drink up the sound, kissing her hard and deep while in the back of my mind a voice shouts for me to slow it down. But fuck, she's amazing. So soft and supple in my arms, kissing me back with eagerness that seems to surprise her. In fact, every time we break apart for air, there's a shine of wonder in her eyes, as if she can't believe we're doing this. Or maybe, that she can't believe she's enjoying it. She looked the same way on opera night—stunned, amazed, and greedy for more.

Hell, if she hadn't been married before, I'd wonder if maybe she was a virgin.

"You're . . . so . . . hard," she breathes between kisses.

Fuck yeah, I am, baby. Except I realize she's not talking about the rock in my pants. Her hands are now tracing my pecs and abs over my shirt, as if she's trying to memorize every plane and ridge of my torso.

"And you're so soft," I breathe back, my hands drifting up to cup her perky tits. Soft, all right. My mouth goes dry at the thought of kissing and licking those soft, sweet breasts. I almost unbutton her shirt right then and there, until she kisses me again and proceeds to distract me by grinding lightly over my crotch.

The heat of her core is an even bigger lure than her tits. My hand is between her legs before I even realize it. Hailey gasps in delight as I cup her, then moans and rubs herself over my palm.

"Fuck," I groan again. "I need . . ." I don't even know what I need. It's been so long since I've done this that my entire body is trembling with excitement. My brain has stopped working. My fingers work just fine, though. They're already popping open the button of her pants, easing the zipper down, slipping inside her panties.

Hailey's eyes go big when my thumb brushes her clit. I did *not* intend to let one kiss lead to *this*—stroking her slick paradise, sliding one finger into her damp heat. But it's fucking happening and it's amazing. Every sound she makes is like a hit off some fantastic drug, fogging my senses and turning me on more and more. Will she sound like that when I'm inside her? When my tongue is flicking against her clit?

The dirty images summon a strangled groan from my throat. Fuck. I'm close to coming and all I'm doing is fingering this woman.

"Matt," she says, a note of desperation in her voice. Her chin rests on my shoulder, her hips moving in time to the slow thrusts of my finger. "I . . ."

"You what, Hottie?" I say thickly. "You want to come?"

She peers up at me and nods wordlessly, and something about her earnest, nakedly honest expression drives me wild with desire. I add a second finger, and holy fuck she's tight. Really tight. And wet. And hot. And . . . yeah, I'm in danger of shooting my load in my pants. I really am. Which means I need to make her come—ASAP. Because at least then we can lose control together.

I lean closer and press my lips to hers, kissing her as I move my fingers in and out of her tight channel. Her breathing becomes shallow, lips trembling against mine as I bring her closer and closer to the brink. My thumb tends to her clit, rubbing slow, gentle circles over her swollen flesh, and her breaths are even more labored now. Yeah, she's close. Any second now, I'm going to feel her pussy convulsing around my fingers as she—

Buzzzzzz!

The loud noise rips our mouths apart.

"W-wha . . ." Hailey blinks in confusion.

"Shit," I mutter. "Just the doorman." I try to ignore it. I give it my best shot, kissing her again.

Buzzzzzz!

Hell. The front desk doesn't bother tenants unless it's

actually important.

We both give a sigh of defeat. With the utmost reluctance, I slide my fingers out of paradise and gently ease Hailey off my lap and onto the cushion. Then I get up in search of the cordless phone I always misplace. I find it on top of the fridge, of all places.

"Yeah?" I'm a tad irritable as I greet the doorman.

"Sorry to bother you, Mr. Eriksson, but you've got visitors," Henry says politely.

My forehead creases. "Who is it?"

"It's your ex-wife and daughters, sir. I know you have a guest, so I asked them to wait a moment. But Mrs. Eriksson is rather impatient to be let up."

What the hell? My gaze swivels to Hailey, who's discreetly fixing her clothing and buttoning her pants.

Shit. What is Kara doing here? She never shows up without calling first.

A sliver of fear pierces me. Are the girls okay? Oh fuck, now I'm worried.

"Let them up," I blurt into the phone.

And then I hang up and hurry to the living room to check my cell.

Shit.

There are five missed calls from Kara, which I didn't see because my phone was on silent. There are also two text messages, which I'm terrified to read. Jesus, if something happened to one of the kids . . .

Pick up your damn phone, Matt! Emergency!

My heart jumps into my throat, but the fear dissipates slightly when I read the second message.

Girls are ok. But I'm dropping them off at your place. You better fucking be there.

As if on cue, the doorbell rings.

"I'm sorry," I tell Hailey, who's still staring at me waiting for an explanation. "My kids are here, apparently."

Her face pales. "What?"

Rather than respond, I head to the door, open it, and find a

STAY

frazzled-looking Kara and two pyjama-clad pre-schoolers.

"Mommy cut her thumb off!" Libby shouts when she sees me.

"Not *off*," Kara quickly corrects. "But I need stitches."

"There was b-blood," June whispers, attaching herself to my legs and hanging on tight. "I don't like blood."

"And Mommy said a bad word!" Libby announces. "But then she said we could have a slumber party with Daddy!"

June holds on to my legs even tighter. "You were gone *forever*, Daddy."

"Just for a week," I say, trying to make light of my absence even though my heart clenches hard.

Kara mutters under her breath, "A week can feel like forever when you're home alone and waiting."

I give her a sharp look, but luckily, I don't think the girls caught that. Still. She can blame me all she wants for the demise of our marriage, but she's not going to fucking do it in front of our kids.

"Can you fix Mommy's thumb?" June asks, bottom lip quivering.

I put a palm on her warm little head. "Okay, calm down, everyone. Let me see that thumb, Kara." She's holding it wrapped up in a dish towel, and I tug her hand toward mine and flip the cloth open.

"What? You don't believe me?" Her brown eyes flash. "Would have sent you a photo if you'd answer your phone."

"I'm sorry. My phone was on silent," I admit. "How did you do this?" There's a deep slice in the pad of her thumb, and when I expose the wound it oozes blood. But, hey. I'm a hockey player. Blood doesn't faze me.

"Daniel and I were julienning organic carrots for the girls' lunch tomorrow."

And he couldn't stitch it up for you himself? Oh, that's right, he's a dentist, not an actual doctor.

I shove the mean-spirited jab out of my head before my mouth can give it voice.

"He's waiting for me downstairs in the car, actually. I

would've left the girls at home with him if I didn't think I'd bleed all over the steering wheel driving myself."

Although I'm inwardly bristling, I choose not to comment on the fact that Kara's boyfriend was at my old house, preparing lunches for *my* kids. At least he's not fucking living there. Yet—but I push that notion aside.

I apply more gentle pressure and wrap it for her again. "Stitches are a good idea."

Kara winces at the thought. I feel a rush of sympathy for her, but it evaporates when she pushes past me into the room. "Girls, your bedtime is in thirty-seven minutes and— Oh. Hello."

I know the moment Kara spots Hailey, because her tone turns to ice. So does her gaze. Gulping, I watch as my ex-wife takes in the scene before her. Hailey's tousled hair and rumpled clothing. The two wine glasses on the coffee table

After a long, tense moment, Kara's head swings back to me. "I see," she says coolly. "So this is why you can't be bothered to answer your phone? Because you're too busy entertaining college girls?"

I frown, while Hailey's cheeks turn beet red.

"Hailey, this is Kara. Kara, Hailey." My tone is as frosty as Kara's. "And I can assure you, she graduated from college a long time ago." At least I think she did. We haven't even discussed shit like post-secondary-school education yet. We're still just getting to know each other. But I'm not admitting that to Kara.

"It's nice to meet you," Hailey says faintly, and I see her edging toward her purse as if she's planning her escape.

"A pleasure," Kara replies, though we all know pleasure is the last thing she's feeling right now. Then she dismisses Hailey with her eyes and turns to me. "I can't take the girls to a germy emergency room. And there's no way to know how long this will take, so I figured the girls would just spend the night here and I'll collect them in the morning. I assume that's all right?"

"Of course," I say tersely. I'm not about to let my children hear me say they aren't welcome. But Kara clearly has no

STAY

qualms about restricting my access to the girls until the moment she needs something.

Kara sets her jaw, then winces as if the action causes her pain. She squeezes her thumb inside its wrapping. "Christ."

Her obvious discomfort thaws some of my anger. She might have been rude to Hailey just now, but she's obviously panicked. "Go," I tell my ex-wife. "Take care of it. The girls will be fine."

Kara stays rooted in place. She stares at the wine glasses again, then at Hailey, and it's easy to guess what she's thinking.

"Don't worry, I was just leaving," Hailey blurts out.

Startled, I glance over at her. "Stay," I find myself saying, even while Kara scowls at me. "We can watch a movie with the girls."

The suggestion goes unacknowledged. Hailey simply slings her purse over her shoulder and sprints to the door. "Thanks for dinner, Matt!" she calls without looking back at me. "I'll just let myself out."

A second later, she's gone.

LATHERBLATHER

Hailey

The next morning, I work for a few hours in peace. With my office door closed, nobody bothers me. And I absolutely force myself not to think about the prior night's disasters. But my solitude goes to hell at noon when Jenny arrives for a twelve-to-nine shift.

At 12:01, Jenny pounces.

"Where did you disappear to last night?" she demands from my doorway.

"I . . ." That's as far as the sentence gets. The truth is that I'm still trying to figure out what happened to me last night. Encounters with Matt always leave me a little befuddled.

For example, did I *really* grind on his lap while our mouths were fused together? And then, did my lifelong crush slip his hand inside my panties and nearly make me come, while I moaned like a porn star? One thing I know for sure—mid-groan, we were interrupted.

With a different kind of groan, I put my head in my hands.

"Oh honey!" Jenny yelps. She shuts the door and flings herself into the visitor's chair. "Tell Auntie Jenny what happened!"

"It was wonderful and terrible," I whine. "Like all my

encounters with Matt."

She makes a sympathetic noise.

"That shopping order he put in was because he wanted to make me dinner," I start, and Jenny squeals with delight. "That part of the night was really fun. I was able to calm down and turn off the . . . what did you call it?"

"The latherblather," my friend says with authority.

"Wait . . ." I say, just noticing the take-out cup in her hand. "You went to the coffee shop without me?"

"Sorry," she says. "If you tell me what happened, I'll run out and grab you one."

"You want me to humiliate myself without coffee?" I grumble. "That's cold."

She removes the top of her cup and hands it to me for a sip. "Now spill. The story. Not the coffee."

Right. I take a single gulp and hand it back. "After dinner, we sat on the couch."

Her eyes light up with glee.

"He could tell that I was terrified. So he made a bunch of jokes to calm me down. Then he dared me to kiss him."

She leans forward, bracing herself on the edge of my desk. "And then?"

"And then I kind of lost my mind. I attacked him like Rufus attacks a doggy bone."

"Whoa!" Jenny's eyes are saucers. "Did you get a *bone*? Right there on the couch? In front of those floor-to-ceiling windows? Was it *awesome*?"

Embarrassment heats my neck as I realize that there *are* giant windows in Matt's apartment. And I don't think the blinds were drawn. Not only did I give him a lap dance but I performed for all of Yorkville, too.

"Omigod, you did!" she shrieks. "You're my hero!"

I shake my head quickly. "No! I didn't. It's a long story. But he makes me *crazy*, Jenny."

"That's the best!"

"No!" I argue. "It isn't. Not at all. You said so yourself—I used to be a confident person. And I need to start dating again.

But Matt is not the guy for someone who needs to go back to Dating 101. He doesn't make me confident. He makes me nuts. When he's in the room I'll say anything. I'll *do* anything." *I'll unbutton any piece of clothing.* Yikes. "I need to date someone who doesn't give me the . . ."

"Sluttyflutters?" Jenny suggests.

"Exactly!"

"On the other hand . . ." she starts.

But she's interrupted by Jackson, who's standing in the doorway to my office. "The slutty . . . what?"

My face heats another ten degrees. "Is it time for our meeting?" I ask my ex, hoping to throw him off the scent of a story.

"Our meeting? There's nothing on the schedule."

Of course there isn't. But I'm desperate here. "Right. Then what did you need?"

"Uh." He gives Jenny the side-eye. "Can we talk?"

My stomach twitches nervously. Those words never begin a happy conversation. "Sure," I say, giving Jenny a pointed look.

With a disappointed sigh, she takes her coffee cup and heads out the door.

I've extracted myself from one difficult conversation only to find myself in another. "About the other day," Jackson says when she's gone.

"I didn't see a thing," I stammer, thinking of the sex toys on my desk.

He frowns. "I know you haven't seen it. That's why I want to show it to you."

"You . . . what?" I rack my brain for a reason we'd be talking about sex toys. I'm obviously missing something. "Wait. What is it I'm supposed to see?"

"A property on Bayview." He frowns at my obvious confusion. "For the expansion."

"But I thought you weren't ready to expand!" I sound hurt even to my own ears. But he's not making a lot of sense right now. "You said it was too soon."

He leans his head back against my doorframe and closes his

eyes. "I don't know, I guess. My dad thinks this lease is too good to pass up. It's right near all those Bridle Path mansions."

"And you want me to see this property?" I'd rather take the carefully sharpened pencils out of my pencil cup, hunt down Mr. Emery, and stab him with them.

"I guess so." He opens his eyes. "What do you think of the idea?"

I hate it. "Any property on Bayview has got to cost a mint. It must be twice what we pay for this place." I throw out an arm to indicate our Yorkville spread, which is only affordable because it's on the second story of a small building, and Mr. Emery is our landlord. "How much is it?"

When he quotes a number, I groan. "And you think this is a good idea?"

"I think . . ." He pauses to chew his rather thin lip. I never saw it as thin until right this second. But just last night I was up close and personal with a set of bossy, bruising—

Focus, Hailey!

" . . . we could do well in that neighborhood," he says slowly. "Just take a look? See it before you decide."

"All right," I agree, managing to keep my tone civil. "But we can't make this decision just based upon a lease opportunity. If you're serious about expanding, I'm going to calculate the ROI based on the density of that neighborhood and the average cost of residential real estate per square foot. Then I have to compare the results to other cash-rich neighborhoods. Like Rosedale."

That will only take me about fifty hours.

Jackson nods. "Fine. But look at the place, okay? I need to get back to my father."

Of course he does. And I'll probably become first woman convicted of office supply murder.

When Jackson leaves, I pull up some data about the Bridle Path. I should really be working on our mobile-app rollout, and the interruption makes me growl at my computer.

"Wowzers," Jenny says from behind me. "That's the sound of sexual frustration."

"Stop," I bark.

"Fine. Is this a bad time to mention that there's a new request from . . ."

My heart leaps.

" . . . Mr. Dick?"

It crashes to the ground again. "What does he want?" I spot the red notification in the corner of my screen and click it. "A *swing?*" I giggle, feeling the tension leaving my shoulders for the first time in hours. I wonder if the Bridle Path has a colorful clientele, too.

"The specs make me think I can find him something at Home Depot. Or a sex shop. But look at the picture. Please?"

I shift my computer browser to pull up the request on the big screen. And then I'm disappointed, because MrEightInches is not himself today. There's no penis in the picture. Only a beamed ceiling, with hooks embedded in one of the beams. "So he'll have a place to hang the thing," I say. "That makes your job easier, I guess?"

"Hailey! Look at the wall."

There is a bit of wall showing. When I squint, I see more hardware bolted in. There's some kind of chain hanging there. And beside it I can just make out a row of . . ."Are those *floggers?*"

"Seems so."

"Are you even surprised?"

Jenny shrugs. "Why didn't you have sex with the hockey god yet?"

The question catches me entirely off guard, so I blurt out the truth. "I would have, but we were interrupted by an emergency."

Her eyes widen, probably because she hadn't expected her sneak attack to work. "What kind of emergency?"

"The intimidating kind," I admit. "His ex-wife showed up looking like a supermodel, with her twin girls in tow. She cut her thumb and declared a national emergency."

Jenny makes a face. "I hate her for interrupting your first night of sex in a million years."

STAY

"Two years," I correct.

Her eyes bug out. "Two? But your separation was only eighteen months ago!"

Well, this is embarrassing. "Next topic, please."

"Oh *dear.*" She looks truly stunned. "No wonder you turn into a gibberflibber every time he turns up."

"But most men don't make me do that," I point out. "Just him. He's obviously the wrong choice to break my dry spell."

"No." Jenny reaches across the desk and smacks my hand. "That means he's exactly the *right* guy. Did Jackson ever turn you into a bumbleberry?"

"No. Just Matt. I humiliate myself nearly every time we're in the same room. And he has two *kids*, Jen. Seriously. There's a whole bunch of people in line for his attention."

Jenny's wince is just proof that I'm right. "The kids are tricky," she admits.

"The whole situation is tricky. This is like . . . deciding I'm interested in doing a little rock climbing, and then flying to Everest for my first excursion."

"The scenery, though!" She fans herself. "Let's talk about how you're really just a big chicken."

"I'm not!"

"You are."

"Am not!"

"Hi ladies," a male voice says from the doorway. Once again my heart leaps and then dives. It's not Matt.

"Hi, Tad!" I greet him with great enthusiasm, because he's interrupted the dumbest argument Jenny and I have ever had. When I bounce out of my desk chair, he looks a little startled. "Weren't we going to have coffee sometime?"

His eyes widen. "I believe that was the plan."

"Is now good? Jenny went for an espresso without me."

She rolls her eyes.

"Now would be *very* good." His smile leaves no room for doubt that Jenny was right. He had been trying to ask me out, and I missed it.

"I'll just get my coat."

We go to the coffee shop on Yorkville Ave. But instead of getting takeout, we have a seat at one of the little tables in back.

Talking to Tad is easy. I don't feel any shimmies or flutters in inappropriate places. It's soothing. We end up discussing television. Turns out we're both excited for a new season of Sherlock.

"A 'season' is usually only a few episodes, though," I point out.

"True," he says, his brown eyes smiling at me. Tad is empirically attractive. He has a good haircut and a friendly smile. He's a little lean for my recent tastes, but he carries himself well, and wears clothes that suit him. With his turtleneck sweater and his hipster glasses, he looks more like a Club Monaco model than a techie nerd.

Also in Tad's favor? I haven't stuttered once since we sat down to talk. I'm perfectly calm the whole time. He doesn't make me stutter or feel sweaty. He's just . . . Tad. I lean forward a little, wondering if the zap of attraction I'm hoping to feel is somehow held back by the width of the oak table between us.

But . . . nothing.

Interesting.

"After Sherlock is over," he says, "there's always hockey. I know how much you love hockey."

I offer a wry smile. "Speaking of hockey, where's your Toronto hat today?"

The tips of his ears go pink. "Flew off when I was running to the subway station the other week. It was either save the hat and miss the train, or lose the hat and make it home on time."

"I would've chosen the hat."

"Of course. The three pennants and the Toronto pencil cup in your office could've told me that."

He smiles, and it's a nice smile, but once again I don't feel a single spark. "I bet if it was your, say, *Boston* cap, you wouldn't have picked the train," I tease.

STAY

His blush deepens. "Damn. Who gave me away?"

"Jenny. But don't worry," I add graciously, "it's all right with me if you want to root for Boston over us. Foolish, but all right."

Tad chuckles, then tells me about the time he had tickets for a Toronto home game against Boston but then got stuck in an elevator in midtown. It's a pretty good story, and I'm a good listener. But as he's telling me how he used his cell phone to call the building security, I suddenly feel it! A flush spreads across my chest, and everything starts to tingle. I feel myself smile a little wider. I sense something important happening . . .

"*Hottie.*"

I jump three inches in my seat, and my forearm knocks over the dregs of my coffee. I flail for the napkin but it goes sailing off the table.

Two seconds later, Matt Eriksson has retrieved my napkin and dropped it tidily onto the modest puddle of spilled coffee. Leaping to my feet, I take him in. In sweatpants and a Toronto jacket, he must have just come from the morning skate. He's the most casually dressed man in the shop and the hottest by a factor of a thousand.

I'm just goggling at him, still stunned by his sudden arrival. And Tad is faring even worse. His mouth has flopped open, and his eyes are the size of the CDs he uses to install new software at our office. "You're . . ." he stammers.

At least I'm not the only one who loses it a little when Matt shows up. Tad might not be a Toronto fan, but he's still a hockey enthusiast, and all diehard fans go a bit nuts in the presence of a professional athlete.

"Hailey," Matt says with a jaw that's tighter than normal. "Aren't you going to introduce me to your friend?"

"This is T-Tad the techie," I blabber. "Tad, this is Matt Eriksson."

Tad pulls himself together. He stands and thrusts a hand into Matt's, pumping it. "It's a pleasure, sir." Hesitating, he glances between us. "So, uh, you two know each other?"

"You might say that." Matt retrieves his hand from Tad's.

Then he uses it to cup the back of my head. He places a firm, possessive kiss on my cheekbone. "We need to have a little chat, you and me. If you have a moment."

"Oh, we're done here!" Tad volunteers with a nervous chuckle. He grabs our cups off the table. "See you back at the office, Hailey!" He's gone so fast I think I see a contrail all the way out the door.

"What was that?" I demand, finally shaking off my surprise. "You chased off my coffee date."

"Date?" he asks, his strong jaw lifting in a way that's so sexy I can practically feel the testosterone rolling off him in waves.

"Well, not a *date* date," I correct. "He's upgrading our servers with a new installation."

"An *installation*, I bet." Matt snorts and takes my hand in his. "Don't go back to the office yet. Unless you have to?"

I simply shake my head because the . . . flutternutters or whatever Jenny would call them have set in again, and I don't think I can string words together.

"Good," he says, his voice rough. He scoops my coat off the chair and tugs me toward the door.

Outside, we're greeted with a blast of early December cold air. Matt stops and pulls the coat around my shoulders. "Come with me."

"Where?" I croak.

He jerks his head down the block, where his apartment building rises up over the busy street. "We have some unfinished business."

"We do?"

He moves fast, backing me against the bricks of the coffee shop's exterior, his chest against mine, his lips brushing my forehead as he speaks. "We have some very *pressing* business to attend to." His hands steal inside my unzipped coat to land on my waist. "Don't you agree?"

A hot gasp escapes my chest as his mouth travels down to my ear, giving it a nibble. I'm clutching his jacket now, ready to do whatever he asks. And right here, probably.

But in a flash, Matt steps back, grabs my hand and marches

me toward his building.

"Good day!" the doorman says as he admits us.

"It sure is," Matt says cheerily as he guides me toward the elevator bank and leans on the button. "And it's about to get even better," he whispers when the doors part.

When the doors close behind us, he backs me up against the wall of the car. I have time to take one deep breath of his freshly showered scent before he attacks my lips with a hungry kiss.

My head thunks against the wood paneling as he deepens the kiss. This Matt isn't taking it slow. This is the same Matt Eriksson who grabs the puck on a power play and makes a press for the net.

My inner goalie tosses her stick away and forgets to worry. I wrap my arms around his generous frame and hold on for dear life as his kisses travel to the sensitive skin of my neck, where his hungry mouth causes goose bumps to rise all over my body. The sweep of his lips toward my ear makes my knees buckle.

"I didn't like that we were interrupted last night," he whispers hoarsely between open-mouthed kisses to my rapidly heating skin. "Went to your office to apologize."

So how'd you find me? I think to ask. But the words don't make it out of my brain, and I just moan instead. His hands have gripped my hips and I can feel myself getting less coherent by the second. My palms wander between the unzipped halves of his jacket and down the ridges of his abs. He hisses, then leans in—

The elevator dings, announcing our arrival on his floor.

He groans and tugs me off the wall. "Let's go, Hottie. Time's a-wasting." He steers me toward his apartment door and punches in the code at warp speed.

Inside, he lifts the coat from my shoulders and drops it on the floor. Then he does the same with his own.

"You need a coatrack," I point out.

"Later," he grunts.

I have one last rational thought: *there are coatracks at Yorkdale Shopping Centre.* But that's it for thinking, because Matt kisses me again, and we're on the move down a hallway. One possessive hand lands on my ass, giving it a squeeze that steals another ten IQ points.

Then the backs of my legs find a bed, and I . . . freeze. I just stop, mid-kiss, and ice runs through my veins where there was only heat a second before. Because I don't know what the hell I'm doing. My lifelong crush wants to have spectacular sex with me, and I don't have a clue what that means.

"Hottie," he whispers, and his hands turn gentle. His fingertips skim lightly up my back and then down again. "What's wrong?"

"Y-you m-make me s-s-so nervous," I sputter.

He smiles, and it's sweet. His knuckles sweep across my cheek and then he kisses that spot, too. "I know. There aren't any drills for this."

"Wh-what?"

His chuckle curls through my body like a flame. I didn't know it was possible to be so turned on and so scared at the same time. "You're out of practice, right?"

"Right." It's just that I'm starting to think I never had any game to begin with. He makes my body light up in ways so foreign to me that it's clear I've been doing something wrong my whole life.

"So let me coach this round. I'll call the plays. You just listen for the whistle."

"Okay," I say immediately.

"Your coach wants you to unbutton that shirt." His smile is a little teasing, but also kind.

My fingers find their way to the buttons on my blouse and begin to obey.

"Good girl," he whispers, sliding it off my shoulders and tossing it onto a chair I picked out at Crate & Barrel. He leans in to place a soft kiss at the juncture of my neck and shoulder. He moves downward, past my collarbone, tracing the line of my white lace bra with his lips.

The goose bumps are back. And the heat. My fingers find their way into his hair and tug his head closer to my breast.

STAY

His lips nuzzle me, and he lets out a groan. "Coach needs you to remove this bra," he says huskily.

I hesitate, because I've always felt pretty underendowed. And it's awfully bright in here . . .

"Coach is waiting, Hailey," he says, kneeling in front of me. "Be a good recruit and lose the bra while I take care of this." Thick fingers find the zipper of my wool trousers and drag it slowly down. The sound of the zipper's teeth makes me gasp. With fumbling hands, I find the clasp of my bra and unhook it.

Matt isn't watching as I ditch the bra onto the floor. He ducks down, his lips finding the skin just north of my bikini panties. He kisses me there and I feel a rush of desire *everywhere*. Then his eyes lift and he groans. "Fuck, Hailey. It's gonna be an effort to go slow." He reaches over his head and grasps his T-shirt by the back collar. "But warmups are important." He hauls the shirt over his head and tosses it aside.

And, oh, the view! My mouth begins to water at my first sight of all that male perfection. He yanks my pants down and then stands up, where I blink at him, my eyes traveling all over his chest.

"That's right," he says. "Now touch me. Both hands."

My greedy fingers leap to do his bidding. I skim my palms over his pecs, and his breath catches. I let my fingertips explore the ridges of his washboard abs. The dusting of brown chest hair thickens as it approaches the waistline of his sweats, and when I run my fingers over it, his stomach tightens.

"Mmm," he growls. And when he lifts his hands to cup my breasts, I let out a whimper that makes him smile. "I know, honey." He strokes his thumb over my nipple, and I clench my thighs together. "Good girl. So responsive to your coach. Now I want you naked and on that bed." He clicks his tongue. "Let's go, trainee."

I scramble to obey, and a moment later I'm lying in the center of his comforter, wearing nothing but my own desire for the god who's prowling toward me on hands and knees. He's down to a pair of black cotton boxer briefs and a smile. I should be cold, but I'm burning up as he looks down at me, his eyes sweeping over my body before he drops his head to take one of my nipples into his mouth. His tongue circles and I moan, long and loud.

He lowers that perfect body down onto mine, his mouth claiming my own. The heavy weight of him is delicious. "Fuck," he groans between kisses. "Your coach is anxious to get this game underway."

I giggle into his mouth. He's hot and hard, and everything is *wow*. I work a hand down his chest again, finally reaching for the ambitious erection that's straining the cotton to its maximum capacity.

We both sigh happily.

"Good girl." He sits up a little. "Take it out."

"Yessir." I push the briefs down and the most gorgeous cock I've ever seen (in my vast experience) springs into view. When I wrap my hand around all that perfection, he lets out a hiss.

I lick my lips as a drop of liquid appears on his tip.

"Taste me," he barks, sitting back on his heels.

I move to my knees and dip my head, my forehead skimming his abs, and the clean, salty scent of him envelops me. I lick the pearly drop from his tip and he growls. Suddenly, a big hand grasps my hair tightly. I'm not expecting it, and a shiver runs through me as my subconscious registers my helplessness in this situation.

For a split second, panic shows its face again. It's the middle of the workday, and I'm naked with my two-hundred-pound client. He's got me by the literal scruff of the neck.

Another hand lands on my upper back, caressing me sweetly. "Such a good girl," he whispers. "The coach is proud of you." And just like that, I melt onto him, his cock sliding into my mouth. "Suck me, honey," he rasps. "Take it all."

I moan as he fills my mouth, the heavy weight of him on my tongue. It's a lot to handle, so I have to back off right away. The hand in my hair relaxes immediately. I take a deep breath through my nose and try again. His moan is so sweet that I want to hear it again. Relaxing my throat, I figure out how to

STAY

take him deep. Before long we have a rhythm, his powerful body rocking forward, fucking my mouth in short strokes.

The hand tightens on my hair, and I'm drowning in my own desire. *Suck me, honey.* The words vibrate through my core. *Take it all.* Nobody has ever said anything so wonderfully dirty to me before. I give a good, hard suck and his rhythm stutters.

"Ungh," he pants, cupping my chin and stopping me. "On your back now."

Dazed, I release him with a pop and blink up at him.

"Glad you were into that, honey. But I have other drills for you. Okay?"

I nod.

"Say, yes coach." He winks.

"Yes coach," I whisper, and he smiles.

Then he reaches behind me and grabs my ass, which he then slaps. "Lie down."

IN A MINUTE, BUDDY

Matt

Hailey spreads herself out on my bed, and I turn away for a minute just to calm down. I make myself busy kicking away my underwear and finding a condom in the nightstand. I open the packet and roll it down over my aching cock.

I damn near lost it when she was giving me head. Every time she lifts those trusting blue eyes I get a little more turned on. Her gaze gets a little hotter every time I issue a command. Hailey wants me in spite of her nerves. And I can sense that she likes it a little dirty, but that the urge confuses her.

Good thing her coach understands.

I turn back to see her lying there, watching me with a heated gaze. As I move toward the bed, she shifts her hips and sighs.

Gawd. The sight makes me crazy. I'm eager to please her, and a little nervous to have sex for the first time since my marriage ended.

But I don't let her know it. "Warmups aren't quite done," I say lightly. "Put your hands on your breasts."

She blinks.

"Right now," I order, putting a knee on the end of the bed. "Touch them."

She raises her hands and cradles her breasts in her hands,

cupping their fullness. The sensation makes her sigh again, and my balls tighten at the sound.

Easy, I tell my dick. Hailey isn't the only one who needs firm guidance right now.

"Tease your nipples," I growl.

She does as I ask, arching her neck and closing her eyes. Her cheeks are stained pink, and I have to wonder if she's ever touched herself in front of a man before. And now I feel like pressing the issue. "Hailey." Her eyelids fly open. I kneel at her feet, and nudge her ankles apart a few inches. My mouth waters at the sight of her wet pussy. "Touch yourself for me."

Her hands grow still on her breasts.

"You heard me." I reach up and take her hand in mine, giving it a squeeze. Then I place it gently on her mound. "Show me where you want my mouth."

Her breath catches and she clenches her thighs.

"Show me," I coax. "It's okay, you pretty thing. Touch yourself for me."

She swallows, and finally her fingers trace the pretty little triangle of hair between her legs. She eases her thighs apart, and then her fingertips dip down to slide over her clit. Then she checks my face for approval.

I approve, alright. In fact, I can't wait any longer. Leaning down on my forearms, I kiss the back of the hand that's slowly stroking her clit. The scent of her arousal tightens my balls again. *Jesus.* I nudge her hand aside with my nose and lick up the center of her.

Her moan is a sob. I take her thighs in both hands and deepen my kiss. My tongue slides without effort. She's so wet and ready that my dick leaks in sympathy. *In a minute, buddy. I'm busy here.* Hailey gasps, arching off the bed, pressing her core closer to me, riding my tongue. It's so hot that I break out in a sweat across my back.

A minute or two later, and she's close already. "Oh, no you don't," I chide, moving my kisses to the inside of her thigh. "Not without me." Her legs try to catch me and hold me close, but I press her hips down into the bed. "Don't get ahead of the coach," I warn, just to keep things light. But I'm dying for it. I kneel between her legs and wrap my hand around my girth. Our eyes lock, and the fog is gone from hers. There's just desire there. It's beautiful.

The anticipation is so sweet that I drag it out one beautiful moment longer. If anyone knows how fleeting intimacy is, it's me. "You are so fucking beautiful, Hailey," I say as I drag the head of my cock through her soft, wetness. "This is perfect." Then I lean down and give her a quick kiss as I push myself inside.

She moans as I fill her. I press back up again onto my hands, so I can watch. Maybe hockey players make shitty husbands, but I'm a great lover. I take a deep breath to keep control of my eager body. Then I give her a nice, slow thrust. Hottie squeezes her eyes closed with pleasure.

"Look at me, baby doll. The way I'm looking at you."

Her eyes open again, and she smiles up at me. All her nerves are finally gone.

"I love this," I promise. I capture one of her silky legs under my arm and pick up the pace. "You feel like heaven, and you look like an angel all splayed out on my bed. You like my cock, don't you."

It isn't a question, but I get an answer anyway. "Yes," she gasps as her back arches toward me again. Her fingers reach out to grip the comforter as I pick up the pace.

"Come on my cock," I urge her. "Want to feel you."

Her hands lift to my chest, and the slip of her fingertips over my heated flesh feels amazing. "I can't come during sex," she whispers. "But I still love it."

Seriously? I slow it down a notch and admire her gorgeous body beneath me. "How do you want to come, then? You want my mouth again?"

"Don't need to," she says on a sigh. "It's all good."

No way. I mean—some women aren't able to get there. It's just that I don't think Hottie is one of them. "Okay," I say, because I don't want to pressure her. Then I pull out. "Coach wants you to roll over."

STAY

Her eyes widen in surprise, but her hesitation only lasts a fraction of a second. And when she turns, I groan at the sight of that killer tattoo all over her back. "You hot thing." I lean down and taste the smooth skin of her shoulder. Then I lift her hips and slide inside again. My mouth is right at her ear now. "You make me crazy," I murmur.

She lets out a happy sigh.

I slip a hand beneath her, right between her legs. "You taste so good right here," I say as she grounds down on my hand. I give her a nice, dragging pace until her breath hitches. "You like that, don't you? Tell me."

"Yes," she gasps.

"Ride my hand, honey. I need to come."

She fucks herself backward onto my cock and I have to grit my teeth as my balls tighten.

"Oh," she pants, and the note of desperation in her voice is beautiful.

I recite the first verse of the Canadian national anthem in my head to distract myself.

"Maaaaatt," she chokes out. And then I feel it—the first sweet pulse of victory. She moans and I curse as my control falls to pieces. I give it to her fast now, my body shaking with eagerness. I wrap my arms around her silky body and shudder as I pour myself out in several energetic bursts.

My mind goes absolutely quiet then. We lay there, recovering our breath. I roll Hottie over and cuddle her, my eyes falling closed. I'm supposed to be napping, anyway. "I thought you said you never come during sex," I slur sleepily.

"Seriously?" Her voice is teasing, and she kisses my shoulder. "You don't strike me as the kind of guy who has to fish for compliments after sex."

I open my eyes and smile at her, because she totally called me on my bullshit right there. But then the smiles slide off both our faces, and we're left looking deeply into each other's eyes. A different kind of warmth spreads inside my chest. "Everyone needs a compliment now and then," I point out quietly.

She tucks her cheek against my shoulder and sighs. "Well, I'm pretty sure I just paid you a big one. Talking about sex isn't my strong suit. But everything about today has been amazing."

I stroke her hair, and she leans into my hand. I'd only had sex in mind when I sought her out today. But the peacefulness of this moment is just as rare, and it's just as sweet. I'm getting something I didn't even know I needed.

"Question," Hailey whispers after a while.

"Mmh?"

"Do you always hum 'O Canada' while you have sex?"

I let out a very unsexy snort, and she giggles. "No. That was special. Only for you."

"I'm honored."

"Tonight when I'm singing it again from center ice, I'll think of you."

"Wait!" Hottie sits up suddenly. "It's game night? Holy crap. I forgot. Get up! You have to beat Dallas! I think you guys can win this one, especially if Coach Hal doesn't monkey with the defensive pairings."

I grin into the pillow. "It's nap time, Hottie. Simmer down."

"No. Now I'm all distracted," she says, poking me in the ribs. "Who's starting?"

I grab her, roll, and pull her onto my chest. "I don't know. You want to come to the game?"

"Am I breathing?"

We cuddle for another minute until my sex-fogged brain realizes there's a problem with the invitation I just extended. "Actually . . . I gave my seats away to a charity. The dog rescue program."

"Dogs? Where's Rufus, anyway?" Hailey lifts her head off my chest. "Is he hiding somewhere from all the sex noises?"

"I took him to the doggy ranch before I went to find you."

"Oh. How *did* you find me?"

"Jenny. She was more than happy to send me to the coffee shop in search of you." I run my hand through her soft hair. I'll have to thank Jenny. I owe her one. "Anyway, I give most of my tickets to charity. They auction off the seats for big money."

"I'll bet," Hailey says enviously. "Those seats are virtually priceless. It's okay. I'll watch you on TV."

"You can still come," I clarify. "But you'll have to watch from the WAGs box."

"Where?"

I chuckle, wondering if this is a terrible idea. But Hottie is the greatest, and I want to do something nice for her. "There's a private box for wives and girlfriends. I can ask the box office to put a pass together for you. But you'll have to come alone. Shall I do that?"

She's quiet for a second. "I'm always up for watching the game, Snipes. I don't care where. But of course I'd love to see it live. That just goes without saying."

I give her a squeeze. It's been a long time since I held anyone, and I'm enjoying it immensely. "I'll get you that pass. Game starts at eight. I need to catch an hour of sleep, though. Lie down."

She sighs. "I can't. If I'm going to the game tonight, I have to finish up everything else first."

"Your loss," I say, trailing my fingers across her lower back. "I'm a good napping partner."

She leans down and kisses my shoulder. "I'll bet."

I get one more kiss and then let her go. Catch-and-release style. "You okay?"

"Peachy."

"Not nervous?" I ask, just because I'm feeling cocky.

"Stop," she says, grinning over her shoulder at me. "Unless you need your ego stroked along with your . . ."

I laugh again. "Good workout today, recruit. Keep up the good work. Practice makes perfect."

She gives me an eye roll and then scoops her panties off the floor. I watch her get dressed with hungry eyes. "I didn't plan this well. Would rather have gotten you into my bed when you didn't have to get out of it right away."

"You are very sweet." She seems to be making a hasty getaway, though.

"Sure wish you could come back over tonight. But I won't get home until midnight, and we're leaving for the airport at five tomorrow morning."

"Ouch." Hottie buttons her blouse. "Beat Dallas, okay?"

This girl kills me. "I'll do my very best," I vow.

PROPERTY OF MATTHEW ERIKSSON

Hailey

I t's a few minutes before eight o'clock when I pick up an envelope from the Will Call window at the stadium. I expect to find a ticket inside, but instead it's a plastic card with my name on it in shiny letters.

"For the use of: HAILEY TAYLOR EMERY" it reads.

Below that it says "Property of: MATTHEW ERIKSSON."

How oddly they've phrased it. *Property of.* I know they mean the card, but it sounds like they're referring to me. There's also a creamy business card which reads only: "Suite 7."

"Good evening, miss," a guard tells me when I show him the card. "Enjoy your evening."

"But I don't know where I'm going."

"Ah." He smiles. "First time? You'll need to take the escalators in that direction." He points. "Your card will activate the turnstile. Then read the plaques on the doors. If you're spending time with the WAGs, you should know that the strawberry daiquiris are strong."

"Thanks," I say, hoping it will make more sense when I find the right spot. I get on an escalator, which slowly lifts me away from the madness in the rest of the stadium.

Since leaving Matt's apartment earlier in the day, I feel I've done a first-rate job of pretending that everything is normal. It isn't, though. Stopping by Matt's apartment for earth-tilting sex is not normal. Even if I kissed him goodbye and nonchalantly pulled on my clothes again, my inner Hailey was still chanting, *Oh. My. God.* And, *Did that really just happen?*

In the office, Jenny had swarmed, trying to get the story. But I didn't yield. I need a little time to make sense of the day's events and how I feel about them.

And then there was Tad! He'd stuck his head into my office late this afternoon. "So you're, like, dating Matt Eriksson?" he asked tentatively.

"I . . . don't really know," I'd admitted. *Even though I just had naked, dirty sex in his bed after our coffee date.* "I'm a little confused about the whole thing."

Tad laughed. "Hope you figure it out, then."

So did I.

As the escalator climbs higher, I try to see today from Matt's perspective. We've been on one date, where we made out at an opera and in the back of a hired car. Then he made me dinner and we were interrupted before he got the big payoff he was probably expecting.

So today he came looking for it. I gave it to him. And tomorrow at five in the morning he's headed to the West Coast for a four-game road trip—the longest of the season. I'd checked.

It's anyone's guess whether he'll still be interested in me when he returns to town after his trip.

The escalator takes me to a long, curving corridor. Then there's a turnstile in my way. I wave the plastic card with my name on it, and the glass barrier slides aside to let me pass. I follow the corridor. Elegant wooden doors every twenty feet or so, each with a brass plaque. The first ones I pass have the names of financial institutions on them. Suite number seven, though, is labeled: WAGs.

Beside the door is a card scanner, the sort you might see outside a hotel room. I hesitate there, wondering who is seated inside, and whether they'll think I'm imposing. That sounds awkward. But it's two minutes to eight, and the thought of missing the start of the game is a great motivator. I wave the card in front of the scanner, and the door clicks open. I glimpse several women standing in the open space, backlit by the glare of the rink beyond.

To my dismay, a dozen heads of shiny hair swivel in my direction all at the same time. Yikes.

"Hi there," I say with a smile. The truth is that I'm not actually a shy person. Not unless Matt Eriksson is in the room. A room full of strangers doesn't really scare me. But this room is paneled in walnut and softly lit by shiny sconces on the walls. There's a thick oriental rug on the floor beneath my feet. And facing the rink are three rows of generously sized plush chairs. A bar and buffet line the wall beside me.

This place is seriously kitted out for the wives of the team, and I'm not sure why Matt sent me here.

"I'm Katie Hewitt!" a woman says, bounding toward me. "Welcome to the WAGs box. You're a guest of . . . ?" The room is silent, and all the women are listening for my answer.

"Matt Eriksson."

There is a collective intake of breath.

"He, uh, donated his seats to the dog rescue. So he told me to watch from here. If that's okay," I add, stupidly. But they're staring at me with fascination.

Katie is the first to shake off her apparent surprise. When she claps her hands together, I swear an entire jewelry store's worth of diamonds flashes in front of my eyes. "Matt? That sneaky Pete! I didn't know he was seeing anyone!"

"We're, uh . . ." I realize I can't finish the sentence. I have no idea what we are.

"Have you known him for long?" she tries.

"At least a year," I say, wondering how to explain the odd beginning to our relationship. "He's a client. I have a personal assistant company called Fetch . . ."

Katie's eyes practically glisten. "And he fetched himself a girlfriend!"

I laugh nervously. "Not exactly—"

STAY

"Katie!" another woman chides. "That sounds terrible."

"I didn't mean it like that," Katie insists. "Fetch is cool. I just used it for the first time last week to find my aunt some tulips to cheer her up. It's hard to get tulips this time of year."

"But not impossible," I can't help but say. "We have all the specialty florists in Toronto in our database."

There's an appreciative murmur. Something tells me these women receive a lot of flowers.

"Hey! You're back!" someone else says, and I turn my head to find Jess Canning, who swoops in to give me a hug. "I, for one, am not surprised to see you here. Girls, Matt was all over her at the opera."

"Yikes," I say aloud. I seem to be capable of anything when that man is nearby.

Katie cackles. "At least someone was having fun at the opera. Hailey, would you say you're more of a hockey fan or an opera goer?"

"Hockey all the way," I confess. "I'm more fluent in hockey."

She beams.

"Let's get you a drink," Jess says, pointing at the refreshments. "We have all kinds of beer and wine. And Katie makes a mean strawberry daiquiri. But pace yourself because if Matt scores tonight you'll be expected to do a shot."

"I will?" I say with no small amount of alarm. I haven't done shots since college.

"Sure, unless you don't drink. This isn't a sorority initiation."

"It's close!" someone hoots.

Having been warned about the daiquiris, I grab a beer. Katie opens it for me with shiny red fingernails, and then the girls steer me toward a seat. The national anthem is underway already. I feel tingly with excitement, and it has nothing to do with the earth-shattering sex I had a few hours ago, and everything to do with hockey.

Because hockey.

There are a few more minutes to wait. They're setting up a

ceremonial puck drop on the rink. I sip my beer and receive a few more greetings from players' wives. I'm good at remembering names—that comes naturally to me. But I wonder if there's any point. These women are being awfully nice to someone who's probably never going to repeat her visit to the most privileged spot in all of Toronto.

But I'm sure going to enjoy it while it lasts.

The door to the suite bursts open, and a short woman with curly black hair arrives like a windstorm. "Girls!" she shouts. "You'll never guess who asked us for a pass tonight!"

"Was it Eriksson?" Jess asks with a grin.

The newcomer's eyes sweep the room and land on me in my comfy seat. "Ah!" she says, tossing her purse onto a side table. "That's what I get for being late to the party. Welcome, Miss Hailey! We're happy to see you. That poor man needs someone to love him right." She looks me up and down. "Are you up to the job?"

Gulp. Her stare pierces me, and I don't know what to say. Loving Matt Eriksson sounds like the easiest job in the world, but I really can't assume that I'm going to get the chance.

"*Estrella*," Jess protests with a giggle. "We don't interrogate people until their second visit, remember? Not until they figure out that we mean well."

Estrella smiles. "Sorry. It's just that he's been through a lot." Her gaze travels over my head to the ice. "Faceoff time!"

My attention whips back toward the rink. The ref drops the first real puck of the evening, and that's it. I'm gone. The WAGs and their questions fall away, and I'm lost to the tug of the game beneath me.

Matt is skating with Wesley and Riley tonight. They look *on*, too, passing amongst themselves with barely a necessary glance. When a line is working well together, it's instinctual. They sense each other's situations effortlessly.

It takes a few shifts of hard skating to shake up Dallas. Our first couple of shots on goal are deflected. Then their defense makes an error around the seven-minute mark that changes the game. Riley steals the puck, using his considerable bulk to box out his opponents. He fires a nearly blind pass to Wesley, who fires it to Matt.

He shoots, and I hold my breath. The goalie dives for it, and my blood stops circulating.

The light on the net is quickly followed by my shrieks of ecstasy. "YEESSSSSS!" I scream. "GET USED TO IT, DALLAS!" I'm jumping up and down. The jumbotron zooms in on Matt's handsome face, grinning behind the safety shield as his teammates congratulate him.

It takes a little more screaming to burn off my zeal, and then I flop back into my seat. My system is a little stunned at all this good fortune. Both orgasms and live hockey games are rare in my life, and having both on the same day is life-changing.

Someone taps me on the shoulder, and I look up to find Katie grinning at me. These women are probably used to having orgasms and hockey in steady supply. The cushy seats and beers are just icing on their gourmet cake of life.

"Here's your shot!" Katie enthuses. She hands me a shot glass with salt around the rim, and a wedge of lime.

Still high on Matt's goal, I toss it back, bite the lime and smile. The room promptly erupts with glee.

But we have a game to watch, and I'm all business.

The speed of play increases down on the ice. I can grudgingly admit that Dallas is a great team. The next portion of the game is tense and non-scoring. I forget my beer and everything else. When there's less than a minute on the clock, Dallas makes one more rush. I hold my breath again as Matt steals the puck. He can't get the pass off before a Dallas player reaches him, and the asshole uses a crosscheck that stuns me.

"Did you fucking see that?" I shout, leaping to my feet. "HEY REF! Clean your glasses or I'll come down there and do it myself!"

Estrella whoops from behind me. "Ladies, we have ourselves a hockey fan!"

I spin around. "Did you *see* that? He raised that stick high enough to play a game of limbo! Asswipe."

There is laughter, but I'm still seeing red.

"Breathe, Hailey," Jess says as the announcer begins to speak. "They gave the jerk a penalty."

Indeed, the offending player is making his way to the box. Matt skates off unharmed.

I sit down, and play resumes for only a few seconds before the buzzer sounds for the end of the period. Jess gets up to refill her drink, then flops beside me again and leans in with a smile.

"You're a blast," she tells me. "Are you coming to the next home game?"

Discomfort ripples through me. "I don't know," I admit, because I guess it all depends on whether Matt wants me to. I lower my voice and add, "I'm not really sure what's going on with me and Matt, if I'm being honest."

Either I don't speak quietly enough, or these women have superhuman hearing, because Katie Hewitt speaks up from the other end of the row. "You're his girlfriend," she says with a grin. "Totes."

I'm even more uncomfortable now. "I'm not. I mean, we haven't had the are-we-dating conversation yet."

Katie rolls her eyes. "Of course you're dating."

I frown. "Why are you so sure of that?"

She waves a manicured, diamond-ring-laden hand around the lavish private box. "You're here, aren't you?"

It can't possibly be that simple.

Can it?

Hailey: Good game! I'm sorta plastered because of you.

Matt: Yeah? I knew it would stink not to be able to see you again tonight. Did you do shots for me?

Hailey: Yap.

Hailey: Yurt.

STAY

Hailey: YES. Stupid phone.

Matt:

Hailey: Problem. Maybe. I mean, not for me. But maybe for you. A problem, I mean.

Matt: Um, help me out here. What?

Hailey: Tonight your teammates' WAGs informed me that I'm *your* WAG.

Matt: They did, huh?

Hailey: Ya. Apparently it's a big deal that I watched the game in their box. Why didn't you warn me?

Matt: Honestly, didn't even think about it. Just wanted you to see the game.

Matt: They didn't freak you out, did they?

Hailey: Not really. But . . .

Matt: But what?

Matt: ?

Hailey: I guess I am wondering what it means. Ugh. I'm being a girl, aren't I?

Matt: It's OK. Girls are hot ;) Especially when they're sorta plastered. Do you really want to have THE TALK over text?

Hailey: I didn't say I wanted THE TALK!

Matt: "I guess I am wondering what it means" = THE TALK. What do you want it to mean?

Hailey: I don't know. Drunk person here.

Matt: Do you like me?

Hailey: Hell yes!

Matt: And I like you. We're dating, right?

Hailey: Yes.

Matt: So that was easy, right?

Hailey: Are we just dating each other, though?

Matt: Ah, gotcha. You want the E-word.

Hailey: Echo? Earwax?

Matt: Exclusive.

Hailey: I wasn't even thinking about that. But . . . now I am. Are you seeing anyone else?

Matt: Nope. And neither are you. Because we're exclusive.

Hailey: LOL Is that so?

Matt: Abso-fucking-lutely. My flight gets in at 7 tomorrow. Dinner and sex around 8? Stay loose, Rookie. The coach needs you limber.

Hailey: Wow. Okay. I'm free then. Anytime, really. For that. I'm going to go now before I latherblather or sluttyflutter. Night!

Matt: I don't know what that means but I like the sound of that second one. Night!

GROWING BOY

Matt

"So when do we get to see Weather Lady again?" Blake asks as we lumber across Pearson Airport, heading toward the exit. "Wanna double date?"

I glance over him. "Weather lady?"

He nods fervently. "Yeah. The hottie from the opera."

"Still not seeing how you got weather lady from that."

"Her name's Hailey. As in, hail. As in, ice chunks that fall from the sky. As in, weather." Blake beams at me. "So she's the Weather Lady."

"Christ, Riley, your nicknames just get worse and worse," I inform him, shifting my carry-on duffel to my other shoulder. "Matty-Cake at least makes sense in some stupid Blake Riley way."

We step out into the evening chill and head toward the taxi stand. There's no line, fortunately, and we get a car in no time, the two of us jamming our huge selves into the backseat. Blake and I were the last ones to get off the plane, so most of our teammates had already hightailed it out of the airport to hurry back to their respective homes before Blake and I even cleared customs.

"My nicknames only get better," he disagrees as the cab

driver weaves out of the terminal in the direction of the highway ramp. "And you didn't answer the question. DD with me and J-Babe?"

"Can I assume DD means double date? One never knows with you." I pull my phone out of my jacket pocket to see if Hailey texted. We have late dinner plans for tonight. "I'll ask her," I say absently, my eyes on the phone screen. "But it might be too early for the double-dating thing."

Blake guffaws loud enough to startle our driver. "Too early? You sent her to the WAGs box, dude. You're practically engaged!"

Shit. I really didn't think things through when I gave Hailey that WAGs pass. I should've known that it would create a flurry of gossip and excitement in our incestuous little circle. But I genuinely wanted her to see another live game—the woman is a rabid fan—and those were the only seats I could score at the last minute.

Except now my teammates and their partners are all on my case. And even Hailey questioned the move by asking me if we were dating. And we are. I mean, of course we are. I'm not seeing anyone else, and have no interest in doing so. But I'm not thinking long term at all, either. I'm just dying to see Hottie tonight and fuck her brains out. I need the release after this last string of road games. My joints ache and so does my dick.

"My Blakey senses are telling me you're scared of the G-word."

I glance over. "The G-word?"

"Girrrrlfriend." He drags out the two syllables, a grin on his face. "But that's dumb. You shouldn't be scared, Matty-Cake. Fear is in the eye of the beholder, you know?"

"One, that's not the correct phrase. And two, it has nothing to do with this situation. I'm not afraid of having a girlfriend."

Okay, I'm lying. Maybe I am a bit afraid. But only because past experience has taught me that I fucking suck at that shit.

I hesitate, then bite the bullet and ask, "What's it like for you and Jess when you're gone? Does she get pissed? Lonely?"

Blake narrows his eyes, and then they widen with

understanding. Blake is so ridiculous sometimes that I tend to forget he's more perceptive than he looks. "Gotcha. I did that, too."

"Did what?" I ask in confusion.

"Compared everyone to my psycho ex. I told you about the psycho ex, right?"

I nod slowly. "The woman you were going to marry after college?"

He nods, too. "She was insecure with a capital insecure."

"A capital I, you mean."

"A capital everything, broski." Blake shudders. "She didn't trust me, and after that relationship exploded I was all like, women are nutso. Get laid and get out, am I right?"

"Right." Although I'm not sure the parallel holds up. Blake's ex was legitimately nutso. Kara isn't. And when she left me, she made some very valid points about how often I'd let the family down.

Blake's expression softens, as if he's thinking about something truly amazing. Which he is, because in the next breath he brings up Jess. "And then I met Jessie and it was, like, boom! This girl ain't crazy, and she trusts me. I'm going all in."

I shift my gaze out the window. All in, huh? Not sure I can do that again. Last time I did, I lost my wife and custody of my kids. Besides, Hailey hasn't said she wants a serious relationship with me, just an exclusive one.

"You'll see," Blake says cryptically. "When the boom's there, it's there. Anyway, double dating. Let's make it happen."

I simply shrug again and repeat myself. "I'll ask her."

For the rest of the cab ride, we each have our noses buried in our respective phones. Blake is sexting Jess, I bet. And while I'd love to be sexting Hailey, we seem to be having a dinner miscommunication.

> **Hailey:** Wait, I thought you were having dinner before we meet up. You said something about a post-game dinner, no?

STAY

Matt: *Post-game press conference. Why would they serve dinner there?*

Hailey: *Shoot. Sorry. Well, I literally just pulled a lasagna out of the oven and was about to sit down to eat.*

Matt: *Then why don't I head over to your place instead of vice versa?*

There's a long delay in which my screen remains blank, and I suddenly remember how she admitted that she still lives in the apartment she shared with her ex-husband. I wonder if it would make her uncomfortable to have me there. But on the other hand, I think it would be a damn good idea. Living with a ghost can't be fun for her. Maybe my presence will help her feel like the place is *hers* rather than some tomb to her marriage.

So I type another text.

Matt: *C'mon, Hottie. Feeeeed me. I'm starrrrrrving.*

I see her typing something.

Hailey: *Stop whining. It's unattractive :)*

I grin to myself. I can't wait to see her. And get her naked again. I'm dying to taste her again. To hear those breathy noises she makes when she's close to coming. Fuck, I need to make her come again.

And she needs it, too. I don't know when it happened, but somewhere between our first kiss and that first fuck, I came to the conclusion that Hailey needs sex. Good sex. And lots of it. I've caught glimpses of her steel, her confidence, her sexiness, usually in our online exchanges. But in person, it's like she's second-guessing herself all the time. The poor girl needs to get her mojo back, and I've decided I'm the man for the job. Just call me Matt the Mojo Maker.

"Later, Matty-Cake." Blake slaps a meaty hand on my shoulder as the cab comes to a stop in front of his lakefront condo.

I nod. "See you later, Riley."

Once he's gone, I give the driver Hailey's address and then we're back on the slush-covered roads, heading midtown. Hailey's building is a low-rise condo, about eight stories tall, with small balconies that face Yonge Street. Damn. Guess there won't be any fucking on the balcony, at least not without giving the bumper-to-bumper traffic on this busy street an eyeful. We'll save that for my high-rise, I suppose.

In the small lobby, I buzz Hailey's apartment. A moment later, the door clicks open and I ride the elevator to the fourth floor.

She answers the door with a hesitant smile. "Hey."

"Hey." Zero hesitation on my end as I kick the door closed and lift her into my arms for a kiss.

Our mouths lock together eagerly, tongues sliding out to say hello. It's the kind of frantic, greedy kissing that sends shockwaves straight to my cock. Hailey gives a tiny whimper and wraps her legs around my hips. Within seconds we're grinding up against each other and I'm harder than stone.

"Whoa, slow it down, greedy girl," I pant as I pull my mouth away.

"I'm the greedy one?" She's as breathless as I am. "You're the one who mauled me the second I opened the door."

"You mauled back harder," I tease.

Rolling her eyes, she gestures to my coat, which I remove and hand to her. She hangs it up and then leads me deeper into the small apartment. There's a dining nook next to the kitchen, and it's giving off the most fantastic smells. My stomach growls when I spot the huge serving of lasagna on one of the place settings.

Wait, only one place setting?

"I couldn't wait," Hailey says sheepishly. "I was famished even before you called from the cab. No way would I have lasted the forty minutes it took you to get here."

"It's all good, but that just means you get to watch me eat."

"Do you want something to drink? I've got water, beer, and wine."

STAY

"Beer me."

Chuckling, she ducks into the kitchen while I take a seat at the round glass table. She comes back with two Bud Lights, twists both caps off, and hands me one. I greedily take a swig, then dig into some of the best lasagna I've ever had in my life.

"Hottie can cook!" I say in delight.

She snickers. "Hottie can order ready-made meals, freeze them, and then nuke them when Hottie is hungry."

I snort and shovel more pasta into my mouth. I demolish the generous serving, then have a second helping while Hailey sits there with wide eyes.

"You're a beast," she marvels.

"Growing boy," I say between bites. "And I didn't get to eat after the game."

At the mention of the game, her expression sours. "That was a bullshit penalty in the third," she grumbles. "Wesley did *not* trip that jerk!"

Actually, he kind of did, but I love how loyal Hailey is to the team. We can do no wrong in her eyes. Though technically we did wrong tonight, since we lost to Philly. That penalty Wes took led to the power play goal that clinched the game for the other team.

"You can't win 'em all," I say, a surprisingly magnanimous attitude considering I fucking *hate* losing. But I think Hailey might hate it more. Jeez—a relationship in which *I'm* the level-headed one when it comes to hockey? Who woulda thunk it.

Not a relationship, I have to remind myself. We're seeing each other and having fun, but I don't envision engagement rings and wedding cakes in our future. I already tried walking that path, and it only led to a dead end.

We keep talking hockey until I finish eating. And that's always fun. But I can't seem to shake the awareness that things are supposed to be a little different between us now. That she's someone I can disappoint if I'm not careful.

I sure don't want that.

She hurriedly cleans up while I wander around the apartment, trying to get a sense of the woman living in it. It's hard, though. There's no art on the walls. The furniture is plain and slightly boring.

"So this was all the stuff you bought with your ex-hubby?" I call toward the kitchen.

Hailey pops out with a frown, following my gaze to the rather boxy, beige couch. "Yeah," she admits. "Jax doesn't like splashy things. He's all about neutral tones and clean lines."

Yet he married a woman with a nose ring and tats. Interesting. I wonder if, deep down, ol' Jack is more adventurous than he lets on, or if his long history with Hailey was the sole reason they ended up together. They knew each other when they were kids, so she wouldn't have had the piercings and ink when she was six.

Did he divorce her because she evolved into something he wasn't comfortable with?

Christ. Where are all these questions coming from? I'm not usually so curious about other people's past relationships. But having met Jackson—and noting how stuffy he seemed—I can't figure out how Hailey ended up with someone like him.

"I should probably get rid of it, huh?" She heaves a great sigh. "It's just so expensive to refurnish an entire apartment."

"I hear ya. I saw the credit card statements after your shopping spree for my place," I tease.

Her bottom lip sticks out as she stares at the rectangular coffee table. It's as sedate and personality-free as everything else in the living room. "We should've gone to your place," she says.

Maybe I'm not the only person experiencing a moment of hesitation. "Why? Because you bought this furniture with your ex?" I wave a hand. "I don't mind."

"I kind of do," she confesses, her blue eyes worried. "It's weird to have a man here who isn't Jackson. Like, I want to ask you to sit down, but I look at the couch and all I see is Jax on it."

I cock a brow. "You two get it on a lot on this couch?"

Pink splotches rise in her cheeks. "No. We only did that . . . um . . . stuff in the bedroom. And I did get a new bed," she's quick to assure me. "That's one thing I couldn't keep."

"Okay, so if you guys didn't bang your way around the apartment—outside of the bedroom—then what do you see when you look at the couch?"

"Jackson reading a book," she answers glumly. She gestures to the bar. "There, I see him reading the morning paper." She points to the balcony doors. "Or I see him out there reading our quarterly statements."

"Your ex did a lot of reading." I'm trying hard not to laugh. I shouldn't find this funny, because Hailey looks so distressed, but the idea that all Jackson Emery did in this apartment is *read* is so damn absurd. Look at who he was married to!

I take a deep breath and feel my own tension fall away. "Hottie. Come here." I crook my finger at her.

She takes a step closer to me, and I pull her in for a hug. Then I whisper in her ear. "How could your ex have his hands on some book or newspaper when those hands could've been on *you*? I don't get that at all."

She looks up, her eyes vulnerable.

"Let's make some new memories. Replace the old with the new," I clarify. "In fact . . ." I waste no time planting my hands on her slender hips and backing her toward the kitchen counter. Before she can blink, I lift her up onto one of the tall stools.

"What are you . . . doing?" she squawks when I sink to my knees.

I grin up at her, happy again because I've got this. I really do. "You said you look at this counter and picture your ex reading the morning paper, right? Well, after I'm done with you, all you're gonna remember is *this*."

I get her yoga pants and bikini panties off so fast that Hailey sputters with laughter. Then the humor dies and her eyes take on a panicky glint as she realizes she's half-naked. She tries to close her legs, but I make a tsking sound and stop her by placing my hands on her thighs.

"Nuh-uh, baby girl. Open up."

"Matt . . ." There's a slight warning there. "This is . . ."

"Hot?" I supply. My voice grows smoky as I stare at the perfect pussy that's inches from my mouth. "You're right. It is."

Then, before she can say another word, I close the distance between mouth and paradise and take a long, languid lick that makes both of us moan.

"Love how you taste," I whisper against her slick core.

"Mmmmmrghh," is her response.

I peek up to see that her eyelids have fluttered closed and her lips are parted in anticipation. Fuck yeah. There's nothing sexier than a blissed-out woman.

My tongue comes out for another happy lick. Hailey gives an answering shiver. I don't even notice the hard tile beneath my knees—knees that are sore as fuck from tonight's game. I'm too busy concentrating on pleasuring Hottie. I plant the softest of kisses on her clit and enjoy the way she gasps, the way she tries to tangle her fingers in my hair to trap me in place.

"Matt," she begs when I deny her what she wants by licking a path away from her clit toward her inner thigh.

"Simmer down," I murmur. "We're making memories here."

A choked laugh heats the air. "You're making me crazy, that's what you're doing."

That's what I like to hear. And so I keep going, making her crazier and crazier with my barely there licks, the hint of suction where she wants it before darting away to taste another delectable part of her. By the time I slide one finger into her tight sheath, I'm sweating with desire and my erection is damn near painful. But the slow, seductive exploration is worth it, because when Hailey comes, the orgasm lasts *for fucking ever.*

Her moans fill the kitchen. Her hips rock as she comes hard against my tongue, as her inner muscles squeeze the hell out of the finger I'm lazily thrusting inside her. When she finally crashes from the high, she pries her eyelids open and makes a soft, contented noise.

"You're . . . good at that."

STAY

"I know." Smirking, I rise to my feet and reach for my belt buckle. "You want to know what else I'm good at?"

Her blue eyes laser in on the bulge in my pants. "I already know you're good at that, remember?"

"Oh, I remember. I remember how tight you were," I rasp. "And how fucking amazing it felt to be inside you. I want to feel that again."

Anticipation shines in her eyes, but it turns to confusion when I take a step away. "Where are you going?"

I give the room a contemplative look. Eventually my gaze settles on the couch. Her ex liked to read books on that couch, huh? Sucker. I'd way rather fuck the goddamn cushions off that thing.

"Up, baby," I order, tugging Hailey onto her feet.

Then, like a caveman dragging his woman into their cave, I haul Hailey to the couch with all the finesse of a horny teenager. Before she's even settled on her back, I have my pants off and my dick covered with a condom. The adrenaline from tonight's game is still pulsing through my system.

"This is gonna be a fast ride," I warn her as I strip off my shirt. "So you'd better hang on."

Heat sizzles in her eyes. "Bring it."

Oh yeah. *This* is what I hoped to achieve tonight—coaxing the badass out of this woman. *I* know she's a badass. She just needs to remember that.

Within seconds, I'm buried so deep in her that I'm seeing stars. Hailey hooks her legs around me and off we go on the ride I promised, and, holy hell, it's fantastic. Each deep thrust threatens my control. Actually, what control? I'm horny and anxious and desperate to finish, and thank God I got her off before, because *finish* is actually what I do. Ten strokes, tops, and then I'm coming with a grunt, in a rapid burst of pleasure that sucks the breath from my lungs.

I sag forward, redistributing my weight to my elbows so my chest isn't crushing Hailey. "Sorry," I gasp against her cheek. "Told you it would be fast."

"Not complaining," she murmurs, wrapping her arms

around my shoulders. Her nails begin drawing little circles in the center of my sweaty back.

"I'll be ready to go again in . . ." Even as I withdraw, my dick twitches at the thought of another round, bringing a rueful smile to my lips. "Well, much sooner than you think."

She laughs, and then we both grow silent for a few moments. When she speaks again, it's with a note of wonder in her vote.

"New memories."

"New memories," I agree, rolling over so that I'm lying on my side with my arm slung across her flat stomach. I add, "I'm sorry I didn't text much these last few days. Hard to when I'm on the road."

Hailey shifts her head so we're eye to eye. "You were working. I get it. So was I."

I swallow my surprise. I expected some condemnation about the fact that I only texted her twice in three days—once to say *hi*, and another to say *tired, hitting the hay*. She sent several messages relating to the games I'd played, but I hadn't responded to them. Not because I was ignoring her, but because road trips are exhausting. I can barely keep my eyes open to punch in the floor number in the hotel elevator, let alone to have a whole text convo.

"You're not mad?" I hedge.

"Of course not." Her brow furrows. "Do you want me to be?"

"Of course not," I echo. Though I'm still a bit confused. If I'd gone three days without constant contact with Kara, the woman would've smacked me. She would've argued that it meant I didn't care about her, that I wasn't thinking about her.

And truth was, Kara would be right. There were plenty of times I wasn't thinking about my wife. Before a game, I get so focused on hockey that it's all my brain is capable of thinking about. Watching game film of the opposing team, prepping myself mentally, working out. The life of a professional athlete is about concentration, hard work, and determination—Kara knew what she was signing up for before she married me.

STAY

Besides, it's not like she even wanted me around half the time. She liked making all the decisions about the kids, the house, the finances.

Maybe because she knew I'd be shit at it?

Damn, the divorce really fucked with my head. It *hurt* when Kara sat me down at our kitchen table and calmly slid those papers toward me. Before that day, I'd never failed at anything so . . . *big* before. Small things, sure. But marriage?

I stifle a heavy breath and gaze at Hailey's face, her eyes still glazed from the sex. I don't want to fail her. I might not be able to promise forever, but I think her divorce screwed her up, too. I think she needs to spend time with a man who can't keep his hands off her, a man who can show her how fucking cool she is.

"Hey," I say suddenly. "What are you doing tomorrow?"

"Research," she answers. "We're thinking of opening a second Fetch location, so I'm looking into possible sites."

"You need to get it all done this weekend or can you take a break?"

"Why? What do you have in mind?"

"I'm taking the girls to the CN Tower tomorrow," I explain, grimacing. "I might need the moral support."

Hailey wrinkles her brow. "Moral support? But you get along great with your kids. You love them."

"Oh, I love them," I agree. "I'll need the support for another reason."

Her eyes fill with curiosity. "Oooh, tell me more."

"Nope." I sit up and cross my arms over my chest. Then I realize I still have my sweater on. And so does Hottie. And that makes me snicker, because we just had crazy hot sex and we both kept our shirts on?

"What's so funny?" she demands.

"Nothing." I bring my attention back to the topic on hand. "So you wanna come along?"

Hailey stares at me. "You're really not going to explain the moral support remark?"

"Nope," I say again, flashing her a cheerful smile.

"Why?" she whines.

"Because it's embarrassing," I answer frankly.

A slight smile tugs on the corners of her lips. "The mighty Matthew Eriksson gets embarrassed? All right. Well, this is one mystery I refuse to let go unsolved." Her smile turns into a full-fledged grin. "I'm in."

MORE THAN A THOUSAND FEET

Hailey

"**S**tay away from the window, Junebug! I mean it!"

Oh boy. I'm witnessing the impossible. Matt Eriksson . . . one of the biggest, toughest hockey players in the league, the man who can slay me with one crooked smile and bring me to my knees with one raspy-voiced word . . . is a wimp.

Okay, he's not a wimp. But apparently my hockey god is human. As in, a human who's deathly afraid of heights.

"But it's so pretty!" Matt's daughter whines. "I wanna see!"

"Me too!" Libby pipes up, dashing up to the huge glass window to join her twin.

Matt looks like he's about to have a coronary. His face is paler than the fluffy white clouds that we're pretty much at eye level with. Yeah, we're in the clouds. This tower is frickin' *tall*. More than a thousand feet, if the brochure in my hands is telling the truth. And is it weird that I've lived in Toronto all my life and never visited its most popular tourist attraction?

"Guys, listen to this," I say, reading from the crisp booklet. "There's something called an Outdoor Sky Terrace one level below us."

Matt makes a sputtering sound, his head swinging toward

me in sheer betrayal. "They let you go *outside?* From this height! Jesus Christ! I'm calling my lawyer."

I can't stop a laugh. "Your lawyer?"

"Yeah," he huffs. "To pre-emptively sue this place for all the murders they're going to be complicit in."

Sighing, I walk over and place a hand on his big arm. He's wearing a gray sweater that showcases every delicious contour of his torso, and faded blue jeans that hug his ass so right that I've already caught several other women ogling him. But it's hard for me to ogle when he's clearly so upset.

"Matthew," I say softly, and his lips twitch at my use of his full name. I stroke my fingers up his arm until they reach the underside of his chin. I firmly meet his eyes. "Breathe."

There's a beat. And then I hear the slightest intake of breath.

"This tower has been here for decades and it's still standing. People fly in from all over the world to see it. The elevators carry a gazillion people to the top every day." I sneak a peek at his girls to make sure they're focusing on the view and not us, then caress the strong line of his jaw. "We're perfectly safe up here. Okay?"

He exhales slowly. "Okay."

"That a boy." I give his cheek an exaggerated pinch. "Now come on, let's move a little closer to the windows. Libby wants to find out if we can see your condo from up here."

Matt crosses his arms over his chest. "You go. I'm good where I am."

Another laugh bubbles in my throat. I manage to tamp it down, though. Truthfully, it's a bit of a confidence booster to know that Matt is afraid of heights. It knocks him a foot or two off the pedestal I've put him on. Plus, it makes me feel like I'm more in control, when normally I feel so wildly out of control when I'm around him.

"Hailey, come see!" June calls. "I think that's a doggy down there!"

I bite my lip in amusement. I'm fairly certain that whatever she's seeing is *not* a doggy. From this height, she'd never be able to make out one measly dog. But I still humor the little girl, bending down beside her, squinting extra hard, and then agreeing that, yes, that teeny black dot hundreds of feet below is *absolutely* a dog.

"Daddy's sweaty," Libby whispers to me.

I glance behind us, then back at Libby's wide gray eyes. "Seems so," I confirm. "It's probably because it's so hot in here with all these people." I gesture to the crowd of tourists all around us. Everyone but Matt is oohing and aahing at the breathtaking view of the city.

"It's 'cause he's a scaredy-cat," Libby disagrees.

A snort flies out. "Well. Even daddies can be scaredy-cats sometimes."

June shifts her gaze from the window to study me. "You're pretty like my mommy," she says frankly.

Heat rises in my cheeks, while discomfort fills my belly. I don't like the comparison to Matt's ex-wife, especially since the former Mrs. Eriksson isn't just pretty—she's a bombshell. "Thank you," I manage. "So are you. And you," I add, smiling at June's identical twin.

"Your nose is shiny," Libby says in response.

It takes me a second to realize she's talking about my nose ring. June decides she needs to touch it, and suddenly two chubby fingers are probing the tiny silver stud, and I don't know whether to laugh or die of embarrassment.

"Does it hurt?" June asks curiously.

"Nope. Half the time I forget it's there."

"Do you have a dog?" Libby asks.

"Do you like ice cream?" June asks.

My head starts spinning as the girls fire seemingly random questions at me, but after the tenth or so inquiry, I realize they're asking me if I like the things *they* like. They're sussing me out, trying to figure out if I'm good enough to be their friend—or rather, if I'm good enough to be their father's friend.

I answer each question honestly, which I think they appreciate. Even though Libby turns her nose up when I admit

STAY

I hate gummy bears, she nods solemnly at the explanation I give—"I don't like slimy things in my mouth."

Matt snickers loudly at that. He's slowly been creeping toward us, not getting too close to the windows, but close enough to eavesdrop apparently.

"That's what she said," he coughs into his hand.

June notices her father and squeals. "Daddy!"

"You guys have enough of this view already?" he asks us. "Because I'm hungry."

"Liar. You're just looking for an excuse to hide in the restaurant," I accuse, and the twins giggle in delight.

He winks at me. "That too. But it *is* one o'clock, which is usually when the girls have lunch. What do you say, kidlets? Lunchtime?"

We end up in a corner booth in the family restaurant at the tower, not the revolving one that would probably put Matt in a straight jacket. As the girls babble to each other while eating chicken fingers shaped like animals, Matt slides one hand under the table and slips his fingers through mine.

"Thanks for coming along," he murmurs.

I smile. "Thanks for inviting me." I give his hand a teasing squeeze. "Though I think you only did that so someone could stand at the windows with your kids."

His answering smile is wry. "I'm sorry you have to witness this. I don't know what it is about heights, but . . . ." He gives an exaggerated shiver. "Man, I hate 'em."

"I like that," I admit.

He arches a brow. "You like that I'm a total pus—wimp about heights?" He shoots a glance at his daughters to make sure they didn't hear his almost-use of *pussy*.

"No, I like that you're not invincible." I reach for my soda and take a long sip. "It makes me feel less inclined to stammer and stutter in your presence, knowing you're such a wimp."

"Ha ha." He studies my face for a moment. "You haven't stammered and stuttered in a while, now that I think about." A grin stretches his sexy mouth. "Could someone finally be warming up to me?"

I warmed up to you the day we met. I melted for you the second you kissed me.

I swallow the urge to voice those thoughts. I have no idea how I feel about Matt, except that I love spending time with him, and, yes, I'm definitely starting to relax around him. Jenny was right—my confidence took a hit after the divorce. But it's slowly coming back. I feel stronger. More self-assured.

"There might be some warming," I concede with mock reluctance. "But I'm not sure I can deal with the scared-of-heights thing." I lean in to whisper in his ear. "Now's probably not the time to tell you that I enjoy skydiving, right?"

He blanches. "Oh God. Please tell me you're lying."

"Afraid not. I try to get a dive in a couple times a year if I can. Biggest thrill *ever.*"

"You're dead to me," he deadpans.

I burst out laughing, then lift my hand from under the table and pat his broad shoulder. "It's okay. I'd never force you to skydive with me. We all have our stuff."

We're interrupted when Libby reaches over to persistently tug at Matt's sleeve. "Daddy. I have to potty."

"Ah. Okay. Let's take care of that, shall we?"

He starts to push his chair back, but I get up instead. "I can take her," I offer. "Saves you an awkward trip to the men's."

He looks grateful. "Thanks, Hott—Hailey," he corrects himself.

"Of course." I hold out my hand to the little girl. "You ready, Eddie?"

She gives a high-pitched laugh. "I'm not Eddie!! I'm Libby!!"

"She's Libby!" June chimes in.

"I know, I'm just teasing you." I ruffle Libby's silky-soft hair and then lead her away from the table. Glancing back, I see Matt sliding closer to June and whispering something that makes her giggle. His rugged smile as he talks to his little girl makes my heart flip over in my chest.

In the ladies' room I make sure that Libby washes her hands after she comes out of the stall. When she shuts off the water,

STAY

I'm ready with a paper towel, which she grabs and swipes across her little hands.

An elderly woman smiles at me just as Libby hands back her used towel. "Your daughter is gorgeous," she says, a smile on her wrinkled face.

The compliment catches me completely off guard. My eyes drop to Libby's pale eyes as I try to see what the woman saw. It isn't often since my divorce that I allow myself to think about having a family of my own. That way lies the abyss. So I take a breath and try to compose a polite explanation. But before I can form the words, "I'm just a family friend," Libby darts toward the ladies' room door. And since I don't want to lose sight of Matt's daughter in the touristy melee, I only get out "thank you" before I chase after her.

After the tower trip, we spend another hour walking past all the department store windows that have been specially decorated for the Christmas holiday. The girls squeal over the glitzy displays, and Matt slips his hand into mine.

Heaven.

So when he asks me to come upstairs with them and stay for an early dinner, I say yes even though I should say no.

"Can I help?" I ask when he goes into the kitchen.

"Nope!" he says cheerfully. There's a slow cooker on his countertop, and I watch him pick up an oven mitt to lift the lid. "It's already done."

After petting Rufus hello, I peek into the pot. "Chili? It smells great."

"My mother's recipe," he says, giving it a stir. "And also gluten free." He takes a piece of paper out of his back pocket, unfolds it and smooths it onto the counter. "*Matthew*—" it begins. Many paragraphs follow in a small font. His finger skims down the page until he reaches a bright yellow section called DISALLOWED FOODS. "Yay. Rice is still legal. I'll make some rice on the side."

"It's still . . . what?"

He makes a face. "Kara has a hundred rules, and I try to break as few as possible."

"This letter is, like, her permanent instruction manual?"

He laughs, but the sound is bitter. "That's just for today. I get a new, updated manual on every visit. She didn't used to print them out and highlight passages, though. So that's new."

I literally bite my tongue to keep from making a comment. Bashing the ex-wife is not something I want to do. But I just spent several hours with Matt and his kids, and he made it all look easy.

After he walks the dog for a few minutes, the girls disappear into their room with Rufus, and I sit at a counter stool with a beer, watching my hot man make rice. My big contribution to this meal is to put napkins and silverware on his table and pour milk into two plastic cups with handles.

"Half full," he cautions. "There are frequent spills."

"Gotcha."

"Rufus loves it when the girls are here."

Sure enough, the dog wags his tail happily from the floor between their two chairs when we all sit down later, waiting for errant grains of rice or whatever else falls from the sky.

Matt's kickass chili is delicious and makes me feel embarrassed to have served him store-bought lasagna. At least the dessert he takes out of the cupboard is store-bought.

"YAY, cookies!" one of his daughters yells. "Mommy will be mad."

"No she won't," he says quickly. "They're organic and low sugar."

"Really?" I whisper as he opens the package beside me. They're coconut macaroons dipped in dark chocolate, and they look delicious.

He gives me a guilty shrug and I swallow a laugh. "They're gluten free, though," he whispers back. "You can't have everything."

He's right. You can't. I've just spent the past couple of hours trying not to wonder how different my life might be if I'd married someone who wanted to stay married and have

177

STAY

kids. Children had always been on Jackson's and my to-do list. Or at least I'd thought they were. But since I'm not even thirty, it was never an urgent matter. And we had a growing business to run.

Matt disappears for a little while to get his girls changed into PJs. They'll do anything to avoid brushing their teeth, it seems. A game of tag breaks out, and then Libby tries to ride Rufus like a horse. His reaction is to yawn and sink down onto the floor.

Then there's a story book on the couch, followed by pleas for more.

"That's all," he says, snapping the book shut. "Bedtime was two minutes and seven seconds ago." It sounds like a faintly sarcastic echo of his ex, and when I smirk, I get a sexy wink from him. "Say goodnight to Hailey."

"G'night, Hailey," they both chime.

"Night, girls. It was fun scaring your daddy earlier."

They giggle, but Matt gives me the side-eye for that. Apparently it's fine for a bossy, alpha male to admit his fear of heights, but only once a day. Matt herds them into their room and reappears a few minutes later.

"I should go," I say reluctantly, rising off the couch.

He lifts an eyebrow. "Like hell you should. This is the perfect evening—all my favorite females under one roof." He kisses my forehead and I feel the warmth trickle through me. "Besides. You just survived seven hours at the Eriksson circus. Now you win a glass of wine and a snuggle on the couch."

I fold like a bad hand of poker. Five minutes later I'm sipping cabernet and watching the highlight reel of the Pittsburgh/Montreal game.

Five minutes after *that*, we're making out like a pair of teenagers right before curfew. Matt's hand is up my shirt, his thumb circling my nipple through the lace of my bra. His muscular thigh parts my legs, and my body practically bursts into flames. I swear I hear the same *whoosh* sound as when the heat kicks on in my apartment. I'm stroking his pecs and rubbing against him like a cat in heat.

He catches both my wrists in one of his big hands and lifts them over my head, pinning my hands to the arm of the couch. Then his mouth lands, hot and determined, on my neck. *Whoosh*, again. Firm, generous lips begin to suck at my skin. *Whooshity-whoosh*. I'm turning to a liquid right here on the sofa.

In front of all of Toronto.

While his daughters fall asleep a few feet away.

"Matt," I pant, lifting my chin. "We have to stop."

His hand releases immediately, and I lose his hot mouth on my neck. "Sorry," he gasps. "Thought you were into it."

"Mmmm," I agree, trying to get a grip on myself. "But . . . your girls."

His thumb circles my nipple again. I knew there was a reason I'd spent my life lusting after hockey players. Matt is really good with his hands. "Hottie," he says, his breath ghosting over my jaw. He pauses to kiss that spot, and I shiver. "My bedroom door has a lock. Let's go use it."

"You sure?"

Instead of answering me, he stands up and shuts off the TV. Then he tugs me off the couch. Leaning in, he murmurs in my ear. "We'll be very quiet, okay?"

I nod to show him I understand the need for silence.

"Walk slowly into my bedroom." His whisper is a hot hiss in my ear. "Then take off your top and your jeans. Wait for me beside the bed."

A shiver runs through me as I nod again. He pinches my butt and tips his head toward the bedroom, getting me moving in that direction in a big hurry.

His bedroom looks different in the dark with the lights of Toronto shining in, bathing the white comforter in silvery light. There's no chance that anyone could spy on us in the darkened bedroom. But it still feels risqué to strip out of my top in front of his windows. There are other apartments lit up throughout the neighborhood. Other Saturday nights in play.

None of them is as great as mine.

The door clicks shut as my jeans drop to the floor. Hands land on my shoulders and turn me around to face his sexy smile in the dark. He lifts his eyebrows and then points at the buttons of his shirt.

It takes me only a split second to understand that I'm the one who's supposed to undo them. My hands rush to do this task. He's warm and solid under my hands as I quickly flick the buttons apart. As soon as I've revealed a portion of his chest, I have to lean in and kiss it. The only sound is his sharp intake of breath when my tongue finds his smooth skin. Two hands give my ass a squeeze that's full of expectation.

There are so many *whooshes* now I lose count.

Somehow I strip him out of that shirt, my eager fingers moving to his fly. "That's it," he breathes into my ear as his pants fall away. He hooks his thumbs in the waistband of my panties and drops them to the floor. Then he does the same to his briefs. "Now turn around."

I expect him to nudge me onto the bed, but he doesn't do it. He just clasps me there, my back to his front, his erection pressed possessively against my lower back. His hand flicks my bra clasp open, and now I'm completely naked. A gasp escapes my lips as his hands slide across my skin, waking every nerve ending and making it sing. One arm clamps across my body, his roughened palm holding my breast. The other palm skates down to my core, cupping me.

His shameless fingers dip between my legs and I bite my lip, eyes squeezed shut, as he discovers how wet I already am for him. I can feel his heartbeat against my back, and I sink down against his hand, my head falling back against his shoulder. I can't help myself. In this room, I'm a different Hailey, the kind whose hips move in time with his strokes. Modesty be damned.

"Look," he orders so silently that the "k" is almost the only sound I hear.

My eyes flip open to see our reflection in the full-length mirror on the back of his closet door. The light is dim, but there's no mistaking my pale, bare skin. His strong arms stripe across my body. I can't decide which one is sexier—the one that's gripping me possessively across the chest, or the big hand working me over below, the tendons flexing in his wrist.

My gasp is loud. Too loud. And his upper hand has to give up my breast to clamp across my mouth. My moan is dampened by his hand, thank God.

This man is going to ruin me.

Matt

Damn she's amazing.

Getting Hottie hotter is my favorite thing in the world. I've blasted the doors off her comfort zone, and the reward is the panting, sexy woman in my arms. It's beautiful to watch her throw away her inhibitions and relax against me, her body supple and willing.

She has no idea how much this means to me. I've spent the last year and change believing myself unfit to be anyone's partner. And maybe it's true. But by spending her day with me—and her night—Hailey lets me believe I'm not a lost cause, that my messy life is worth sharing, at least when I can manage it.

Now it's my turn to show her how sexy she really is. Helping her feel that is the best thing ever.

My dick is as hard as the CN Tower statuettes we saw in the gift shop a few hours ago, but I let this moment linger, teasing her pussy with my fingers, kissing her neck. When I can't take the anticipation anymore, I guide her to the side of the bed, but not onto it. Instead, I nudge her onto her knees on the rug beside the bed. I place each of her arms onto the mattress, palms down. "Don't move," I whisper.

She lays a cheek on the cotton comforter and takes a deep, steadying breath as I grab a condom out of the nightstand. I roll it on in a big fat hurry. But then I take an extra second to adjust the closet door a few inches, leaving it ajar, the mirror aimed at the place where Hailey leans over my bed.

When I sink down behind her, I run my hands over her

silky back, cupping her ass cheeks. I nudge her knees further apart. "You ready for me?" I ask. But I know she is.

Hailey nods eagerly, eyeing me over her shoulder.

I lift her hips gently, tucking my cock beneath her body. When I rub the head against her slickness, she sucks in a breath. I position myself at her entrance, then pause.

Her body is tense with expectation. But I'm waiting for something important. She shifts a fraction of an inch, offering me her body.

I wait, throbbing with want.

Finally it happens. Her eyes flick over to the mirror. She's trying to figure out why I'm not fucking her yet. But as soon as our eyes meet in the mirror I push inside.

Her chin lifts, her mouth falling open with desire. It's fucking gorgeous. I take her tits in both hands and pinch the nipples. "Watch," I growl. "See how beautiful you are?" In the mirror I see the sexiest woman I've ever met, her small body bouncing as I thrust. She's tight and hot and I feel a wave of lust roll through me, until I have to close my eyes before things get out of hand.

She's magnificent, and I do my best to make it last. I give it to her nice and steady while her heart beats wildly in my hands. Then I slip one hand down between her legs and finger our connection, which makes her whimper.

"Shhh," I whisper, and her breathing becomes even hotter.

When I don't think I can last much longer, I pull out and climb up on the bed, settling on my back. She follows eagerly, seating herself on my cock. I've made her forget her inhibitions entirely now. We're face to face, her eager body riding me like a champion. "That's it," I urge. "Take what you need."

Her big blue eyes are heavy with lust, the pupils blown. I pull her down onto my chest, taking her mouth in a rough kiss. With a moan, she strains against me, desperate to find her release. I suck on her tongue as she reaches the finish line, her body quaking over mine. My hips pump on their own volition and I'm spilling and moaning and holding her tightly.

"Shhh!" she chides when I give one last, loud grunt of

satisfaction. Her small hand slips over my lips.

I kiss it, then nudge it aside with a clumsy hand. "S'okay," I say, then suck down the oxygen that I need. "They sleep like the dead, Hottie."

"Then why were we silent?"

"Because hot," I mumble, my eyelids heavy.

"Seriously?" she says at a normal volume, and I just grin up at her with my eyes shut. "You're so . . ."

"Sexy?" I offer.

She smacks my shoulder and then collapses onto it. "Yeah. Fine. You win."

I squeeze her body to mine, just feeling lucky.

CRUMBS

Hailey

Waking up in Matt's bed is startling.

It's not his naked body beside me that's a surprise. I felt his heat all night long. Best thing ever.

The startling part is the light knock on the door. "Daddy! Time for waffles."

"Grrmf," he says into the pillow.

There's a moment of silence before the knocking begins again. "I'll make 'em if you don't!"

That gets him moving. I get a quick kiss and an apology. "I'll start the coffee. Take your time," he insists. "Take whatever you want from the medicine cabinet."

"'Kay," I manage.

After he disappears, closing the door behind him, I get up and hurry into his bathroom. I decide he won't mind if I borrow his fabulous walk-in shower, with three jets and a heated towel bar.

I shower and braid my hair so it doesn't resemble a sex do. His medicine cabinet has a few of those airline toothbrushes, and I help myself.

When I'm nearly presentable, I put on my jeans. But my top is crumpled like a tissue on the floor. I should have hung it up last night. It looks ridiculous so I peek into his closet (the mirror causing me to blush) and borrow a flannel shirt.

And it smells like him. Gah! I'm such a goner.

"Nice shirt," he says quietly when he hands me a cup of black coffee a few minutes later.

"Mine looked like hell."

He smirks at me. "That looks better on you than it ever looked on me." He kisses my neck surreptitiously, and it reminds me of last night, when we were . . .

"Hailey?" Libby asks me. "Can you braid my hair like yours? Daddy can't do girl stuff."

"Oh. Sure," I say, stepping away from her daddy before I maul him. "Do you have a hair tie and a comb?"

She runs off to find them.

"You don't have to do that," he says, breaking an egg into a mixing bowl.

"I don't mind at all. Easiest thing in the world." I clear my throat. "They don't seem to mind that I'm here."

"Of course not," he assures me.

When Libby comes back, I sit down on the couch with her on the floor in front of me. Rufus comes bounding over, his leash in his mouth. "Do you need me to take him out?" I ask Matt, who's whisking waffle mix. There is nothing sexier than a shirtless man cooking. Yowza.

"I owe him a walk," he says. "But it will wait until after breakfast."

It takes me two tries to braid Libby's hair because she can't hold still. But I manage a decent braid in her silky hair. Then June asks, so I do hers, too. Then everyone eats waffles and sausage at Matt's table.

The waffles are . . . awful. When I give up on mine, I glance at Matt to see that he's abandoned his, too. "Gluten free," he mouths at me over his coffee cup, then scowls.

His daughters don't seem to mind, though. They scarf theirs down. When they're done, Matt's ready with a wet washcloth to get the syrup off their sticky fingers. Then they beg him to read him a chapter of *Ramona the Brave*. "Before Mommy comes to get us," June adds, looking sad.

He checks his watch. "After I finish my coffee," he promises, parking his feet under the table beside mine.

Surreptitiously, I offer a bite of waffle to Rufus.

After a single sniff, he turns his nose away. But then, since he has my attention, he picks up his leash again and eyes me pityingly. *"Can't you see me?"* his eyes say. *"I'm right here!"*

"I'm going to take Rufus out for a little walk," I announce.

"You don't have to . . ."

"I know!" I say, snapping the leash onto his collar. "Read to your girls."

"Thank you, honey," he says, his gray gaze warming me.

"You're welcome. Go."

I put on my jacket and take out the dog. When we pass the coffee shop, I have an idea. A barista I know is behind the counter, and I wave frantically until he spots me. "Can I get two chocolate croissants to go? Sorry for making you come over here."

"No prob, Hailey. One sec." He takes my money and brings back my pastries in a bag, and change. "That your dog? He's cute."

"He's a friend's," I say. "See you tomorrow."

We're not gone for very long, because I plan to leave the croissant for Matt and get gone before his ex comes to fetch the girls at ten. I re-enter the lobby at 9:30 and scamper for the elevator doors, which are closing.

"Thanks," I gasp when a hand holds them open.

But when I step inside the elevator, I realize my mistake. It's Kara, Matt's ex. And now she's eyeing me as if I were the carrier of a nasty disease.

"Good morning," I say, wishing I'd taken Rufus out for a very long walk.

"Morning," she says tightly.

Rufus tries to greet her, too, but she pushes his feet off her camel-colored coat. So I tug him back, clicking my tongue.

Neither one of us pleases her, apparently.

It's the longest elevator ride ever. I try to think of

STAY

something nice to say, but the doors part before I've worked out what that might be.

I let her get off first, and she walks ahead of me to Matt's door with a posture so regal the queen could take lessons. When she knocks, he opens right away. "Hail— You're early, Kara," he says quickly. Then his eyes lift to find me bringing up the rear.

I make an apologetic face, but his only looks amused.

"Are those waffles?" she asks by way of a greeting.

"Gluten free," he assures her.

She sniffs anyway. "Let's go, girls."

"We were going to read another chapter!" Libby whines.

"Go get your clothes on," she barks. The girls are still in their PJs.

"Isn't my braid pretty?" Libby asks, twirling around in front of her mother. "Hailey did it."

Kara's lip curls, and I don't really blame her. She doesn't know me, and it looks as if I've tried to remake her daughters into my two little clones. "Please put on your *clothes*. Leave your PJ's on the bed. They stay here. Matt," she snaps. "Help them."

He opens his mouth and then closes it again, trying to decide what to do. I lift my chin slightly. *Go on. It's okay.* He trots off toward the girls' room while I drop to a knee and unclip Rufus. Then I rub his belly. Last time Kara showed up, I ran away like a frightened bunny. I could do that now, but why? The damage is already done. And I'm not afraid of her anymore.

It is what it is.

Matt reappears, holding a little pink duffel bag. "All set," he says, handing the bag to Kara. When I stand up, he steps closer and rubs my back.

Kara actually rolls her eyes. "We didn't discuss the girls spending time with your hookups."

Matt practically growls. "Hailey is not a hookup," he spits. "We're dating."

"Uh-huh." Her irritated gaze swivels to me. "It won't last, you know. He's never around. The women hurl themselves at him on the road."

"Which doesn't matter," he says through clenched teeth. "And never did."

Whoa. Nothing like a little post-marital spat on Sunday morning.

Luckily, June and Libby have made it back into the room, calming everyone down. I drift out of sight, taking myself into Matt's bathroom to wash my hands while he says goodbye to his children and sees his ex out the door.

A couple of minutes later I hear him enter the bedroom. "What's in the bag?" he asks.

"Chocolate croissants," I say, handing them over. "One for each of us."

"Fuck yeah." He sets the bag on his dresser. "I'm topping up our coffees. Let's eat 'em in bed."

My first impulse is to worry about crumbs. Then I check myself. "Yeah, let's."

Matt

"**Y**ou look hot in my shirt," I tell Hailey. I've just fucked her in the middle of my bed. I'm naked and she's wearing only the shirt.

"Mmh," is all she can manage, since she's still breathing hard.

We cuddle for a few lovely minutes. "Thanks for not freaking out when my ex-wife was a bitch."

She chuckles. "I get it. I really do."

"I'm always the bad guy," I tell her. Telling Hailey my troubles isn't my MO, but sex has loosened my tongue. "She has a boyfriend. I'm sure he spends the night more often than not."

"The dentist, right?"

"Good memory. I didn't say a word when he entered the

picture. I thought—Kara is so fucking picky about every goddamn thing. But she knew him in high school, and if she's brought him into my children's lives, he must be a good guy. I gave her the benefit of the doubt. But I don't ever get that with her. Everything I feed them is questioned. I don't get a say on what school they go to next year, or where they should spend Christmas."

"I'm sorry," Hailey says, stroking my chest. "You're such a good dad. They're lucky to have you."

"I do okay," I mumble. I've whined enough already.

She raises herself on one elbow. "I'm not kidding. You're the best kind of parent. You listen when they talk. You don't correct every little thing that comes out of their mouths. You just *appreciate* them."

"That's what anyone would do."

"Not true."

There's something vehement in her tone that gives me pause. "Sore spot?"

She snorts. "Maybe. My mother spent every day of my childhood making sure I knew I'd already let her down. My dad left when I was five, and she told me it was my fault."

I sit up fast. "What the fuck, Hailey? Who says that to a child?"

"I know." Her smile is wan. "Maybe I don't have the parenting bar set very high. But you're good with them, Matt. Don't ever let her convince you otherwise."

Flopping back on the bed, I let out a grunt. "The co-parenting thing is hard."

"I know," she says quietly. "I can't even imagine the stresses it adds. What did you say to your girls when you moved out?"

"Well . . ." I try not to think about that day if I can help it. "Kara sat 'em down and told them, '*Our family will work better if Daddy lives somewhere else.*' And I just kinda sat there and nodded, like that made any sense at all. I think she got it out of a parenting book on divorce. The girls weren't even three, though. And I already traveled so often that I'm not sure it sunk in for a while."

That whole month is a blur to me now. But it still hurts, goddamn it. I never wanted to do that to my kids. And I was never given a choice.

"Do you miss Kara?" Hailey asks softly.

"Fuck no," I say, and it's the truth. "Things weren't great between us. But I don't give up like that. I made a vow, and I wasn't going to let a shitty game schedule mess it up, you know? She hated the lifestyle. She said, 'Being divorced won't really be any different most of the time.'"

Hailey makes a noise of distress. "That's cold."

"And short-sighted," I point out. "I'll be retired before the girls need braces. We said *forever* at our wedding, but she can't count." I laugh, but it's bitter.

She strokes my hip with soft fingers. "Sorry for your troubles."

"Not having any troubles right now. Except for croissant crumbs in my bed." Time to lighten up this conversation.

"That was your idea, big guy."

I roll over and kiss her.

STICKS & STONES

THREE WEEKS LATER

Hailey

The holidays pass blessedly fast. The good thing about owning a business like Fetch is that everyone and their mother is overwhelmed by last-minute holiday bullshit, which means I'm able to bury myself in work so that I don't have to think about *my* holiday bullshit and mother.

She didn't even send a card. Not that she ever does, but it still bothers me. Some people like to believe that parents love their children no matter what, but I realized at an early age that that's not the case.

My mom doesn't care about anyone but herself. My dad . . . heck, I don't even remember what he looks like—that's how fast he ran out the door.

I didn't get to spend Christmas with Matt, because he flew to Tampa with the girls to visit his parents. He asked me to come along, but there was no way I could abandon Jackson during Fetch's busiest season. Jax invited me to Christmas Eve dinner at his folks' place, which I politely declined. Deciding who I'd want to spend time with the least—my selfish mother or Jackson's horrible father—would be an impossible feat. In the end, I went to Jenny's family's place for dinner and spent the whole night bouncing Jenny's adorable infant nephew on my knee.

Now, the holiday craziness is behind us, Matt is back in town, and I'm excited to see what this new year will bring. Good things, I hope. And lots of hot sex. But the sex will have to wait until later tonight.

"Weather Lady!" Blake Riley bellows as I approach the back booth of the bar. He's so ridiculously loud that his voice carries over the din of the crowded room, causing a dozen heads to turn in my direction.

This will be the third time I've hung out with Blake, so you'd think I'd be used to his bellowing by now. Yet it startles me every time. And don't get me started on the Weather Lady nickname. Still makes no sense to me, but Matt keeps advising me to ignore it.

Speaking of Matt, my big, sexy hockey god rises from his seat to greet with me a suffocating hug and a toe-curling kiss. And now we're attracting a different kind of attention, in the form of curious stares from patrons and catcalls courtesy of Blake.

"Leave the poor girl alone," Jess Canning chides from her perch on Blake's lap. There's plenty of space for her to sit on the actual bench, but I've noticed that every time Blake and Jess are in the same room, he insists she be draped over him in some fashion.

Me, I sit down next to Matt like a good girl, even though I'm dying to be a bad one and maul him like a hungry lion. I haven't seen him in three days because of road games, and he had to cancel our last two dinner dates because of team events. I would have gone to his place last night to welcome him home, but he got in super late and I had to be up super early, much to our equal displeasure.

It's weird being Matt Eriksson's girlfriend. Or, at least I *think* I'm his girlfriend. He hasn't said the G-word, and I only use the B-word in my head when I'm thinking about him. But I know we're exclusive, and I'm pretty sure we're together.

Jenny teases me that we're in a relationship with a capital R. All I know is that I love every second I spend with Matt. He's so . . . real. Warm and gorgeous and funny and how the hell did I ever get so lucky?

"Aw, Hails doesn't mind," Blake is saying to Jess.

"Yeah, I'm sure she's thrilled every time you announce her presence to the entire bar and then make howling cat sounds while she kisses her man," Jess grumbles back.

I grin at the couple. "I don't mind that part. But the Weather Lady nonsense is another story."

"Nonsense?" Blake looks outraged. "Took me for-fucking-*ever* to pick the perfect nickname for you, WL. You oughta be more grateful."

I swipe Matt's beer bottle from his hands. "Uh-huh. I'm so very grateful, Riley." I take a sip, then hand the bottle back, earning me a crooked smile from Matt.

"Yours is right here, you know," he says wryly, gesturing to the bottle directly in front of me.

"Oh!" I say, reaching for my favorite local beer. It's hard to find in most bars, which is why I was thrilled to discover it's actually served at Sticks & Stones. I knew this place was a hockey bar, but since it's not close to where I live, I'd never been before until Matt brought me here for the first time a couple weeks ago.

And I'm blushing happily as I reach for the beer. He must've ordered it when I texted him after I got off the subway, because it's still cold. My boyfriend is thoughtful like that.

"I'm glad we're finally making this happen," Jess says, gesturing around the booth with her beer. "Blake's been babbling about this double-date idea for ages."

"I do not babble," Blake protests.

"Yeah, sorry it took a while to get it done," Matt says, and there's a guilty flicker in his eyes.

I pat his thigh under the table. The last double date we tried to schedule was one of the things he had to cancel, because

STAY

he'd gotten held up at an interview he was doing for *Men's Health*. I ended up going out with Blake and Jess alone, and the next time I saw Matt, he wouldn't stop apologizing for missing dinner, an unhappy look on his face the entire time. I tried to assure him that it was no biggie, but the man seems to think that canceling on me is a cardinal sin. I suppose I should be flattered that he's so determined not to let me down.

I decide to change the subject before Matt starts apologizing some more. "So how was morning skate?" I ask the guys, even though I'd already spoken to Matt earlier on my lunch break. But I love hearing any and all details relating to the team.

Hell, I love the team in general, and not just because nearly half of Matt's teammates are now using Fetch's services. I don't know who got the ball rolling, but somehow over the past few weeks, our clientele list has grown to include Blake, Wesmie, Ben and Katie Hewitt, the team captain Luko and his wife Estrella, and several other Toronto players and their spouses.

Oh, and my ex-husband's jaw nearly hit the floor when a request came in from none other than Coach Hal. Turns out Coach Hal and his wife have a sweet tooth that needed to be satisfied at four in the morning the other night. Jackson was on night duty, and when I came in the following morning, he spent fifteen minutes raving about how he *personally* delivered tiramisu to our city's favorite coach.

I almost gloated and said, "See! Dating a hockey player is good for business, huh, Jax?" But I restrained myself, because Jackson and I agreed not to discuss our love lives.

"Morning skate was amazeballs," Blake answers. "They got this new coffeemaker in the facility kitchen, and it's fancy as shit. It spits out little cups of heaven. It's like drinking a cloud."

Jess furrows her brow. "I don't think you can drink clouds."

"And why would you want to?" Matt inquires.

"You haven't tried this coffee," Blake tells us. "Trust me. Cloud-like."

"That didn't answer my question," I point out. "What does your fancy coffee have to do with morning skate?"

Matt rolls his eyes. "What does anything Riley says have to

do with anything?"

"True," I agree, and Jess snickers.

I lean closer to Matt, enjoying the warmth radiating from his sturdy chest. His arm is draped across the back of the booth, fingers loosely hanging over my shoulder. Sometimes it feels like we're a real couple. I mean, we're on a double date right now—isn't double dating something only couples do?

"But yeah, morning skate was fine," Matt says. "Except for O'Connor and Lemming's little scuffle."

I frown. Will O'Connor seems to engage in a lot of "scuffles." "What now?"

Both Matt and Blake shrug. Jess, however, wears a frown that matches my own.

"I swear, that kid has a chip on his shoulder," she remarks. "Why is he always causing trouble?"

"Probably because he hasn't learned how to keep his pants zipped," Matt says flatly.

"Wait." Jess pauses. "You said he got into it with Lemming? Isn't Chad, like, his only friend on the team?"

"Pretty much," Blake confirms. "But like Matty-Cake said, OC's got a zipper problemo. Or maybe a dick problemo—as in, the little bugger can't stay behind the zip. I guess that's okey-dokey when the dick doesn't interfere with Lemur's conquests, but supposedly last night it did."

My head is spinning. Blake's made-up Blake language is hard to understand on a good day, but when I've had a few sips of beer? It's incomprehensible. From what I manage to glean, though, it sounds like O'Connor hit on his friend's girl.

Jess reaches the same conclusion. "So Will hooked up with someone Chad was interested in?"

"Hard to hear what they were saying over the sounds of fists smashing faces, but yeah, I think that's what happened," Matt says with a sigh.

"Coach shit a brick," Blake adds. "Sent them both home."

"Wouldn't be surprised if neither of them are on the starting lineup tomorrow night." Matt looks annoyed as he reaches for his beer.

STAY

Eek, I hope not. As troublesome as O'Connor is off the ice, he's shaping up to be one of the best forwards on the team. The guy is lightning fast. And Lemming is one of our most solid defensemen.

Across the booth, Jess sees my expression and snorts. "Oh shit, guys, Hailey's been replaced by the Hockey Fanatic. And the Hockey Fanatic does *not* like the idea of losing Will and Chad tomorrow."

I glare at the smirking blonde. "Damn right I don't! We need all our guys on the ice if we're going to win the Cup!"

"Hear hear!" a random college-aged guy shouts from the next booth.

Err. I guess I said that louder than I intended. Oh boy. I'm turning into Blake.

With a deep chuckle that I feel all the way down to my toes, Matt leans in and brushes his lips over my cheek. "Don't worry, babe, we can survive one game without the Duelling Dicks."

Babe. I love it when he calls me babe.

I tip my head to meet his ice-gray eyes, and as usual, I get totally and completely lost in them. They have these gorgeous flecks of silver around the pupil, and, in some lighting, specks of baby-blue too. His eyes are as beautiful as the rest of him.

Fuck. I'm a goner for this man. Our relationship might not be "official," but holy hell, I *officially* feel *all* the feelings for Matt Eriksson.

"Let's order nachos," Blake announces, reaching for the stack of menus in the center of the booth. "I'm thinking . . . eight orders?"

"*Eight?*" Jess squawks. "There's only four of us here."

"I'll eat at least four," Blake assures her. "You guys can battle it out for the rest. Oh!" He suddenly snaps his fingers. "Storm Chaser!"

I'm busy studying the menu, so it takes Matt clearing his throat to alert me. "I think he's talking to you," Matt murmurs.

Setting down the menu, I glance over at Blake. "I'm Storm Chaser now?"

He beams at me. "You could be. Do you like it better than Weather Lady?"

I think it over. "Sure, what the hell."

"Perfecto. Anyway," he continues, pointing one stern finger at me, "you got a TV?"

I'm flummoxed. Blake jumps topics so fast, it gets confusing. "Um . . . yes . . . ?"

"Good. Make sure you watch *Mornings with Matilda* tomorrow. I think it's on at eight?"

"Nine," Jess supplies.

Blake jabs his finger in the air. "Nine. Right. Watch it, Storm Chaser."

I have to bite my lip to keep from laughing. "Any reason why I need to watch a cheesy morning show?"

His dark eyes twinkle mischievously. "That's for me to know and for you to find out."

With an arched brow, I turn to Matt. "Spill."

He holds up his hands. "Hey, I have no fucking idea what he's babbling about. This is news to me—" Matt stops abruptly, and because we're sitting so close to each other, I feel his pocket vibrating. He reaches in and pulls out his phone, then frowns. "Gotta take this," he apologizes. As he raises the phone to his ear, his tone immediately takes on a stiff note. "Kara. What's up?"

I stiffen too. And damn, I think Jess notices, because a flicker of sympathy flashes in her brown eyes. Okay, so maybe I'm not entirely comfortable with Matt's ex-wife. Since our awkward run-in the morning after the CN Tower excursion, I've made a point to stay away whenever I know she's due to pick up the girls. I don't like the way Kara looks at me, as if I've committed some major offense for *existing* near her children.

At least my ex is cordial when Matt happens to show up at the Fetch office. Jackson has never been anything but polite to Matt, and he's never, ever mocked him about being nothing more than a hookup.

But Kara's the mother of Matt's children. I can't be rude to her, and I definitely can't criticize her to Matt. That has *"jealous new girlfriend"* written all over it.

"What do you mean?" Matt sounds aggravated. "But we agreed I'd have them for two days next week."

I hear Kara's voice on the other end, but I can't make out what she's saying. Whatever it is, Matt doesn't like it. The tips of his ears turn red, a clear sign that he's pissed.

"Kara." He speaks quietly, but there's menace there. "You can't just rearrange our schedule to suit you. We—" He stops again, glancing around the booth as if remembering where he is. Then he squeezes my shoulder briefly and mutters, "Excuse me. I'll be right back."

I slide out of the booth to allow his escape, and then Blake, Jess, and I watch as Matt marches toward the restroom area with the phone glued to his ear and his shoulders set in a tense line.

"Exes, right?" Blake quips.

The comment is meant to break the tension, but all it does is make things more awkward.

"Have you met her yet?" Jess finally hedges.

I nod. "She's . . . all right."

Blake snorts.

Thoughtful, Jess reaches for her beer and takes a sip. "I've never met her myself—she was before my time—but the WAGs don't have a lot of nice things to say about her."

I don't have a lot of nice things to say, either, but I try to tamp down the urge. "She's the mother of his kids," is all I say, and I manage a careless shrug.

Jess continues to eye me sympathetically. I know she can see right through me.

I turn away from her steady gaze and focus on Blake instead. "So . . . nachos?"

The next morning, I keep my promise to Blake and make sure to have the TV on in the break room while I brew another pot of coffee at the small counter. I'm on my third cup already, and it's not even nine. That's what happens when you stay up very, very late having sex with a very, very hot hockey player. I was a bleary-eyed, sex-haired mess when I dragged myself out of Matt's bed at seven a.m. Luckily, I brought a change of clothes, so I was able to shower and dress at his apartment and make it to work at eight without a hitch.

Jenny wanders into the room, holding a travel mug and a stack of mail. "Morning!" she says breezily.

"Morning," I mumble.

"Someone's grumpy."

"I didn't get much sleep last night," I answer as I pour myself some coffee.

Jenny grins. "Oh you poor thing! Stayed up all night having sex! How *dreadful*."

I flip her off while taking a huge gulp of my caffeine fix, then settle in one of the chairs around the table. "That today's mail or yesterday's?" I tip my mug toward the stack of envelopes.

"Today's." She heads to the coffeemaker. "Mostly bills, from the looks of it, but there're a couple things for you and Jackson."

Setting down my cup, I reach for the mail and begin flipping through it. One item catches my attention. It's a white envelope addressed to me, with a familiar logo printed on the return section. Huh. It's from the Toronto Women's Business Association. I hope I didn't forget to renew my annual membership fee. It's a really useful organization to join for a female business owner, particularly for all the free workshops they run every month.

"Also," Jenny is still chattering behind me, "you missed out on an epic Mr. Dick request last night. He ordered a hundred packages of Jell-O. Who needs that much Jell-O?!"

"Maybe he was hosting one of those naked Jell-O wrestling parties," I say absently, sliding my fingernail under the flap of the envelope.

"Oh God! Imagine? I'd love to be a fly on the wall of his pervazoid house." Jenny joins me at the table, lacing her fingers around her mug. "What's that?"

"Don't know yet." I extract a single sheet of paper and unfold it. A small placard falls out of the paper. It's printed on lovely, thick cardstock and done in calligraphy. It seems to be an invitation to the annual TWBA awards banquet. At first I'm bewildered, because I didn't know the TWBA even gave out awards.

Then I'm stunned, because apparently not only do they give out awards, but . . . they're giving one to *me*!

"Oh my God!" I squeal so loudly that Jenny jumps in her seat. "Oh my God, Jen! Look at this!"

I shove the paper and invitation across the table. Jenny quickly puts down her coffee and reads both, then lets out a squeal of her own.

"Holy shit! This is so awesome!"

Grinning like idiots, we both do a little happy dance—while still fully seated. Of course, Jackson chooses this exact moment to enter the break room. His eyes bug out as he looks from me to Jenny, taking in our happy squeals and gyrating arms.

"Um. Okay." My ex-husband smiles as he goes to get himself some coffee. "And what are we celebrating?"

"Me!" I blurt out. I hop out of my chair and pat myself down for my cell phone. Crap. I left it in my office. But I *have* to call Matt and share this news. "I'll be right back," I tell Jenny and Jackson. "Don't change the channel! I'm waiting for *Mornings with Matilda*."

I'm pretty sure I leave two confused people in my wake, because they've both known me a long time, and not once had I ever expressed interest in morning television.

In my office, I grab my phone and pull up Matt's name. He answers on the fourth ring, sounding groggy as hell.

"Hey, Hottie."

"Hey, Snipes. You awake?" I can't wipe the silly grin off my face as I stare at the piece of paper in my hands. I probably should've left it in the break room so Jackson would know what the heck I was freaking out about, but Jenny can fill him in.

"Barely. *Someone* kept me up last night." I can almost hear the smile in his husky voice.

"Well, wake up for just one minute," I beg. "Let me just tell you my news and then you can go back to sleep."

"News?" I hear the bedsheets rustling, as if he's sitting up. "What news?"

"Have you heard of the Toronto Women's Business Association?" I'm practically bouncing up and down now, and it has nothing to do with the three cups of coffee I drank.

"No, but I'll take your word that they exist," he jokes.

"They do. And they're one of the most influential networking organizations in the city for Toronto businesswomen." I bounce some more. "And they're giving me an award! I've just been named Entrepreneur Innovator of the Year."

"Seriously? Fuck, Hottie, that's incredible! Congratulations!"

"Thank you." I can't quit smiling. "And there's this huge gala next week for the awards ceremony. It's black tie, open bar." I hesitate, only for a beat, before continuing, "It's on Wednesday night. Will you go with me?"

There's no hesitation on Matt's end. "Hell yeah I will! Timing works out great, huh? My flight from Nashville lands Wednesday afternoon, so that should give me plenty of time to throw on my penguin suit and be your plus one."

Happiness ripples through me. "This is the coolest news ever, Matt. I honestly didn't expect it."

"The best things in life are the ones you don't expect," he says softly.

I hold those words close to my heart as we say goodbye, and I head back to the break room. Just in time, too, because the moment I walk in, Jenny shrieks and points to the television mounted to the wall.

"He just mentioned Fetch! ON LIVE TV!"

"What? Who?" I hurry over to her and Jackson, both of whom look shell-shocked. On the screen, I'm startled to find Blake Riley sitting on Matilda Morgan's beige upholstered couch. He's wearing a gray wool suit with a Toronto jersey

STAY

under the jacket instead of a dress shirt. And either I'm imagining things, or Blake really is talking about our company.

"Miracle workers," he's saying. "Like, you realize how easy my life is now, Matilda? All those things I used to want at three in the morning and couldn't get because I was a Lazy Lou? I get 'em all now."

The bleached-blond, Botox-faced morning show host giggles loudly. "Well, Mr. Riley, you can't just tease our viewers like that and not offer some details. What *does* a professional athlete require at three in the morning?"

Blake's expression is solemn. "Pie. I always crave apple pie at night. Oh, and once I ran out of puppy food for Puddles." He winks at Matilda. "But this is why I use Fetch now, feel me?"

The host changes the subject to Blake's childhood, but my brain is still stuck on the previous topic. Did Blake Riley just endorse our company on live television?

"Did Blake Riley just endorse our company on live television?" Stunned, Jackson voices my exact thoughts.

I slowly turn toward him. "I . . . think he just did."

NOT THE CHOCOLATES' FAULT

Matt

I have a box of chocolates clutched in my hand, and I'm sitting on the team jet, hating them.

It's not the chocolates' fault, though.

I cancelled another date with Hailey tonight. Third time this month. The team was supposed to get back to Toronto at six, which should have been plenty of time to make it to the bowling alley and wow her with my horrible bowling. It would have been fun.

But we were late to the Denver airport, and we lost our takeoff time. Then it started snowing on the Rockies, and the whole airport got backed up because of visibility issues. If that weren't enough, Toronto airspace is too crowded, and now we're actually circling, waiting to land.

All the chocolates in the world aren't enough to make up for dating a guy who stands you up every time he says he wants to take you out to dinner.

My brooding is interrupted by a howl of victory across the aisle. Chad Lemming has just defeated Will O'Connor at whatever video game they're obsessed with this week.

"You got owned, OC!" Blake says, peering over their seats from the row behind. "I'm up next, right?"

STAY

O'Connor gets up and sidesteps, parking himself in the empty seat beside me, allowing Blake to take his place. "What's up with you, E?" he asks, signaling the flight attendant for a drink.

"Nothing much." I sigh, checking the time yet again. I wonder what Hailey is doing right now. I hope she took me up on my offer to head over to my place and wait for me.

Except . . . ugh. Waiting. That's the very thing my ex hated about being with me. And she let me know pretty damned frequently during the last year of our marriage.

O'Connor accepts a diet soda from the flight attendant and gives me an appraising glance. "Something wrong?"

Yeah. But I'm not whining to this youngster about it. "You and Lemming were brawling just the other day," I point out, changing the subject. "Did you kiss and make up?"

"It was a misunderstanding," O'Connor says, stretching his neck.

I snicker. "Lemming just *misunderstood* your intention to move in on his conquest?"

"Yeah he *did*." O'Connor narrows his eyes. "I took that girl home and walked her to her door. Handed her off to her parents."

"*Parents?*" Jesus.

"Yeah. She was underage and lying about it. I saw her real driver's license when she took out her fake ID for the bartender. Lemming didn't believe me. He was drunk and horny. And the girl was working it *hard*."

"Shit."

"Exactly. She was a high school girl, and that's not cool. I like to have my fun, but everybody has to be a consenting adult, you know?"

"Hell," I say. "I'll be retired from the league by the time my girls are dating. But I'm planning to keep up with my bench press. The first time a boy comes to take one of my girls out for a date, I'm gonna ask the kid to spot me while I bench three hundo. Just so the kid knows I can take him."

O'Connor laughs.

"So you patched things up with Lemming?"

"Yeah." His smile fades. "Told him he needs to be more careful. And I promised I'd be the best wingman he ever met the next time we're out at the bars. Like, Top Gun level."

"Ah." I'm a little stunned at this burst of humanity from our team's resident asshole. But I guess it's good to know he has a heart beating in there somewhere. My phone buzzes with a text, which means the jet's Wi-Fi is back on. "'Scuse me," I say. "Gotta do some groveling because we're so late getting home."

O'Connor lifts his eyebrows, and I brace myself for another helping of his cynicism about relationships, but it doesn't come. He tips his head back against the headrest and closes his eyes.

I unlock my phone, and the message is from Hailey. She's responding to my profuse apologies from earlier.

Hailey: Don't worry about it. I used the extra hours to keep my head above water at work.

I'm sure that's true. It's just that one of these nights she'll look up from her work and realize how much more fun it would be to date someone who was around more than two randomized nights a week.

Matt: And now? Are you at my place?

It takes a second until I get a response. But then my screen fills with a shot of Hailey's bare feet crossed on my comforter. Her toenails are painted pink, and wouldn't you know it, but Rufus's nose is lying across her ankle.

Matt: Once again, I'm jealous of my dog. He's not supposed to be on the bed, by the way.

Hailey: He's good company.

Ouch.

Matt: I can't wait to take his spot.

Hailey: :) You don't need to sleep on my ankle, though. It's okay if you use the pillow.

STAY

Matt: *You know what would be fun?*

Hailey: *Three straight wins in a row this week? I thought you had excellent footspeed last night, BTW. Good hustle.*

Matt: *Um, thank you. You know what else would be fun? If you were naked in my bed when I got there.*

There is no response for a couple of minutes.

Hailey: *Rufus has been relocated to the dog bed in the living room. And I made myself more comfortable.*

My groin tightens with expectation.

Matt: *How comfortable are you?*

A photograph appears on the screen. It's a shot of Hailey's naked breast in profile, the nipple rosy. Holy crap. Hottie sexted me! That's out of character for my shy girl. As I look at the photo, I harden up just imagining how much I want to put my mouth there.

Matt: *That is the best sight I've seen in a really long time. Can't wait to put my mouth on you.*

Hailey: *It's really warm in here, suddenly.*

She adds a few flame emojis, and I'm grinning at my phone. Hailey is cute and sexy and I'm getting all kinds of turned on.

Matt: *I love sucking on you. Makes you so wet. I'm going to run my tongue all over your tits, honey. Just how you like it.*

Hailey: *Wow. They really don't make emojis to express how I feel right now. Think: Niagara Falls.*

Matt: *Put your hand on your breast. Tease your nipple.*

I sit there, imagining it, getting hornier by the second. And a minute later I'm treated to another photo of her, and this time she's pinching that tasty little peak. *Gawd.* I look around to make sure nobody else can see this. But the guys sitting behind me are sleeping. Across the aisle, Blake and Lemming are still locked in battle over their video game on Lemming's laptop. And Will O'Connor has nodded off beside me.

Fine.

I stealthily unclip my seatbelt. Then I use one hand to gently tighten the wool of my trousers, until the obvious bulge is easy to spot. With my other hand, I snap a quick picture on my phone.

Five seconds later I've hit send, refastened my seatbelt and put a magazine over my boner. The picture takes a while to upload.

"Dude. Did you just take a photo of your package?"

"No!" I say too quickly, even before I get a look at Will O'Connor's evil grin. *Fuck.* "I was just . . ."

The grin widens. "The guys are gonna be very amused."

"Christ. How much will your silence cost? I'll buy you a beer."

"Forget the beer." He's ready with another blackmail request, but it isn't anything I'm expecting. "Tell the trainer I've been working hard at sprints," he says. "They're nagging me about my skating."

"We all need a little technique refresher at some point. It's easy to form bad habits." Nothing to be ashamed of, either. But a young hotshot like O'Connor might be the sort to assume he can't afford to admit he needs the extra coaching.

Sure enough, he makes a face.

"Hey OC!" Lemming yaps from across the aisle. "You're up, my man."

Will takes his soda and moves seats again.

As soon as I'm alone, I open my phone again. There's a text waiting.

Hailey: *Someone misses me.*

STAY

Matt: *As if there was any doubt.*

I *hope* she doesn't doubt it. Kara always seemed to, though. And I miss Hailey like crazy.

Matt: *Please tell me you're completely naked in my bed right now.*

Hailey: *Would you like proof?*

Matt: *Would I? Does the pope wear funny hats? Is hockey the best sport ever? :)*

A minute later my proof arrives, and it's the very best kind. The photo is a black-and-white shot from above of Hailey's naked torso, with one hand tucked demurely between her legs, covering my view of the good stuff.

Matt: *Unngh, Hottie. I'll be hard all the way over the Great Lakes, and it's totally worth it.*

Hailey: *My work here is done.*

Matt: *And I love that you don't include your face in these shots, honey. Because that means I don't have to instantly delete them in case my phone goes astray. Gonna hang on to this one, that's for sure.*

Hailey: *Where's my no-face picture of your hot self, then? I'm way out on a limb here. But I find myself there a lot because of you. I never took a naked photo before. I also never did it on the kitchen counter. So thank you for checking that off my list last weekend.*

Matt: *Did I mention I'm dying here? In the best way. Thank you for going out on that limb for me. I'm honored to be the one who takes you there.*

This is a hundred percent true. And when Hailey confides in me that way—like I matter—I'm able to feel for a few minutes like I'm not the worst boyfriend ever.

Naturally our Wi-Fi cuts out right in the middle of this sexy, heartfelt exchange. There are no more messages from Hailey, and every other player is cursing up a storm about their lost connections, too.

Eventually we land in Toronto. Since I've spent the last hour thinking of all the things I want to do with naked Hailey, I'm stiff as a pipe as I deplane. We've got maybe ten minutes before our luggage arrives on the carousel, so I tuck the chocolates into my carryon and go into the men's room in the charter terminal to brush my teeth.

Wes and O'Connor are having a conversation at the sinks, so I duck into a stall instead. I unzip and take out my phone. Hottie was right that fair is fair. I grip the base of my aching cock and frame the shot. It's the perfect expression of how much I'm looking forward to an hour from now when I let myself into the apartment. I depress the shutter.

And the flash blinds me.

Shit. Maybe nobody noticed.

I tuck the phone away and zip up. Then I flush the toilet casually.

"Did you just take a selfie of your dick?" O'Connor asks as I emerge.

"No." I walk over to the sink and wash my hands.

"Then why'd the flash go off?" Wes asks, looking amused.

"No idea."

Blake Riley emerges from a stall. "What do you call a dick selfie?" he asks, his big face frowning thoughtfully. "*Delfie* is kinda awkward."

"You ladies have a nice night," I grumble, getting the hell out of there.

Their laughter follows me out the door.

An hour later I'm tapping the code into my security system. I drop my luggage on the floor, and then jump about a foot into the air as I see an unfamiliar shadow looming in the darkened corner.

Luckily I realize what it is before I give myself a coronary.

It's a coatrack. Hottie's coat is the only thing on it. I laugh quietly in the dim light. She got me a coatrack, because I'm obviously too dumb to remember to source one myself.

God, I love this woman.

Usually that offhand thought with—you know—the L-word in it would freak me out. But right now I don't even have time to stop and worry about it. I just toss my jacket onto the new coatrack and toe off my shoes. Then I sprint toward the bedroom, still lit by warm lamplight. Rufus lifts his nose from the dog bed as I go by. But I'm in a hurry.

And . . . Hottie is passed out cold in my bed, facedown in the center of the bed.

Ah, well.

I brush my teeth. Now that sex is off the table, my body relaxes. I yawn as I towel off my face. Dropping my suit, shirt and tie onto the armchair, I crawl into bed, pulling Hailey's warm body into my arms. God, it's nice. She makes a sleepy, purring sound. My dick wakes up immediately, but her limbs are heavy. And I'm not going to pester Hailey for sex if she's too tired after a long day.

And yet she's pressing back against my chest, her sigh deep and soft. *Mmm.* I tilt my hips, pressing my cock against her very fine ass. Her body reacts, legs shifting, creamy skin seeking mine. My lips find her neck and I'm lost to kissing her sweet skin. This woman in my bed, she's been waiting for me. My heart beats a new rhythm. *Grateful. Grateful. Thank you.*

I try to turn her around, but she resists with a shake of her head.

"You want me to take you from behind?" I ask, my voice gravel.

She presses back against me in answer.

"Say it, honey." I just want to make sure she's awake and completely onboard with the fun we're about to have.

"It's hard for me," she whispers, the arch of her foot tracing my calf.

It's very *hard*, my body agrees. I want her so badly. "You mean it's hard . . . to say the words aloud?"

She nods, so I know she's really awake.

"Dirty talk weirds you out a little."

"I *love* it on you," she says, and I smile in the dark.

"Well." I lift her knee and slip my cock between her legs, just brushing her sweet pussy to tempt her. We both groan, because she's already wet. "Tell me what you want and I'll give it to you." I roll her nipple between my fingertips to make the point.

"Mmm," she whimpers. "*Fuck* me. Do it right now. You have morning skate and I have work and you sent me that dick pic, you fucking tease."

"Delfie," I whisper, running my cockhead over her clit.

"Give. It. To. Me," she whines.

As I am not a stupid man, I don't make her ask again. I lift her knee high, and she gasps as I push inside her tight heat. And now I'm gasping, too. We had a quick chat about birth control and health status last week, but this is our first time together since. And it's heaven. With a groan, I start to thrust. She grips the covers and pushes back against me. We find our rhythm, and my shaking hand snakes around her hip so I can touch her. My fingertips meet soft, supple flesh and she moans my name.

Fuck, I'm a goner. She feels so good around my aching dick. I give it to her hard and fast, and I'll bet it's not sixty seconds later when I feel my body gather in on itself. "Jesus, baby," I groan into her ear. "Gotta come right now."

She squeezes her legs together and turns her face toward mine. Our tongues touch for the first time in a week as I burst inside her, moaning and rutting like the desperate man I am. And she shivers and shudders, her pussy clenching around me as she follows me over the edge.

A minute later she's turned to flop onto my chest. We're both panting like sprinters. We *are* sprinters tonight. I think I set a land-speed record for sex. The taxi that brought me home from the airport probably hasn't made it out of Yorkville yet.

STAY

I start laughing, and it bounces Hailey on my chest.

"What's so funny," she slurs.

"Us. Quickest quickie ever."

"Good hustle," she says against my pec. "Good foot speed. Dick speed."

I laugh some more. I'm totally beat but totally happy, too. "Sorry we didn't talk much this week. I hope you know it's not because I don't care."

"Not exactly sitting around watching reruns here, babe. I worked twelve-hour days. Have you ever been to Niagara Falls?"

"Mmm?" I'm sleepy, and the change of subject has confused me.

"I keep forgetting you're not from around here," she says. "The falls are really impressive. The biggest torrent of water you've ever seen. That's what business at Fetch has been like since Blake made his TV testimonial. I've never seen anything like it." Her voice is sounding further and further away. "Matt? Honey?"

Sleep takes me away.

M att is in California now. That quickie we had last week was one of our few moments together. I went to his home game with Jenny, sitting in his row-D seats. But I was on call, and when two Fetchers called in sick afterward, I had to do a night shift for the first time in months.

The team is playing San Jose tomorrow night, so they're in California already. They're eating an early dinner somewhere gorgeous tonight, and Matt just texted me a shot of him and Wesley at a dockside restaurant, munching on shrimp and sampling wines.

I'm spending the evening with . . . data. Lots of data.

Instead of shrimp, I have granola bars. Instead of wine I've got . . . water. Even coffee is out of the question because I hit my caffeine limit hours ago.

It's not glam, but I'm not bitter. I love data. I really do. It's infinitely interesting and it never misses your dinner reservation. It doesn't whisper sexy things into your ear from afar, but then end the call suddenly when the charter jet is about to take off.

All right. Maybe I'm just a little bitter. But not at Matt.

If I were going to blame anyone for my twelve-hour workdays, it should be Jackson. Even though we're full-tilt right now, he's the one who won't let this crazy expansion idea die. He gave me a spiel about how the property was going to get snapped up if we didn't act fast. It sounded like an infomercial. It sounded like his father, damn it.

Unfortunately I voiced this opinion a couple of hours ago, and it didn't go well.

"What's the hurry?" I'd pressed when my ex came into my office to ask me what I thought of the idea. Again.

Jackson had rubbed the back of his neck, as if in pain. "He wants us to get the spot, that's all."

"Jax?" I asked carefully. "Does your father own that building?"

His frown deepened. "Yeah. But so what. He owns this one." Jackson spread his arms to indicate our current office space.

"But this one is cheap," I pointed out. "Why's he so desperate to get us into that pricey spot?" I don't trust that man. And worse—I don't trust Jackson to stand up to him.

"He can't hold it for us forever. That's all."

I studied Jackson, the same way I had since we were kids. He was still fussing with his neck, and he ran his fingers through his hair. He looked as jumpy as a man who had fleas.

"I'll give you an answer by Tuesday," I said slowly. "There's still work to be done."

That had satisfied him. Or maybe it hadn't, but at any rate he'd disappeared.

STAY

Now it's nine p.m. and I'm rolling around in data, trying to get a handle on the question of my company's future. Plenty of promising businesses have put themselves on a collision course with the sun by trying to grow too fast. I don't want that to happen to this company that I love. Although a little part of me—the part that's sitting here alone and pathetic on a Friday night—is tempted to take the half-million dollars Mr. Emery wants to give me and walk away. To let Jackson run this place into the ground.

Ack. No. That idea fills me with horror. That's a solution for people who don't care. But I do care, damn it.

So here I sit at my desk, building the mother of all spreadsheets. Now that we've been open for four years, our customer records are a treasure trove of data. I've decided that I need to know more about our clients before I can decide what our expansion should look like. I've made a density map of their locations. But then I realized I needed to know more about our *best* clients. Since a quarter of our active clients provide *three*-quarters of our revenue, those are the people I need to understand.

Unfortunately, understanding them has proven to be a tedious process. I've spent the last few hours opening up client files and tagging them with various attributes. We have people who use Fetch for their business needs (for document delivery, office supplies, client entertainment.) Then we have what I'm calling the Busy Moms (diapers, organic food) and the Swinging Singles (wine selection and delivery, catering and gift-giving.)

Someone has to think about these things, and tonight that someone is me.

I started at the front of the alphabet and now I'm up to the E's. I smile when I click on *Eriksson*, but then I realize that it's not Matt's account. It's Kara's. That's not a huge surprise now that I think about it. He'd told me once that he learned of Fetch from his ex, who'd grown to depend on us when the twins were younger.

Checking out her charges feels a little weird, but I have a job to do tonight, and it won't take long.

I quickly scroll back through her lengthy list of requests and see that she belongs in the Busy Moms category. Lots of diaper deliveries in her early days. She also gets a tag for Concierge Services because she has Fetch make a lunch reservation for her every Friday, under the name of Dr. Daniel Bryant. The reservations happen exactly once a week, rain or shine. The choice of restaurants varies a great deal, but the consistency is admirable. She's been lunching with Dr. Daniel Bryant every Friday for . . . I keep scrolling. For two years.

Well. Kara obviously found what she was looking for—a Steady Eddie. Matt said she hated his travel. Hated the Hockey Wife lifestyle. She wanted a dentist to lunch with like clockwork. And she got one.

I close that account after tagging it and move on. The next one in alphabetical order is Matt's. I don't need any time looking at the list of charges, because I've seen them all before. Tagging him is tricky, though. He doesn't fit any of my tidy categories. I scroll back through the long list, wondering where to put him. The charges start eighteen months ago, but I don't let myself pull up any of our old text messages because I'll be here all night rereading them and missing him.

Eighteen months ago, when he was separated. I already knew the date, because he and I were leading parallel lives and didn't know it. Our spouses asked for divorces only a couple of weeks apart.

That's when the hair stands up on the back of my neck, and goose bumps climb my arms. Matt's marriage was over a year and a half ago. His wife has been lunching with Dentist Dan every Friday for *two years*.

With a pounding heart, I open up her account again. It's right there. Two years ago last month, she made her first Fetch reservation request—a lunch date at Sassafras. Table for two. Under the name Dr. Daniel Bryant.

There must be some mistake I'm making. Maybe that Daniel isn't her boyfriend. Maybe it's her dad.

But who dines at fancy restaurants with her dad every week?

STAY

I Google Daniel Bryant, pediatric dentist, and he pops up immediately. His website shows a picture of him wearing scrubs with teddy bears on them. I check the hours.

His office doesn't open until three p.m. on Fridays. Plenty of time for lunch and a quickie.

Holy shit.

ALWAYS ON MY MIND

Hailey

"**O**h my God! She was cheating on him! *Really?*"

Jenny's shriek of outrage makes me wince. We're in my room. She was sprawled on my bed before I dropped my Kara bomb. Now she's sitting upright, eyes wide and mouth gaping open.

Jenny doesn't come over often, but she's here this evening to do my hair and makeup. I'm got to be at the hotel in an hour, and normally I wouldn't make such a big fuss about my appearance, but I'm getting an award tonight. It's a big deal. And I want to look like a big deal.

We haven't quite made it to the getting-ready part, though. The discovery I made earlier this week has been weighing on my mind, and I finally caved and told Jenny about it, since I can't very well tell Matt. But even though I'd just laid out the facts and Jenny came to the same conclusion as I had, I can't help but play devil's advocate.

"Not necessarily," I answer. "Maybe she was meeting this guy for a weekly friend lunch."

Jenny arches one eyebrow. "But aren't they together now, the ex and the dentist?"

I nod.

STAY

"Um, then they're not friends now and they sure as booger-sugar weren't friends back then." She flops back against my pillows and crosses her arms over her chest.

"They might've been," I say weakly.

"Bullshit. Even if they weren't hooking up, they were still having an affair—an *emotional* affair. I mean, come on, Hailey. A married woman doesn't meet the same man for lunch for *six months* if she doesn't have feelings for him."

I agree, but I hate the idea that Kara was actually doing that to Matt. For some dumb reason, I want to give her the benefit of the doubt, even when she can't give me the same courtesy. From the second we met, Kara assumed I was a one-night stand or a casual hookup. Even after months of me dating Matt, the woman continues to turn her nose up at me whenever she sees me. So, yeah, Kara is a bitch. But if she was seeing some dentist behind Matt's back during their marriage, that's beyond bitch. That's cruel.

"Are you going to tell him?"

Jenny voices the question that's been hounding me for days. I'd spoken to Matt a few times this week but didn't once mention that I think his ex-wife was a Cheating McCheaterson. There's no good way to bring that up. *Yeah, I miss you too, can't wait to strip you naked. By the way your ex cheated on you, good game tonight!*

"I don't know," I admit. "A part of me is, like, hell yes, he deserves to know. But another part wonders if I'll just be needlessly hurting him. They're already divorced, so obviously the marriage wasn't working. What will knowing do, besides hurt him?"

Jenny flashes an evil grin. "It'll make him hate the bitch."

"Exactly. But she's the mother of his kids," I say softly. "Is it right of me to create a rift between them?"

Her jaw drops. "You're not rifting them. *She* did!"

"Yeah . . ." Then something occurs to me. "Maybe he knows, Jenny. It's embarrassing, right? Maybe he knows, and he didn't tell me. It's sort of private."

Jenny flops onto the bed. "I dunno. You say he blames

himself for their breakup. Would he do that if he knew?"

She makes a good point. I know he blames himself, thanks to the offhand comments he's made about being a shitty husband and a failure. But he didn't cheat on Kara. And if she'd truly gone behind his back with another man, then maybe all the reasons she'd given him when she'd asked for a divorce were just a way to excuse her own awful actions.

"Or . . . She wanted to leave him but didn't want to look like the bad guy," Jenny tries, drawing the suspicions out of my head and giving them voice. "So she blamed his schedule and his hockey career and whatever else and made it seem like that's what destroyed their marriage. That way she wouldn't have to take responsibility for being a cheater."

"*Maybe*. But again, is it any of my business?" I counter.

"It's *literally* your business, Hailey! She used your business to cheat."

I falter, one hand rising to rub my cheek. Yikes. She's right. Kara utilized Fetch's services to make those lunch appointments with her dentist lover. If Matt is the kind of man to check credit card receipts, he would've just seen "Fetch" on all those statements, rather than the name of the restaurant where she was meeting Dentist Dan.

"Oh boy." I raise my other hand and start massaging both my temples. "I just thought of something."

Jenny eyes me warily. "What?"

"Are we cheater facilitators?"

There's a beat of silence. Then she bursts out laughing. "I'm sorry—what?"

"Fetch is a cheater's paradise," I explain with an unhappy moan. "You want to buy sexy lingerie for your mistress? Use Fetch, and then your wife doesn't see sexylingerie.com on the credit card statements. We also give clients the option to remain completely anonymous. Are we aiding the immoral?"

Jenny rolls her eyes. "Okay, we are *not* getting into a morality debate right now. These are grownups—if they want to use a delivery service so they can get their secret golly-jollies, let them. Besides, there are lots of ways to conceal shady credit card charges." Another laugh pops out. "We're not cheater facilitators, weirdo."

I drop my hands and wipe them against the front of my yoga pants. My palms feel clammy for some reason.

"Anyway, back to Matt," Jenny says. "You guys are dating. Don't you think he deserves to know?"

"Yes. No. God, I don't know. I just don't want to hurt him. And even though he's over Kara, I *know* this will still hurt him." A groan slips out. This is why I don't like it when people tell me their secrets. I can't take on these kinds of burdens.

And yet I don't think I can keep this from Matt.

I'm falling for him. All week I've thought of nothing but him. The sexy texts and hurried phone calls we exchanged haven't come close to satisfying my Matt cravings. Fortunately, tonight I'm going to be on his arm. He'll be wearing his sexy tux, smiling at me from the audience as I get up to accept my award. We'll feed each other hors d'oeuvres and slow dance and, if I'm lucky, maybe sneak off and hook up somewhere in the hotel. Jess told me that coat closets are all the rage. That could be fun, a covert quickie in a coat room . . .

"Um, please don't tell me you're thinking sexy thoughts about the ex. Are you batting for the other team now?"

Startled, I lift my head. "What?"

Jenny snickers. "You got all blushy, which means you're thinking about sex. But we were talking about the cheating ex, so . . ."

It's my turn to roll my eyes. "Um, no. My brain decided I don't need to be thinking about that horrible topic anymore." I pause, feeling heat creep into my cheeks. "I can't wait to see Matt tonight."

She's quiet for a moment, a slow smile playing on her lips. "Wow. You're really into him, huh?"

My cheeks get hotter. "So much."

"Curling iron's ready!" she chirps. "Sit." She drags me to the chair she'd set up in front of the wall mirror in my bedroom. "And elaborate while I make you extra gorgeous."

"There's nothing to elaborate on." I shrug. "I like him."

Jenny grabs a handful of hair clips from the dresser and begins sectioning off my hair. Then she takes one small chunk and twists it around the hot iron. Steam rises up for a moment, and I say a quick prayer that she doesn't burn my hair off. I've actually never seen Jenny do anyone's hair before, come to think of it. But her long locks are always perfectly curled, so I'm hopeful that she knows what she's doing.

"You like him," she echoes. "What else?"

"I don't understand the question." Our eyes meet in the mirror, and we both start laughing.

"You're the worst gal pal ever," she declares. "I want *details*, Hailey. Like, is the sex still awesome after three months? Has the marriage word come up?"

"Marriage?" I squawk. "He hasn't even referred to me as his girlfriend yet!"

"Really?" A frown mars her lips. She slides the curling iron down and a perfect spiral of dark hair bounces on my shoulder. As she unclips the next chunk, her frown deepens. "Do you think maybe this is just a fling for him?"

"I don't think so," I admit. "But don't ask me *what* it is, because I'm still not sure." A sigh heaves out. "All I know is that I get it now."

"Get what?"

"Passion," I say frankly.

Jenny giggles and tackles another section of hair. My reflection in the mirror shows loose, bouncy curls that, paired with my bangs, give me a flapper-girl vibe. I like it.

"Seriously," I insist. "I honestly didn't get it before. I thought that what Jax and I had was normal—pleasant missionary sex a couple times a week, I-love-you's instead of dear-god-I-want-to-fuck-you, no orgasms more often than not . . ." I shrug. "It's different with Matt. I swear, I want him *all the time*. I wish I could carry him around in my pocket and take him out whenever I'm lusting for him."

She throws her head back and laughs. "Um, we all wish that. But you'd never get any work done if you had a Pocket Matt."

"Work's overrated."

STAY

As Jenny finishes my hair and moves on to my makeup, we chat some more about the sheer hotness of Matt Eriksson. Anticipation burns hot in my blood. I cannot wait to see him tonight.

"Oh wow!" Jenny exclaims thirty minutes later when I exit the bathroom in my dress.

"It's not too racy?" Biting my lip, I step up to the mirror and examine the deep vee neckline of the long, silky gown. It's black and has a high back to cover my tattoos—I don't usually try to hide them, but I'm not sure who'll be at the event tonight and how open-minded they are. The TWBA has been around forever, and some of the women who sit on the board are . . . old.

Oh brother. Am I being ageist right now?

"It's a perfect combo of classy and racy," Jenny assures me. "The future Mr. Hailey will drop dead when he sees you." She bites her lip. "Wait, that's not a good thing. You want him to be alive for your wedding." She thinks it over for a second, then beams at me. "The future Mr. Hailey will come in his pants when he sees you."

I sure hope so.

The gala is being held at the Fairmont Royal York Hotel, a luxury hotel near Toronto's Harbourfront. It's insanely fancy-pants and I can't believe I'm actually being honored here tonight. I walk into the lobby alone, marvelling at the impossibly high ceiling, the shiny floors, and the old-timey clock that stands between two spiral staircases. Near the check-in counter is a small area with two long tables and a sign for the Toronto Women's Business Association. I make a beeline for it, greeting the woman at the table with a nervous smile.

"Hailey Taylor Emery," I say, gesturing to the name cards lined up on the tables.

She checks her clipboard, scribbles something down, and then finds my name among the thick cardstock nameplates.

"One of our honorees!" she crows. "Congratulations!"

I feel myself blushing. "Thank you. I'm a bit nervous."

"Don't be. Everyone here is thrilled for you. We're lucky to have you as a member."

I fight the urge to twirl around happily. "Thank you,'" I say again. "I'm proud to be one."

"You're at table three," she tells me, before referring to the clipboard again. "It says here you have a plus one."

"Yes, he'll be here shortly." I haven't spoken to Matt since this morning, but he confirmed earlier that he'd meet me at the Fairmont. His flight time had changed from three p.m. to five. But we'd anticipated this. In order to make sure there wouldn't be any snafus, Matt left his tux in the car at the airport just in case there wasn't time to go home beforehand. And it's only a ninety-minute flight from New York, with clear skies tonight.

"I'll just wait in the lobby until he arrives," I tell the hostess.

"Of course." She sets down the clipboard and smiles. "You still look nervous."

"I still am," I answer with a weak giggle. "I've never received an award before."

She winks at me. "Don't worry, it's not as nerve-wracking as you think. The speeches take up hardly any time. Our chairwoman, Barbara Dubois, will give her intro speech at eight, the awards are handed out at eight thirty, and by nine everyone'll be on the dance floor."

That relaxes me a bit. I wrote a short speech, but I'm afraid it's not good enough. Or that it doesn't sound grateful enough. I am, though. Growing up with a mother who was impossible to please, I tend to overcompensate when it comes to my job. I work my ass off, and sometimes I wonder who I'm doing it for. If I'm chasing success for *me*, or if because I'm still, subconsciously, trying to silence that critical voice that told me I'd never amount to anything.

Those thoughts are too damn dark to delve into right now, though. All I know is that I'm proud of myself. Which, I guess, answers those Deep Questions. I'm doing this for *me*. Because building this little business from the ground up has brought me a shit ton of joy.

STAY

My other source of joy, however, is nowhere to be found. I stare at the front doors, willing Matt to walk through them. He's ten minutes late, but we've got time. The ceremony starts at eight, and the lobby clock says it's only seven forty.

Plenty of time, I assure myself.

Several more people stream into the hotel. Matt isn't one of them.

I fish my phone out of my black satin clutch, but there's no message waiting for me. I take a calming breath. Hopefully he's parking his car and will be here any second.

I wander over to the lobby doors and watch the night traffic zoom by on Front Street. Three different cars stop at the valet stand in front of the hotel. Matt doesn't get out of any of them. I check my phone again. It's seven fifty. He's twenty minutes late. Damn, I hope he didn't get held up in customs at the airport.

"Ms. Emery?"

I turn to find the woman from the check-in desk standing behind me. "Everyone is being urged to take their seats," she says softly.

"Oh. Right." Torn, I glance at the huge windows again. Crap. I need to get inside that banquet hall. But Matt's still not here.

The woman follows my gaze. "I'll tell you what—why don't you leave me your guest's name? When he arrives, I'll personally escort him to your table."

It's a compromise I'm not thrilled about, but I don't have much of a choice. I can't stand out in the lobby forever. The idea of walking in right in the middle of Barbara Dubois's speech and causing a scene as I tiptoe to my table turns my insides to knots. That would be mortifying.

"All right. My boyfriend's name is Matt Eriksson."

Her expression doesn't change, which tells me she's not a hockey fan. Probably for the better. That means she won't fawn all over him when he shows up.

I follow the signs toward the banquet-hall doors, while quickly keying a text message into my phone.

Hailey: *Had to take my seat. Lady out front will bring you to table 3.*

I wait for the typing bubbles to appear, but the screen stays silent. No response.

Hailey: *Where are you??*

The banquet hall is packed. I walk in and all I see are sparkling chandeliers, round tables with elaborate centerpieces, and a sea of well-dressed women. Several of them smile at me as I shuffle to my table. I smile back, and excitement builds again. Holy shit. I recognize a few faces belonging to prominent female newscasters and television personalities. There is *a lot* of high-powered estrogen in this room. The women outnumber the men two to one, and it looks like many of them didn't even bring dates. There's something seriously awesome about that—ladies doing it for themselves and all that jazz.

I find table number three and awkwardly sit in one of the two empty chairs. I introduce myself to everyone and discover that this table is reserved for all the awards recipients and their dates. Unlike the solo women I saw at the other tables, this bunch all brought dates. I'm the only one without a plus one.

He'll be here.

Of course he will. There's no reason for him not to be. I checked the forecast only an hour ago and didn't see any storms or weather events that would delay his plane. He didn't have any mandatory press events in New York. He literally has to step off the plane, change, and get in a cab. Maybe traffic over at the airport is worse than usual?

"So. Hailey. What do you do?" the woman to my right asks politely. She's in her mid to late forties and introduced herself as Maryann Winston, but she didn't say what kind of award she was receiving.

"I own a business called Fetch," I answer, feeling oddly shy.

Maryann's husband leans across her to flash me a big smile. "Well, what do you know! I use your services all the time!"

Maryann raises her thin, blond eyebrows at her husband.

"You do?" she says in surprise.

He nudges her slender arm. "Sweetheart, I've had flowers delivered to our house at precisely six twenty-nine a.m. on your birthday for the last three years—how did you think I managed that?" He chuckles. "I certainly wasn't roaming the streets early in the morning, banging on flower shop doors and begging them to open."

"Six twenty-nine a.m.?" I ask, fighting a smile.

Maryann blushes and glances at me. "That's when I was born."

I melt a little. Oh wow. This man loves his wife so much that he arranges for flowers to be delivered at her exact time of birth? That's so damn sweet.

Maryann reaches out and lightly pats my upper arm. "I'm glad businesses like yours exist, Hailey. If only to prove that true romance still exists."

And to facilitate cheaters . . .

I shove the thought aside. This is a happy night. I can't think about Kara. Though I'd be a lot happier if Matt would get here already.

We schmooze for a few more minutes while we wait for the ceremony to begin. I check my phone every other second, until Maryann finally calls me on it, her expression awash with sympathy.

"Your husband is late?" she says.

"Boyfriend," I reply, giving a worried nod. I really hope everything is okay. It's not like Matt to not text or call if he's running late. Out loud I say, "He'll be here soon."

"Of course." She turns to her husband, but not before I catch a glimpse of the pity in her eyes.

Oh my God. She doesn't believe me. She thinks I've been stood up.

But I haven't been stood up. He'll be here. Matt will absolutely, totally be here.

I *haven't* been stood up.

I've been stood up.

Matt never showed. This might not be so soul-crushing if he'd called. Or texted. Or *anything*.

It's nine o'clock and the ceremony is long over. I'm leaning against a column, the dregs of my drink in my glass, feeling awful. The strap of the tiny little purse I brought tonight (because hello, fancy dress!) is gouging a trough in my shoulder. My award is sticking out of the top. It's a trophy of a seated woman with a thoughtful expression, her quill pen poised over a ledger book. She looks lonely. And she's surprisingly heavy.

I feel low. And to make it worse, they're playing "Always on My Mind" for the couples on the dance floor. That's my sad song—the one I listen to when I need a good mope. The Elvis version.

When my award was announced, everyone clapped as I stood to walk to the podium. I felt shaky as I quickly gave the brief acceptance speech I'd rehearsed. This was supposed to be a big moment for me. I thought I'd feel . . . settled. Successful business. Sexy boyfriend. Happy night.

God, I'm so lonely instead. After the ceremony I made some small talk with the other members of TWBA. But there's nobody in this room who really knows me. I'm turning thirty this summer and all I have to show for my life is a business that my ex wants me to leave, and a man who doesn't call when he's late.

Okay, that's probably not fair. It's not like Matt to blow me off so completely. But if I'm not pissed off at him, the alternative is *worry*. What the hell happened to him that he couldn't send a text? Even if his phone died, he's on a plane with two dozen buddies.

Maybe the jet's Wi-Fi died. Unless he was in a car accident! Shit!

You were always on my mind . . .

I have to get out of here before I lose my ever-loving mind.

In the lobby it takes me only a moment to retrieve my coat. Then I'm hailing a cab and jumping in the back, even though public transportation would be cheaper. Screw it.

My phone rings, startling me.

Matt?

I scramble, but the darned trophy is in the way. I set her on the seat of the cab and grab the phone. And it's him!

"Matt?" I answer breathlessly. "Where have you been?"

"I'm sorry." His voice is a scrape. "We were delayed. I'm in a cab heading downtown."

"You didn't call! And I . . ." *Assumed the worst.* Okay, it's probably a bad idea to describe the bloody accident I'd conjured with my worried brain.

"I missed your speech," he mumbles. "Really wanted to hear it, too."

"That's okay," I say automatically. But no, maybe it isn't okay. "Actually, I wanted you to hear it, too. I was really looking forward to tonight. And well, it was . . ." I choose my words carefully, trying to process my own flood of emotions. "A disappointment."

His sigh is weighty. "Can you come over so I can try to make it up to you?"

"I didn't pack a bag," I admit. "The morning walk of shame in this dress would be brutal. Can you come to my place?"

"Sure," he says, his voice gruff. "On my way."

My cab ride takes too long. They're doing some late-night utility work on Yonge Street. But eventually we pull up in front of my building. And by the time I pay the driver, a black sedan pulls up, too. As my taxi slides away, Matt's handsome form unfolds from the backseat of the car. He's wearing his suit pants and a white shirt—not the tux I thought I'd see tonight. His face is tired, and he's thrown an old zippered sweatshirt over his clothes. In other words, he's a mess.

And he's still the best-looking man I've ever seen.

Something softens in my soul when our eyes meet. "Hi babe," I say, a smile beginning to form.

But his mouth looks tight. He gives me a head-to-toe sweep of his gaze, and then reaches up to rub his face. "Shit," he says from behind his hands. "You look amazing. But I was supposed to say that about four hours ago."

"Well . . ." Sadness—and about ten feet of pavement— separates us. I pull my wrap a little tighter against the chill. "I wish you'd called so I wouldn't watch the door all night."

"I fell asleep." His eyes close tightly, as if he's in pain, and then open again. "I crashed out when the jet was on the tarmac in New York. We sat there for more than two hours, but I didn't wake up until we touched down."

"Oh," I say slowly. That explains why he hadn't warned me. "Just come inside, okay? Let's put it behind us."

He doesn't step away from the car, though. In fact, he keeps a hand on the open door. "I shouldn't, Hailey."

"What?" He came all the way over here. How ridiculous to change his mind now. "You have an early skate?"

Sadly, he shakes his head. "No. But it's always going to happen like this. I show up for everything just after it's too late. This is how it goes with me."

"I don't mind," I say, suddenly afraid. "Well, I mind a little," I babble, trying to get a handle on the situation. "But I'm allowed to be frustrated once in a while, right? It doesn't mean I don't lo . . ." *Whoops.* The L-word almost slipped out. Now is not the time. "Nobody's life runs smoothly all the time, Matt. I don't blame you."

"Right." He looks at his shoes. "You will, though. Maybe not tonight or next week. But it builds up quick. And maybe that's just the way it is. You deserve a guy who can show up when it matters."

"Matt," I say firmly. "Let's get some sleep, okay? Things won't look so grim in the morning."

"No, baby. I can't do this again." He lifts his chin, and his eyes are pained. "Don't want to be that guy who makes promises he can't keep. I've been that guy. There's not enough of me to go around. And you'll only end up hating me."

His words are starting to sink in. It's dawning on me that he's serious about saying goodbye. I become unstuck from my spot on the walkway to my building and hurry to where he's standing. "Matt. It's not that bad, honey." I take his hand in

STAY

mine and give it a squeeze. "Come inside with me."

He takes a step toward me and lifts a hand to my cheek. Yes! Then soft lips graze mine. I close my eyes and wait for the rest of the kiss.

But it doesn't come. Cool air meets my face instead. He drops my hand and moves back. When I open my eyes, he's heading toward the car.

"Don't do this," I say quickly. "It's just been a shitty night. You didn't call, and it freaked me out. So I said I was disappointed, but . . ."

"I'm sorry, Hailey," he says, cutting me off. "You're great. But I can't do this again."

Then the car door shuts.

And the car slides away.

The taillights disappear as I wonder what the hell just happened. I'm standing on the sidewalk like an idiot in the cold, and Matt is *gone*. The winter chill gets me moving, at least. Numb, I shuffle up to my door and let myself into the small front lobby, then ride the elevator upstairs to my apartment. Dropping my purse on the coffee table, I survey my lonely little apartment. In the bedroom, makeup is still strewn around from Jenny's ministrations.

The conversation I had with her a few hours ago feels like another lifetime.

My phone is ringing in my purse, and I kick off my heels and run for it. I desperately need it to be Matt. *That was stupid of me*, he'll say. *I've snapped out of it and I'm standing outside your door right now.*

The number isn't one I recognize. But hope springs eternal, so I answer the phone.

"Hailey?" a female voice asks.

"Yes?"

"This is Katie Hewitt. From the WAGs?"

Of course I know who Katie Hewitt is. "Hi, Katie! Um, this is . . ." *a really bad time.*

"Oh, honey. Did he miss it?"

"Miss what?" I say, swallowing hard.

"Your awards ceremony! They had that awful delay with the jet in New York. At poker night in Philly, Matt said tonight was important to you, so I've been worrying about you all evening."

"You . . ."—*gulp*—"were?"

"Oh, yeah. Always. We WAGs have to look out for each other. I'm sorry you didn't have a date tonight."

"Well, I probably could have gotten over that disappointment if Matt didn't just *dump me*."

"WHAT?"

"He said . . ." I sniffle. "He couldn't do this again. That I'll end up hating him." Now I'm pouring out my heart to a stranger who's known him longer than I have.

"Oh, Matt," Katie tsks. "You idiot. TAXI!" There's the sound of breaks screeching to a halt. "Yeah, take me to twelve-eighty Yonge Street."

"Katie?" I say, confused. "That's my address."

"I know, sweetums. I'm coming to see you."

"You are?"

"Of course! I told you WAGs have to stick together. Now go into the kitchen and tell me if you have any wine. Daiquiri mix is my usual go-to, but I realize this is an emergency."

"Um . . ." I wander into my kitchen and open the freezer. "There's, uh, two of those cans of frozen margarita mix. My friend Jenny left it here a while back."

"Perfect. So I'll get Estrella to bring a bottle of tequila."

"Uh . . ."

"Be there in ten." *Click.*

I spend the next eleven minutes panic cleaning—stacking mail and hiding my laundry pile. But at least there's no time to think about Matt. I don't know whether I want to stab him with a pencil or throw myself at his feet, weeping.

When the doorbell rings, I open it to find Katie and Estrella on the other side.

"Omigod!" Katie shrieks. "You look amazing!"

I look down, realizing I'm still wearing a fancy dress. "Thank you. I do need to change."

"First we want to see this award!" Estrella says, gliding into the room. "So exciting. I've never won an award."

"Well, it's nothing. It's just . . ." I look down at the coffee table where my purse is. No statue. "Oh, shit."

"What's the matter, honey?"

"I . . ." My award was on the seat of the taxi cab. I forgot to pick it up again when I got out. "I *lost* it." And for some reason that's the last straw. So I burst into tears.

"Oh!" Katie cries, running over to hug me. "Rough night, sweetie. They happen. Quick, Estrella! Margaritas!"

The other woman goes running into my kitchen.

"R-rough . . . n-night," I echo, shaking. "The roughest I've had in a wh-while."

"You'll be okay." She rocks me against her generous, sparkly bosom. "Next week we'll all be celebrating in the WAGs box again. This too shall pass."

I pull away. "I won't be. He was pretty clear about that." And I realize something awful. "Katie, you guys should be at home tonight. You haven't seen your husband in eight days! Aren't you missing out on some sexy times?"

She gives me a sweet smile. "Ben was so tired when he stumbled through the door that I just pointed at the sofa and brought him a pillow. After a three-game road trip, sometimes he needs to sleep it off before he can get me off."

"Preach, sister," Estrella says from my kitchen. "Luko staggered in the door as grumpy as an ogre. They landed at the wrong airport, you know."

"What?"

"There was a signaling problem at Pearson, and the jet was diverted to Porter. Luckily our car wasn't parked at Pearson."

"Matt's was," I say slowly. "With his tux in it."

"I thought of that," Estrella answers, carrying two margaritas into my living room. She'd found my martini glasses. "Drink this. It's medicinal. Scares off the dementors."

"I thought that was chocolate," I say, taking a glass.

"Pffft," Estrella replies, handing one to Katie. "You can't tell me those grownup witches and wizards weren't hitting the hard stuff after a rough day with Voldemort."

I smile for the first time since my fake smiles at the podium tonight. These women are awesome. I really am going to miss them.

There is a burst of rapid knocking on my door, and my heart lifts. But then the voice I hear from the other side is female. "Girls! My hands are full here!"

I lunge for the door, opening it to find Jess Canning on the other side. Her arms *are* full—there's a bakery box in one hand and a bunch of roses in the other. "I come bearing cheesecake!" she announces. "And these are for you. Congratulations!"

"You didn't have to . . ."

"The WAGs stick together," Estrella says, trading Jess a margarita for the cheesecake.

"But I'm not a WAG," I argue. "Though I really appreciate you guys tonight."

"You are, though," Katie says. "The way Matt looks at you? There is no chance it's over." She leaves the room, returning a moment later with my cake server. Which is a miracle, because I couldn't have told you where that thing was. It's been ages since I served a piece of cake to anyone.

"I'll get the plates," Jess offers, sipping her drink.

I open my mouth to argue and then shut it again. With the WAGs, I've learned you have to just roll with it.

"Everyone sit," Estrella orders. "Wait—Hailey, go change. I'm cutting the cake."

There's no point in resisting. So I go into my room and take off the dress. I toss it onto a chair without another glance. No point in moping over tonight anymore. I'm going to eat cheesecake and get a little drunk with the WAGs. One last time.

Back in the living room, I drag a floor pillow toward the coffee table and take a seat there, leaving the couch and a chair for my guests. Jess takes the chair and eases into it with a sigh. Then she takes a sip of the drink Estrella made her.

Katie narrows her eyes. "Took you a few extra minutes to get here."

STAY

"Traffic," Jess says, reaching for her cake plate.

"Your hair is messy," Estrella says. "Don't tell me Blake rallied while the rest of our men fell apart tonight."

She chews her lip, looking guilty. "Apparently they all took naps on the plane." She clears her throat. "The Blake Snake was feeling quite perky when he came through the door."

Katie drops her fork. "You bitch."

Jess grins. "It's not like I was bragging. You brought it up. We had a welcome home quickie. So sue me. He's probably passed out in the massage chair now, drooling on his chin."

"Where did this quickie take place?" Estrella pries. "I know you two rarely make it to the bed."

"Things were extra urgent tonight," Jess says, cutting a bite of cheesecake with her fork. "I ran to kiss him in the front hall, and we ended up doing it on the welcome mat. It's not the first time. The downside, though, is that Puddles watched the whole time, because he felt slighted. When Blake rolled off me, the dog licked his face."

I choke on a sip of my margarita and then sputter-laugh while the other women howl. "Blake's dog is a perv," Katie giggles. "How fitting."

"No surprise, really." She takes a bite. "This is damn good cheesecake. I can say that because I didn't make it myself."

"You could say that even if you did make it yourself," I argue.

"Damn straight," Katie agrees. "We have to give ourselves some credit, right? Starting with you, Hailey. Tomorrow morning you need to storm the gates. Tell that man he's an idiot for saying he'd leave you."

"Yeah." She's right, of course. Matt might leave me anyway. But I can't slink off into the shadows like a kicked puppy. He matters to me. If I don't stand up for us, what does that say about me?

"You look better, Hailey girl," Estrella observes. "I can see your wheels turning."

"Oh they are. I think his ex did a number on his self-confidence."

"But he can't say it out loud, because he's a macho man." Jess rolls her eyes. "They like to suffer in silence."

"She convinced him he wasn't enough," I say, and it sounds ridiculous out loud. "But I don't think she was entirely honest about her feelings."

"Even if she was!" Katie argues, slapping her knee. "She's *wrong*. I mean, we all have shitty nights when the men are on the road. They happen. There's no getting around it."

"Amy had a C-section during the playoffs," Estrella says, shaking her head. "Sully was a thousand miles away trying to punish Tampa when their son was born. Important stuff gets missed. But on the other hand, the highs are pretty high . . ."

"They are!" Katie agrees, lifting her drink for emphasis. "The best guys in the world. The best sport in the world. And we have front row seats. The highs are like jet-stream high! And if we're honest, the lows aren't so damn low. I mean, if Amy was married to a guy who had to work three jobs to support their new baby, he could have missed the birth pouring coffee at Tim Hortons on a double shift."

"And let's not forget that we live like queens," Estrella points out. "Mi abuelo dug ditches to pay the rent. I know what struggle looks like. It would be some seriously bad juju to complain about your man's hours when you're crying in your thousand-thread-count pillowcases."

"Like Kara did," Katie adds, giving voice to the thoughts in my mind.

"When things get rough, we do this." Jess waves at the cheesecake and the margaritas. "Then we remember that life is good."

Her comment resonates with me for the rest of the night. I can do that. I can weather any storm, face any low that comes our way. I'll do it for Matt.

If he lets me.

WE NEED TO TALK

Matt

I t's eight in the morning, and I'm sitting on my couch feeling hollow.

At six thirty I picked up Rufus from the doggy ranch. Then I took him out for a walk so long he was giving me pleading looks by the end of it. Now we're on the couch, his chin on my knee.

I didn't sleep last night. Taking a four-hour nap and then calling it quits with the girlfriend is a bad recipe for a peaceful night's sleep.

Right now I want to call Hailey so badly. I just want to hear her soft voice. But I refuse to give her mixed signals. When I said I couldn't do this again, I meant it. The slow grind toward disillusionment and divorce is fucking awful.

What can she possibly see in a guy who's never around?

There's still two hours until I have to be at the rink to watch video of our next two opponents. I should make coffee, but the weight of Rufus's head on my knee is a comfort, and I stroke his head while I brood.

But then he lifts his chin suddenly, his ears perking up. A moment later there's a knock on my apartment door.

Hailey. I know it's her even before I get up and cross the room. When I open the door, she's standing there in a suit and heels, two cups of coffee in her hands.

"Hi," she says. "I heard everything you said last night, but there's something you need to know."

For a second I don't do anything. I don't greet her or widen the door or even get out of the way. I'm too busy taking in her sweet face, its tentative expression so dear to me. I'm tongue tied. I feel like she did the first few times we were in a room together.

Rufus picks up my slack. He gives a little woof of recognition and then dances his two front feet against the floor, as if to say, "Well, don't just stand there, come in already!"

I manage to step backward finally, my intention clear even if I haven't found my voice.

Hailey walks into my apartment, her long legs silky in a pair of sheer hose, her tight skirt tempting me. She walks right over to the sofa, sets the coffee cups on the table and takes a seat. "Come here, Matt," she says in a clear voice. "We need to talk."

Well. Who's schooling who these days? I do just as she asks, taking a seat at a respectful distance, giving her my full attention.

She hands me a cup of coffee and pops the lid on hers. "I know your wife told you that waiting around for you was torture. Well, I'm not Kara. My life is set up differently. And we're not the same person. But there's really no way I can predict the future."

"I know," I croak. "I'm probably an idiot for trying to."

She lifts an eyebrow, but a smile hovers at the corners of her mouth. "You are, sir. But we'll get back to that in a minute. I need to ask you something specific. Did your marriage end for any reason you haven't told me?"

"No?" I try to imagine what that question might even mean. "She said she'd had it and asked me for a divorce. Seemed pretty straightforward to me."

Hailey's hands get fidgety on the rim of her coffee cup. "I spotted something that I think I should tell you, even though it feels selfish."

Selfish? "Hailey, honey—you strike me as the least selfish person I've ever met."

Her eyes lift to mine at this compliment. "Not so sure about that." Our gazes lock, and her restraint falters a little. Her eyes turn begging, but then she gives her head a little shake as if to clear it. "You know I've been doing a lot of research on our client database."

"Yeah. Trying to figure out if the expansion makes sense."

"Good listening." She gives me a sad smile. "Your wife's account came up on my file search. She's a long-time customer of Fetch."

"Right. That's how I knew about Fetch in the first place."

She nods. "Well, Kara has a standing lunch date on Fridays."

"Yeah, with her parents and the girls. God forbid they miss a Friday lunch with Grandpa and Grandma."

"No, Matt." Hailey bites her lip. "Kara goes out to lunch with Dr. Daniel Bryant every Friday at noon. They like Sassafras. But sometimes they mix it up at the Greenwich Bistro or the restaurant at the Drake Hotel."

I try to picture it. "Okay. So they take the girls to their grandparents, and Kara and Dentist Dan eat out? I didn't know that. But it makes sense, right? She wants a man who can keep a lunch date."

Hailey sighs. "They're really good at keeping their lunch dates. They've been having them for over two years."

"Over . . ." I do the math. "That doesn't sound right."

Silently she takes her phone out of her pocket and taps on an app. She taps again and scrolls. "I should probably fire myself for this indiscretion," she mutters. Then she hands me the phone.

And it's right there on the screen. Reservations going back two years. "They're in his name. How stupid is my ex-wife? Jesus Christ." I hand the phone back quickly because it's tempting to crush it like a gum wrapper. "She *cheated?*"

"I don't really know," Hailey says quickly. "It might not

have been like that originally."

My head throbs suddenly and I rub my temples. "What am I missing?"

"Maybe nothing." Hailey gets up and moves closer to me. She puts a warm hand on my back and strokes. Fuck, that feels good. I need her touch. "But I wondered about Kara and her dentist. Maybe the reason she convinced herself you weren't a good partner was that she was in love with someone else."

"Oh my God." The last few months with her were so hard. Was there even a point to all the fighting we did? I was trying to save my marriage, and her demands grew by the day. Maybe it couldn't be saved no matter what. "They . . . she went to a high school reunion. He was there. It was, I dunno, a year before I moved out."

"They knew each other in high school?"

"She dated him. I don't know the whole story."

"Well . . ." Hailey hesitates. "I don't know Kara, and I don't want to guess what happened. But I thought you should know that maybe some missed nights at home weren't the only problem."

I cling to this idea. I *love* this fucking idea. I'm so tired of feeling like a jerk and a failure. "My head is kind of exploding here."

She puts a hand on the back of my neck and gives the muscles a nice squeeze. "I know. I didn't know what to do with that information. It's really none of my business."

"Sure it is." I look at her, and all the hesitation is back in her expression. And that's my fault. "I want it to be your business, Hottie. I really freaked out last night. But staying away from you was never going to work."

Her hand leaves my body, and she scoots a few crucial inches away from me. "I need to go to work. You don't have to figure out your whole life this morning, okay? Call me if you want to talk more."

But that's not good enough. "Wait." I catch her in my arms before she can make her getaway. I draw her in and hold her against my body. "If I promise not to freak out like that again . . ." I take a deep breath of her sweet scent and sigh it out. "Can you forgive me? I'm not usually such a drama llama."

Hailey laughs. "I'm not going to pressure you. I'm not going to beg. But I really don't want to break up, either."

I beam at her. "Then let's not." My arms wrap around her for a tight squeeze, and she lets out a shaky breath.

We're going to be okay. *I'm* going to be okay. I truly believe that now.

PORN, SWEETHEART

ONE MONTH LATER

Hailey

'm sitting at my desk, trying to read through a list of ideas for springtime promotions that Jackson sent me. But I can't concentrate, because I saw Mr. Emery come in about forty-five minutes ago, closing Jackson's door behind him.

What the heck are they doing in there for so long? Best-case scenario—they're playing a Scrabble death match. Worst case, they're plotting my exit from the company.

Two weeks ago I finished my expansion report. I really nerded out on it, too. The data show in very crisp terms that the Bridle Path expansion is not the next move for us. My research proved we could grow faster as a company if we first grew our margins here in Yorkville, and then expanded somewhere a little less insular. Like Rosedale.

To make my point, I'd created charts in four colors, a killer appendix of data, and an infographic that kept me up half the night to create. If I thought it would have made me more persuasive, I would have written the report in iambic pentameter or choreographed an interpretive dance to get my point across.

Okay, maybe not that last thing. I have my own dignity to consider. But I will not allow this company—my baby—to be stretched to its breaking point by an unwise expansion.

My high-tech office chair creaks as I shift in my seat for the tenth time in an hour. I feel as if I'm at a big turning point in my life, and it isn't entirely comfortable. Dating Matt is the exciting part. Taking a big risk there is paying off. I poke my phone just to see the new photo on my lock screen—a selfie of Matt and I after last week's victory against Denver. We're partying at Sticks & Stones with the team, and I have a red "T" for Toronto painted on my forehead, and he's kissing my cheekbone.

I could stare at it all day.

But life doesn't let you choose only the changes you want. I feel my work life coming to a boil in the other room. Jackson and his dad aren't making any noise that I can hear all the way in my office. But I feel a disturbance in the force. Something's coming.

"Hailey! You've got to see this! Stat!" It's Jenny's voice yelling from the bullpen.

Stat? Well, then it *must* be important. I pick up my coffee cup and duck out of my office toward Jenny's desk. I find her sitting in her chair, staring at the computer screen with eyes so bright you'd think it was Christmas morning.

"What's up?" I ask, coming up behind her.

"This!" She points a perfectly manicured finger at the screen.

I bend closer, and gasp. "Oh my God."

"Oh my God," she confirms.

"Oh my God," I say again, my jaw half open.

"Oh my God," she repeats.

"Guys," Dion calls from his cube/desk. "We just got an emergency request from a priority client. Should I—"

"*We've got this!*" Jenny and I shriek in unison. Then we look at each other and burst out laughing.

Softening my tone, I glance over at Dion. "Don't worry,

we've got it covered. Jen and I have been handling this account personally for months."

And our hard work is finally coming to fruition, because either I'm misinterpreting this email, or . . . we actually get to *meet* Mr. Dick this morning.

Subject line: *Lubrication needed ASAP*

MrEightInches: *Yo, need a bottle of lube, preferably in the next hour. Willing to pay extra for rush order. Extra-large 64 ounce bottle, warming lube, edible preferred but not necessary.*

The address he provides isn't to the building we usually deliver to, where we just leave his mysterious packages with the doorman. And he included a cryptic set of instructions: *"Tell the guard at the door you're there for Thomas. I'll come out and meet you."*

Jenny is practically bouncing in her chair. "He has a name! His name is Thomas! Thomas! And he's coming out to meet us! We're going to meet him!"

I scan the rest of the form. He didn't include a picture this time, but it sounds like maybe he was in too much of a panic to take the time to pose for us. Who can blame him? Lube emergencies sound stressful.

Jenny won't stop giggling as she hops out of her chair and grabs her purse from the bottom desk drawer. "I am so excited right now," she declares.

Honestly, so am I. We've been responding to this guy's sex-obsessed requests for months now. I am *dying* to put a face to the eight-inch package. I wonder if being this excited to meet some random man is considered cheating. No, right? I mean, Matt can't fault me for wanting to meet such an infamous client, can he?

"You think Matt will get mad that I'm meeting a man who likes to show me his dick?" I ask Jenny as we leave the office to track down a cab. Normally we'd ride the subway, but Mr. Dick needs his lube in the next hour. We can't let him down.

"Um, no. I don't think Matt is capable of getting mad at you," Jenny replies, waving at an approaching taxi.

A few seconds later, we're in the backseat and directing the driver to the nearest sex shop, because I don't think a

STAY

drugstore will have the extra-large, warming, edible lube our client requires.

"Seriously, that man worships the ground you walk on," Jenny adds.

I feel myself blushing. I think she might be right, though. Ever since The Night of Many Disasters, as we call it, our relationship has been awesome to the degree of amazeballs. We see each other as often as we can. We have the greatest sex imaginable.

He even referred to me as his *girlfriend* the other day. In front of his daughters! Yup, the other night when June tried to snuggle with me on the couch while we all watched a Disney movie, Matt teasingly swatted her little hand away and said, "Hailey's my girlfriend, Junebug. Find your own." But we all ended up snuggling together, anyway, Matt's daughters curled up between us while he flashed me sweet, tender smiles over their heads every other second.

I like what we have. No, I *love* what we have. And I think he does, too. The only dark spot in our otherwise bright lives is the growing tension between Matt and his ex. After I told him about Kara's possible indiscretions, I thought for sure he'd confront her. He didn't.

No, Matt refuses to discuss the potential affair with his ex. He claims he doesn't want her to blame me or Fetch for breaching client confidentiality, and that he doesn't want any hostility to affect their relationship as co-parents, but . . . the hostility is there. I feel it in the air every time she comes to pick up the twins. I see it in Matt's eyes every time he's around Kara. It's like a thick thundercloud hanging above our heads. Or rather, *Matt* is the thundercloud.

The resentment is growing inside him, and I'm terrified that one of these days it's going to explode in the mother of all confrontations.

For now, all I can do is hold my breath and hope that he lets go of that resentment. It doesn't affect our relationship in the slightest, but I worry that his daughters will start to pick up on the tension.

"By the way, how fun was the game on Saturday night?" Jenny raves, turning to grin at me.

I'd brought her along to the WAGs box, which I later found out isn't normally allowed. But Katie Hewitt made a special exception when I told her I could just sit with Jenny in the stands. For some reason, Katie and the others have really taken to me. I want to say it's because I'm awesome, and I'm sure that's part of the reason, but I've honestly never had so many women clamouring to be my bestie before.

"It was a blast," I agree. "How potent was Estrella's mango margarita?"

Jenny groans loudly. "Oh Lord. Potent as hell. My stomach was doing the mango-tango the entire day afterward. I think I'm dating my toilet now."

I snort. "Speaking of dating, what happened with that guy you were seeing? Hank?"

"Frank," she corrects, then sighs. "I cut him loose. He was sending too many dick pics. Seriously, it got annoying. I mean, you've seen one dick, you've seen 'em all, right?"

The cab driver twists around to grin at us. He's in his late fifties, I think, with a shaved head and white teeth that sparkle as he smiles. "Amen, sister."

Jenny and I exchange a look, neither of us quite sure what he meant by that. Luckily, we've reached our destination. The cabbie waits outside while we duck into *Naughty by Nature* to purchase our client's lube, and then we're back in the taxi heading toward an industrial area near the lakefront.

Jenny claps her hands happily when we arrive at the address provided. "Do you think he's cute?" she wonders.

"Why? You angling to date him? Because you literally said five minutes ago that you're tired of dick pics," I remind her as we get out of the car. "And this guy is the king of the dick pics."

"King of the Dick Pics would make a great self-help dating book, warning women of the dangers of online dating," Jenny muses.

I can't help but snicker. "Tell you what, you write it, and I'll sell copies on the Fetch website."

"Deal."

Like two giddy schoolgirls, we dart toward the entrance of a sprawling, one-story warehouse with a gray exterior and a single metal door. Several feet from the door, Jenny stops and grabs my arm, bringing her mouth close to my ear.

"Do you think we're about to get murdered?" she whispers.

I jerk my head toward our waiting cab. "Don't worry, our driver will save us if we need help."

"Amen, sister."

We bust out laughing, and we're still giggling as we knock on the door. It swings open to reveal a tall, muscular man wearing a tight black shirt and sunglasses. He was wearing sunglasses inside. Weird.

"Hi," I say in my most professional voice. "We're here with a delivery. For Thomas?"

The man pops the Ray Bans onto his forehead, his eyes filling with relief. "Oh, good. They've been waiting for this."

They?

I'd expected Mr. Dick to come outside like he'd stated in his request, but Muscle Man gestures for us to step inside. Jenny and I share a wary look, until he smiles reassuringly and says, "Nothing to worry about in here, ladies. Tommy just can't come outside right now. He's naked."

With that, he turns around, leaving me to gape at Jenny. "Did he just say naked?"

She nods vigorously. "He said naked."

Dear God. What the heck are we walking into?

Despite our apprehension, we follow Muscle Man into the warehouse. Which turns out to not be a warehouse. It's . . . a studio, I realize as I take in the lighting setup and various cameras. And the set. There's an actual set, designed to look like a classroom, complete with teacher and student desks and a chalkboard.

"Fetch saves the day again!" a deep, jubilant voice shouts.

The next thing I know, a very, very, very naked man jogs toward us. He jogs naked. *Jogs.* Which causes his impressive man parts to swing around jauntily as if they're waving hello to us.

"Oh. My. God," Jenny breathes.

Her dazed response matches my own. At least she's able to get words out. Me, I'm speechless. And staring. Yes, I can't help but stare at Mr. Naked as he approaches us with a big smile on his face and an even bigger erection down below.

"Ah. Sorry." He notices us staring and glances down at his junk. "Viagra just kicked in." When we continue to gape, he offers a shrug. "It's an eight-hour shoot, you know? Gotta stay hard or there's nothing to pump."

"Pump?" I say stupidly.

"You know, pump the pussy." Now he's the one staring at us. "What do you think we're doing here?"

My mouth falls open. "Um. What *are* you doing here?"

His grin dies. "Porn, sweetheart." He waves a hand around the large, well-lit space. "Falcon Studios—I own this company. You never heard of us?"

"No," I answer, at the same time that Jenny says, "Yes."

I swing my gaze toward her. "You've *heard* of them?"

"Of course," she says airily. "Their teacher-student scenes are top-notch." Jenny steps closer and pats Mr. Dick on his thick, oiled-up arm. "Good work. And everything makes so much more sense now."

He cocks his head to the side. "It didn't make sense before?"

"We, uh, get it now," I stammer as all the puzzle pieces fall into place.

He's still frowning. "All this time you didn't know those deliveries were for a porn-production company? I put that information into my client file at Fetch."

Jenny and I exchange a loaded glance as I realize that my strict approach to client confidentiality has its downsides.

"But your account is set to private, sir. The people working on your requests don't have access to those notes. Maybe that's, uh, a flaw in the system," I admit. "Sorry."

"Well, hell," he says, his smile returning. "I made a lot of those pictures extra silly on purpose. I thought if you were in on the joke, it would be funny." He chuckles ruefully. "But if you're not in on the joke, it's just kinda awkward."

"I loved the joke," Jenny insists. "And we brought your stuff. Sixty-four ounces."

"Thanks!" His smile warms. "I really appreciate you getting here so fast."

I'm about to hand it to him when a naked woman strolls past us. She's got long red hair, a pair of double-D's, and legs I'd kill for. "Where are the horn-rimmed glasses? I thought we were doing a librarian scene?"

"Hailey," Jenny hisses.

I snap out of my stupor. "What?"

"The man needs his lube," she prompts, gesturing to the bag in my hand.

"Oh. Right." I jerk my arm out. "Here you go, sir." Sir? For Pete's sake. You'd think I'd never spent time on a porn set before.

Um, because I haven't!

Mr. Dick, a.k.a Thomas, a.k.a. Porn Star accepts the bag gratefully. "Thanks again." Then he spins around and marches toward the teacher's desk, providing us with a candid view of his tight, round ass.

"Great ass," Jenny murmurs to me.

I finally manage to close my mouth. "Can't argue that."

I'm still flushed from laughter when we get back into the office. My giddiness lasts about two minutes. Maybe three. I'm just diving into my email inbox when Mr. Emery sticks his bulbous nose into my office. "Miss Taylor," he barks.

I make myself count to three before I look up, just to piss him off. For the record, he referred to me as "Miss Taylor" for the duration of my marriage to his son. His refusal to acknowledge me doesn't even make the top fifty of the crappy things he's done to me, though. So I brace myself.

"Is there something you need, Herbert? Where's Jackson?"

"Handling a client emergency." He steps in and closes the door, and my stomach dips.

Here it comes, my jumpy gut warns.

And my tummy has called it correctly, because his first words are, "I want to buy you out of Fetch."

"You, what?" Ugh. *Smooth, Hailey.* "My half of Fetch is not for sale." I'm flustered already, damn it.

"Everything is for sale," Mr. Emery says, proving himself to be a walking cliché as well as an asshat. I'm pretty sure I heard that line in a gangster movie this past weekend. "For a half million you could walk away a very rich girl."

"If you think a half million makes me 'a very rich girl,' then you haven't noticed that the price of real estate in Toronto is pretty cray-cray," I snap. Also, I'm a little old to be a girl. But I keep that to myself.

"Five hundred and fifty grand," he says quickly. "My final offer. Take a vacation, Hailey. See the world. And you'll be well compensated for letting my son run his business the way he sees fit."

"*His* business," I echo, my tone flat with disbelief. This man is the most tone-deaf human I've ever met.

"His idea. Therefore his rightful business. Take the cash, Hailey. If he doesn't want you in his bed, why do you suppose he wants to see you at work every day?"

SPLAT. That's the sound of my patience bursting against the four walls of my office, just like my Aunt Linda's pressure cooker did all over her kitchen one Easter.

"You are a pushy . . . *jerk!*" I yell, reigning myself in just in time. Obscenities will only make me sound coarse. Since he's always believed I'm not good enough for his darling boy, I'm trying not to help him prove his point. "I built this place right alongside Jackson. It's half mine because I show up here every day and work my . . . hiney off! So please remove yourself and your suggestions from my office. Right now!"

The door flies open, and Jackson is standing there. "What the hell, Dad? Why is Hailey demanding you leave her office?"

"No idea?" The asshole shrugs and stands up. "She's out of

line. All I did was suggest that she should take a buyout from me. The company should be back in the family where it belongs."

Jackson's face flushes with anger. "I told you I didn't want to buy her out!"

"You're not. I am."

"No *effing* way," my ex-husband sputters, and my heart lifts. "There is a zero percent chance that I'm partnering with you. You'll just try to steamroll me at work the way you steamroll me everywhere else."

"Jackson Herbert Emery! That is seriously ungrateful. You know I've been a businessman about twenty-five years longer than—"

"Doesn't matter!" Jackson interrupts. He's on a serious roll. I don't think I've ever seen him so upset. "You and I are not running a business together. Ever. And Hailey isn't going anywhere. Stop pushing her around. Stop pushing *me* around. And we're not renting that overpriced spot on the Bridle Path! Enough already!"

His face is bright red and I'm getting a little scared for him. I grab a file folder off my desk and fan some fresh air in his direction. "Breathe, honey."

Mr. Emery gives me a glare, grabs the file folder from my hand, and throws it against the wall.

Then he storms out, tossing my door aside with such force that the papers from the folder skitter across the floor. My office looks as if a literal storm just blew through. And I suppose one did.

"Wow, Jax," I say a moment later, still trying to get over my shock. "You didn't have to do that."

"Yeah, I did," he says, sagging into the visitor's chair. "That was a long time coming. And I apologize I never did it sooner. Like, five years ago. I can't have him insulting my best friend."

My throat is thick all of a sudden. "Best friend?"

"Of course! Christ, Hails, we've known each other since we were six years old. Maybe we weren't meant to be lovers. But we sure as hell are meant to be friends."

"And . . ." I clear my throat, trying to sound casual. "Business partners?"

He lifts his hands. "Well, duh. Otherwise I don't know what we're been doing these past five years." His forehead crinkles. "You don't think I'd seriously want to buy you out, right? That's nuts."

Oh, shit. My eyes are watering now. Because I did think he wanted that.

"Hailey!" He jumps out of his chair and comes around my desk. "Jeez, Hails." His slim arms wrap around me. "I don't want you to go! Shit. You think I want to run this place myself? What fun is that?"

I gulp back what might have been a sob. "I heard him say it months ago. Thought maybe you were actually considering it."

"I swear that's the worst idea I ever heard. No way."

"No *effing* way," I say, and it's a half laugh, half hiccup. "You really showed him with that e-bomb."

"Shut up." Jackson pinches me. "That's me going wild."

I giggle.

He giggles, too.

"This year is all about going wild, I think."

"Yeah. It's the best." He smiles at me, and the smile is a little crooked. It's so familiar my heart aches. "You're, uh, going wild dating a hockey player. Am I allowed to bring that up for a second?"

"Sure. And it's still going great. There's an event next week—family skate. I'm going to skate with the whole team."

He squeezes my shoulder. "That sounds amazing."

"And you're going wild with . . ." Suddenly a memory of the sex toys from that box I unpacked leaps into my brain. "Uh, I'm glad you're . . . having fun with Melinda."

He straightens and sits on the edge of my desk. "She's adventurous," he says, his ears reddening.

"That's . . . great," I say, fighting laughter. "Those handcuffs . . ."

"Let's never speak of this again."

"Right!" I agree quickly. "Let's talk about springtime

promotions instead. They're going to be awesome."

"The springiest," he agrees.

"In springy colors like . . . pink leopard print," I say.

"Hailey!"

We both break up laughing. Again.

WHAT AN AMAZING TURNOUT

Matt

"**B**LAKEY! WE'RE HERE!"

I cringe at the ear-splitting arrival of Blake Riley's mother. As every single person in the practice arena turns in her direction, Mrs. Riley steps onto the ice in a pair of scuffed-up black skates, pumps her arms, and goes flying toward her son, who's leaning against the boards with Jess and Jamie Canning.

"Did you bring ear plugs?" I murmur to Hailey, who's gliding to the left of me. Her gloved hand is laced through Junebug's, while Libby is holding on to mine.

"Hush," Hailey chides. "She's a lovely woman."

I'm not saying she's not a lovely woman. But Mrs. Riley also happens to be the loudest woman on the planet and probably in the whole galaxy. She makes up for that by being our biggest fan. Or, at least, giving Hailey a run for her money in the biggest fan department. I don't think I've ever met two women who are more obsessed with hockey.

This morning, there're no sticks or pucks in the rink, only people. The team's hosting a joint charity event for three children's charities in Toronto, two that aim to help inner-city, at-risk youth and one for the Children's Hospital.

STAY

The latter means that several of our attendees can't actually be on the ice at once. Many of the kids are too sick to skate, so they're bundled up on the bleachers, sitting under the heaters. Two or three at a time, my teammates are bringing them out onto the rink on sleds and towing them around so they can get a feel for how much fun it is to fly across the slick surface.

Will O'Connor skates toward me, the rope of a sled around his waist. Behind him he's towing a child of indeterminate age. A hat covers what I believe is a bald head. And the boy's legs are a lot longer than my girls', but this poor kid seems not to weigh any more than my preschoolers. Even so, he's smiling up a storm as O'Connor glides past us, waltzing like a polar bear. He's even singing.

Apparently everyone's caught a case of the jollies today. Even our resident manwhore. While the children wait their turn, other teammates are skating around in front of the bleachers, showing off. Selfies and autograph signing will come later.

For now, I get to enjoy the chill against my cheeks as I skate with my three favorite girls. This is an intimate event for players, their families, and the kids from the charities, along with some hand-selected members of the press. It's my favorite kind of mandatory function. No penguin suits, no schmoozing, and lots of fun.

"WHAT AN AMAZING TURNOUT!"

"She's *loud*," Libby whispers, gazing up at me with wide eyes.

I chuckle under my breath. "She sure is."

"Who's that girl skating with Jess?" Hailey asks curiously, touching my arm.

I follow her gaze toward the laughing, vibrant teenager next to Blake's girlfriend. "Oh wow. I think that's Layla," I say after a moment, startled when I recognize the girl. "Remember how Jess was saying she works in the pediatric cancer ward as part of her nursing program? That's one of the kids she met there. Riley said the girl was pretty damn sick for a long time, but she's in remission now."

Hailey's eyes get watery as she stares at the pretty teen. I love how sensitive she is, how much she cares about people, even strangers.

"Daddy!" Libby interrupts. "Let's skate!"

I grin down at her. "Sure. How 'bout we race each other to the boards?"

Her expression brightens. "Okay! *One . . . two . . .*"

The little imp shoots forward before the count of *three*, and I pretend to growl in displeasure as her pink-jacket-clad body whizzes across the shiny surface. Still, we both know I'm letting her win. When it comes to my kids, I'd lose any day of the week if it means putting a smile on their faces.

Even with me skating in slow motion, Libby's still not much faster. She's got tiny legs but a lot of grit. Her arms pump fiercely as she picks up speed. I hang back even farther, wait until she's a yard away from the boards, and then pretend to skate my legs off.

"You're fast!" I reach her a good ten seconds later, panting as if I can hardly breathe. "When did you get so fast?"

She smirks at me. "When I turned four."

A laugh pops out of my mouth. God, my kids are fun. Hailey and June lazily skate our way, and my laughter turns into a different kind of smile. June's wearing the same jacket as Libby's, except hers is bright purple. And Hailey's decked out in a gray wool sweater, skinny jeans, and a thick red scarf draped around her neck. She looks fantastic.

Sometimes I still can't believe she's mine. And I sure as shit can't believe I was prepared to throw this all away. The embarrassment of missing her awards ceremony still haunts me, and I definitely feel guilty about the fact that I can't spend as much time with her as I'd like. But we're making it work. We text a lot, see each other whenever I'm home, and we've even talked about her flying to Dallas next week for our road game. The team's return flight doesn't leave until late afternoon the next day, so that'd give us an entire night and most of the morning to fuck like bunnies in my hotel room.

"Matt . . ." There's a warning note in Hailey's voice.

STAY

I meet her gaze and realize that she's read my dirty thoughts. The naughty twinkle in her eyes confirms it.

"What?" I blink innocently.

"Nothing," she chirps back, but then she idles closer and whispers in my ear, "This is family-skate day, not undress-Hailey-with-your-eyes day."

"Can't I do both?"

"Both what?" Will O'Connor—without the sled this time—does a hockey stop in front of us, spraying me with ice shavings.

"You jack . . . rabbit." I stop myself just in time.

Instead of giving me grief about the improvised curse word, he puts his hands up in front of his chest like rabbit paws and starts jumping around like a bunny in skates. It's the dumbest thing I ever saw in my life, but naturally my daughters find this *hilarious*. Even Hailey giggles. O'Connor has a way with women of all ages, apparently.

"I wouldn't have guessed you'd be good with kids, O'Connor," I remark.

"No?" He stops hopping and does a goofy spin. "I'm immature. Ask anyone. How does that not compute?"

"Good point."

"I need the potty!" June announces. "Do I gotta take off my skates?"

"Thankfully, no," I say, since there's black rubber matting all the way back into the locker rooms.

"I'll take her," Hailey offers. "I could use a pit stop myself. And this way you can keep losing races to Libby."

My other daughter beams up at Hailey. "I'm faster than Daddy!"

"I saw!" Hailey ruffles the top of Libby's head. "Keep that speed up and maybe you'll play pro hockey yourself one day."

"No," Libby announces, her gaze drifting beyond Hailey. "I wanna be *that!*"

We all follow her gaze to the other end of the rink. There, a young woman in black leggings and a bright green sweater has taken up the job of entertaining the waiting children. I don't recognize her. On one leg, she sweeps in a backward circle. Then she plants a toe and leaps into the air, spinning at least two full revolutions before landing neatly on the surface again.

I whistle under my breath. "Wow. Who is that?" I ask my teammate. When O'Connor doesn't answer, I check his face.

It's ashen. And then it's bright red. "Holy f . . ."

"Fudge," Hailey says quickly. "You know her?"

O'Connor's mouth opens and then shuts again. He does that twice more before frowning angrily. "I'm out of here. See you all later." Then he skates off in the opposite direction, his shoulders drooping, his hands in fists. No more bunny hops.

Hailey gives me an inquisitive look, but I just shrug in response.

"I really need to go," June says, crossing her legs.

Hailey snaps to attention. "Sorry, Junebug, got distracted by the pretty lady. C'mon, let's get you taken care of." I watch as Hailey leads my daughter off the ice, and my heart damn near overflows in my chest. She's so damn good with my girls. *For* my girls.

It just figures that Kara isn't Hailey's biggest fan. My ex has taken to lecturing me about how it's inappropriate for Hailey to spend so much time with our daughters. Even worse, she's tried to weasel time with my girls away from me. In fact, she was adamantly against the girls coming to family skate today, claiming it'd be too "dangerous."

I pointed out that the team owners weren't about to hand all the kids hockey sticks and let them duke it out. For fuck's sake, this event is for vulnerable children. Eventually Kara calmed down and agreed to it, though she scowled pretty damn hard when she found out Hailey was coming, too.

It's taken every last drop of my patience not to argue with her lately. Kara's boyfriend spends even more time with my kids, and you don't see me putting up a fight about it. Besides, Kara has no fucking right to talk about what's *appropriate*. She fucking cheated on me. Or at least, she probably did. I've been trying so hard not to think about it—the weekly lunches between Kara and Dentist Dan, the ones that started long before she and I signed those divorce papers . . .

"Daddy! Let's race again!" Libby begs.

An indulgent smile lifts my lips. "You got it, Libby-Lu."

And so we run through the same routine again—Libby cheating to get a head start, and me pretending I don't know how to move my legs on skates.

"Kid's a natural," Wesley remarks, skating up to us. "Ever thought about signing her up for some hockey lessons?"

"I think she's more interested in figure skating," I admit. Once again, Libby's eyes are glued to the pretty brunette and those graceful spins. "Who is that, by the way?"

"Remember Hal said we're getting a new skating coach? That's her."

"No way!" It's hysterical, really. Half the team will have their tongues hanging out, because the young woman is really something to look at. And the other half will get all bent out of shape at the idea of a female figure-skating coach telling them what to do. "This is gonna be interesting."

"I know, right?" Wesley snickers.

As we watch, a guy I've never seen before skates out and takes her hand. The two of them do a graceful arc of back crossovers. Then she spins in closer to her partner and he lifts her off the ice, tossing her into the air. The children clap when she lands on one foot, gliding backwards as if it required no effort at all.

"Daddy! Let's do that!" Libby says, tugging on my hand. "Throw me, kay?"

"I'm *not* throwing you," I say as Wesley chuckles at my fearless kid.

"Why?"

"In the first place, Mommy will have a cow . . ."

She isn't listening, though. Libby abandons my boring adult explanation in favor of skating as fast as she can in a circle. She tosses her arms out and tries to spin, but her feet get tangled up and she goes down hard.

"Honey!" I say sharply. "Don't . . ."

"S'okay!" she says, getting up quickly enough. She skates in a circle again, picking up speed, her hair streaming out from under her wool hat. "Look how fast I can—"

Wesley and I watch it happen in slow motion. One minute, Libby is tearing around, her little white skates kicking up ice shavings. The next, one of the sleds crosses her path. She doesn't stop. I open my mouth to call out a warning just as she tears toward the ropes between my teammate Lemming and the sled he's pulling.

Libby hits the ropes and I brace myself. Instead of bouncing backward she sort of vaults over them. My heart is in my throat as her head angles toward the ice. But then she keeps rotating, landing on her side instead of her head. She's crumpled on the ice, kicking her feet and wailing louder than Blake Riley's mother at a home game.

Fear and adrenaline surge through my blood, propelling me to action. I leap forward and race toward my little girl. I scoop her off the ice before Lemming can even turn the sled around and stare at us.

"Oh God!" my teammate bellows. "What happened?"

It isn't his fault, of course. I don't even answer. I'm too busy checking Libby's tearful face. "Where does it hurt?" I demand.

"My . . . a-arm . . ." she cries.

And holy shit—arms aren't supposed to bend where hers is bending. It's like a parody of a broken arm.

I have exactly two more thoughts before I snap into fix-it mode. One: I hope my daughter isn't about to see her father cry. And, two: Kara is going to murder me.

BECAUSE OF RADIATORS

Matt

"**W**hat did you do to our child!!!!"

I brace myself as Kara's shout of terror-laced accusation echoes off the hospital waiting room walls. Her high-heeled boots click impatiently across the linoleum as she marches in my direction. She's followed by Dan the dentist, who can barely keep up. I glance across to the far corner of the waiting room, where Hailey is seated with June. They're splitting a bag of peanut M&Ms and flipping through a magazine together.

"Kara." My voice has a warning in it. Not that she'll heed it. "Take it easy."

"I will NOT take it easy!" she shrieks. "I leave her alone with you for *two* hours and—"

"*Stop*," I bark. It comes out louder than I intend, and several heads turn in our direction. Ignoring our audience, I look at Kara—*really* look at her. She's as impeccably dressed as always, but her eyes are red and her mouth is a tight line of stress. She looks completely frazzled. "I know you're scared," I say, my voice low. "But Libby is going to be fine."

"Never again," she hisses. "I told you this was a bad—"

I hold up a hand. "Don't. Don't pretend I'm some

incompetent babysitter who doesn't know how to take care of my own child. I'm her *father*, and accidents happen."

"Not to *me* they don't," Kara snaps.

Knock wood, you stupid . . . I take a deep breath and dig deep, looking for my last reservoir of calm. I can face down any opponent—go chin to chin with a six-four bruiser on skates, and still keep my cool. But Kara makes me nuts. And not in a good way. "Let me tell you what I've learned, okay?"

"You don't, though!" she shrieks. "You don't learn. They're never going to one of your team events, ever again."

These last couple of months it's been a real struggle to be civil to Kara. I've tried to pull out of the rut I'm in with her. But when she lays down the law like this, I know I have to end it right now.

"*Enough.*" The word is like an anvil dropped onto the floor. "I'm tired of letting you pretend to take the high road. I'm *done*, Kara." Several more heads turn in our direction. I don't want a scene, even if Kara is willing to make one. I lower my voice. "You're better than this. If I'm such a shitty dad, why are the first words out of your mouth about me? If today was reversed, and I ran in here, the first words out of my mouth would be, '*Where is Libby?*' But not you, right? You attack me first. You throw down that gauntlet, and you don't even have time to slow down and let me tell you that Libby is having an x-ray right now."

My ex-wife gulps, trying to maintain her equilibrium.

Watching her, I feel like my eyes are finally all the way open. "Thing is? You're not a shitty parent, even though you're acting like one right now. You've been playing this game for so long you're not even yourself. *Blame Matt. Demonize Matt.* Try not to think too hard about why you wanted a divorce."

Her eyes widen, and her cheeks turn bright pink.

"Yeah, I know. We're going to get to the bottom of that real soon."

Sensing trouble, Dentist Dan moves closer, his eyes narrowing. "What if you saved the threats for another time?"

I can't stand the sight of his face right now, and I basically snap. "Are you good at saving things for later?" I ask, equally cold.

He blinks, having no clue where I'm going with the question. But Kara gets it. She never was a stupid woman. Her mouth begins to open and close like a fish's.

"Tell me this," I press. "How many Fridays did you take my wife out for a fancy lunch before I even knew I was getting a divorce?"

Dan's mouth falls open, too. They're twinsies, as Blake would say. But where Kara has flushed, he pales. "I . . . I . . . Uh . . ." He can't even string two words together.

I smile, and it isn't even a little bit friendly. "That's what I thought. Did you cheat?" I point this question at Kara. "If you want to name all my flaws right here in this waiting room, why don't we look at yours, too?"

"No!" she gasps.

"Seriously?" My voice rises more than I wish it would. "Not sure I believe that. Who has lunch once a week with a male friend *for months* and never mentions it? You *lied*, Kara. Fridays with the grandparents."

"I . . ." Her voice is shaky from her tears. "I lied. But it wasn't like that."

"What was it like?" I snap. I see Hailey scoop up June and carry her toward the elevators. She gives me a reassuring nod over her shoulder to tell me everything is fine with her. I watch the two of them disappear down the hallway, and it calms me down to see them.

"It was . . . lunch," Kara whispers. "We'll talk about it later."

"Later? It's already later. I spent a year and a half thinking our divorce was all my fault. That I'm a shitty guy nobody will ever want. You did that to me."

She claps a hand over her mouth, and two fat tears roll down her cheeks.

"Meanwhile—you feel so fucking guilty about falling for someone else . . . ." I give her dentist a mean glare, just because I can. "You keep piling the bullshit on me. 'Cause if you stop, you won't know what to do with your guilt."

STAY

"I'm so sorry." Her tears are a river now. "I didn't mean to hurt you."

"You got a shitty way of showing it," I say, but the words aren't cruel. I'm running out of anger very suddenly, the way a car runs out of gas. One minute running strong, the next coughing to a stop.

"Nothing happened between us," Dan says, deciding to speak up. "I want you to know I didn't touch . . ."

"Save it," I mutter. "You're both cowards. Could have spared us a lot of trouble by owning up to it in the first place."

"I'm sorry. I'm so sorry," Kara babbles.

The set of double doors I've been guarding suddenly open and Libby appears, pushed in a wheelchair by a nurse wearing teddy bear scrubs. "Mommy!" Libby yells. "Don't cry! I'm getting a pink cast. People can write on it with Sharpie. Do we have Sharpies? What's a Sharpie?"

I watch my ex-wife pull herself together in that freakishly fast way a mother sometimes needs to. She smiles widely and sweeps the heels of both hands across her cheeks. "What color pink?" she asks. "Sharpies are markers and we can buy some on the way home!"

"They had to cut my shirt!" Libby exclaims. "I was very brave."

"Oh, I think you're the bravest," Kara says, and a fresh bunch of tears runs down her face. "Can I come with you when you get your cast?"

"A'course," Libby says. "Daddy was with me but they wouldn't let him stay in the x-ray place because of radiators."

"Radiation," the nurse says, fighting a smile. "Come right this way, Mrs. Eriksson."

"I'll go hang out with June," I say.

Kara whirls around. "Where is she?"

"With Hailey. Who you need to be nicer to," I say, even though it's not the right time. But I'm finally feeling my own power. This woman has had too much control over me for too long.

"We'll come and find you," Kara says, looking sheepish.

"I'll count on it."

The nurse, Libby, and Kara all disappear behind the double doors again, leaving me with the dentist.

"I just want to say . . ." he tries.

"Save it," I snap. "I need to find my kid and my girlfriend."

I walk away, not caring what he or anyone else thinks. And I go looking for my girls.

Hailey

"He's really bald," June says, pointing at the last baby in the row.

"She," I tell her. "The sign says baby girl. What are we naming this one? It's your turn to start."

"Hmm," June says, and I shift her slightly to give my hip a break. I have to hold her up so she can see into the baby nursery and continue our game. "Jenny."

"You named someone Jenny already," I point out. "Her." I point to a baby in the back row.

"There can be two Jennys," June points out. "There's two Ashleys in my pod at school."

"Hear you. But let's think of something else for her. She doesn't look like a Jenny to me."

"No?" June's little brow furrows with concentration as she studies the baby. "You're right. She's not a Jenny."

"Yeah. Let's call her George," I suggest.

"What?" June yelps, appalled. "That's a boy's name."

"Georgia is a girl's name."

"Georgia doesn't have a hockey team," June says with mild disgust, causing me to burst out laughing. Once in a while Matt's girls sound just like him, and it slays me. Every time.

Speak of the devil. Matt appears at the end of the hallway, his phone in hand. I'd texted him where we were, so he wouldn't worry. Now he smiles at me, and my insides just melt.

STAY

Not because he's handsome, though he's hotter than blazes. But because of the way he looks at me—like we're sharing a joke and we're the only two people on Earth who know the punchline.

He looks at me like he loves me.

It's a huge effort to remember I'm in the middle of a conversation with June. "How about Henrietta?" I offer.

"Nope. Too much like Henry."

"Anne Marie?"

"Meh."

"Beelzebub?"

"Hailey!" she giggles.

"Hepzibah? Zebedee?"

"Jeanmarie," June tries.

"That's almost like Jenny."

"Too bad," June says and I snort with laughter. "Daddy!" she says, catching sight of Matt. "We're naming babies."

"All right," he says. "You named 'em all Matt, right?"

"Nope." June kicks her legs, making it harder for me to hold her.

Matt reaches for his daughter and lifts her in one smooth motion. "They should all be Matts. Even the girls."

"Daddy—"

"Your real name is Matt. Did you know that? So is your sister's." His arm comes around me while he teases his daughter. "We just call you June so we don't all get confused."

I lean my head against his shoulder and smile. A thought prods my consciousness as I listen to his deep, masculine voice converse with June. If I had a baby, what names would Matt like? *Whoa there*, I tell myself. *Now is not the time for that.*

Now is not even close to the time for that. Moving on.

"How is she?" I ask.

"Getting a pink cast and bossing people around," he says, kissing my jaw. "Sorry this day became such a sh . . ." He stops himself.

"Shit show?" June guesses.

He grunts. "Junebug . . ."

She blinks innocently. "What?"

"It's okay," I tell him. Maybe we didn't have quite the afternoon we bargained for. But I'm weirdly happy and calm these days. I almost don't recognize myself. "How do you feel about the name Mandy?" I ask June.

She peers through the glass. "I'll think it over," she says after a long, serious pause.

We stand there naming babies, and I can't think of anywhere else I'd rather be.

She blinks innocently. "What?"

Matt takes June to the bathroom a little while later, and it's then that Kara appears. As she comes closer, she's looking right at me, and I remember Matt finally spilled the beans about her lunch dates. I'd heard their argument begin, and that's when I picked up June and put some distance between myself and Kara.

It was fine with me for Matt to tell her. I'd already said so. But I don't want us to have a showdown in the hospital waiting room right now.

Although I might not have a choice. She's walking toward me with purpose in her step. She tosses her ridiculously pretty hair. "Hailey," she says, determination in her voice.

Gulp.

"Thank you for all your help today."

I blink. Wait, what?

She doesn't say anything else, so I finally find my voice. "All I did was tag along to the hospital," I say carelessly.

"No, I mean what you did in the waiting room." There's a defeated air to her, but I guess when your ex-husband confronts you about your cheating ways, you're not exactly going to feel victorious. "You took June to the vending machine when Matt and I were . . ." She trails off.

"Arguing?" I supply.

She nods weakly. "I really appreciate you doing that. Matt and I try to never raise our voices in front of the girls, but we both sort of lost our cool back there."

STAY

I manage a shrug. "It was no problem. I enjoy hanging out with the girls."

"And they enjoy hanging out with you," she answers. When my eyebrows shoot up, she goes on in a grudging tone, as if she really, really doesn't want to be saying this. "Elizabeth loves the way you braid her hair. And June says you do great voices when you read their bedtime stories."

Warmth flutters in my belly. I don't know why, but I like hearing that Matt's daughters talk about me when they're with their mother. Not because I'm angling to take Kara's place, but because it means they view me as part of their family. God, I hope they do. I've fallen for those twin girls almost as hard as I've fallen for their father.

"Like I said, I like spending time with them." I glance around the empty corridor. "Where's your boyfriend?"

Discomfort creases her forehead. "I asked him to leave. There was nothing for him to do here." Kara hesitates. "I suppose you already know about . . . ?"

She obviously doesn't want to finish that sentence, and I take pity on her by not forcing it. "I do," I say carefully.

"I never cheated on him," she whispers.

I don't respond.

"Not physically," she adds. "Dan and I dated in high school, breaking up when we went off to college. I saw him at a reunion and . . ." She shakes her head. "I didn't mean for it to happen." Then she gazes at me with guilt-ridden eyes, and damn it, now I feel more than pity. I feel genuine sympathy.

As the WAGs can attest, not every woman is cut out for the hockey lifestyle. Some, like Katie and Jess and Estrella, are made of steel. They can withstand those long absences because the time apart only makes the times together all the sweeter. Other women, like Kara, grow bitter and jealous and, oftentimes, seek comfort in the wrong places. Or the wrong lunch date.

I don't think Kara is a malicious woman. I think her guilt drove her to attack and blame Matt because she couldn't stomach her own actions. But she still hurt him deeply, and damned if I'm going to let her get away with that.

"Emotional affairs are still affairs," I say quietly.

Her teeth dig into her bottom lip. "I know."

"You need to talk to Matt about it, Kara. And you need to apologize to him. What happened at the rink today wasn't his fault. It was an accident, and it could've happened to anyone. Libby could break her arm falling from the jungle gym when you take her to the park. In fact . . ." I pause meaningfully. "Just the other day June told me she took a spill off the monkey bars at preschool. No broken bones, but there could've been. Did you lay into her teacher for that?"

Another flicker of guilt passes through her eyes. "You've made your point, Hailey."

"I hope so. Because Matt didn't deserve the way you reamed him out before."

"I *know*." Shame clings to her tone. "I'm going to apologize to him, I will. I just . . ." Her gaze drops to her expensive heels. "I don't know what to say, how I can even explain it."

"Well, you should figure it out fast . . ." I jerk my head beyond her shoulder.

She follows my gaze to see Matt striding down the hall with Libby in his arms and June walking beside them.

"Girls!" I say cheerfully. "I know you're eager to get out of this place, but your mom and dad need to have a quick talk, so why don't the three of us go down to the cafeteria and pig out on some snacks?"

Kara shoots me an evil look.

"Gluten free," I add quickly, fighting a smile.

Her shoulders sag once again in defeat. "All right. Girls, go with Hailey. Your dad and I will be right down."

Matt gently sets Libby on her feet, and I swiftly take each little girl by hand. The look that Matt gives me is laced with misery and a trace of *you traitor*, but I know I'm doing the right thing by leaving him and the former Mrs. Eriksson alone to work through their shit. Matt and Kara don't love each other anymore, but they also don't hate each other. And even if they did, they share two amazing, lovable daughters who deserve two parents that can be civil to each other.

Trust me, as the child of a woman who did nothing but bash my absentee father, I know firsthand what it's like to have toxic parents.

So I simply give Matt an encouraging smile and lead his daughters toward the elevators.

OPPOSABLE THUMBS

Matt

"**I**s that Libby again?"

I can hear the smile in Hailey's voice as she snuggles close to me. It's only nine o'clock, but we had a long day and decided to turn in early. Of course, the second we slid under the covers, we forgot about the sleep agenda and went straight to the fucking-each-other's-brains-out plan. Now we're warm and naked on my big, comfortable bed, and there's nowhere else I'd rather be.

"Yeah." I chuckle at the voice message my daughter just left me—the third one tonight. "She wants to know if Rufus can sign her cast when she's here next weekend." I start to type a text. "How do you explain to a four-year-old that dogs don't have opposable thumbs?"

"Here, let me." Hailey sits up, the sheet falling off her slender shoulder. She grabs the phone, types something, and hands it back.

She wrote: "*Of course he can!*"

I groan out loud. "Way to make promises on my behalf, Hottie. Now I've got one week to teach a dog how to use a Sharpie."

She giggles. "I have faith in you. Besides, you know I can't ever say no to your kids. They're too darn sweet."

I give her a stern look. "Well, you better learn how to say it. If we ever have our own, I can't be the mean dad all the time because Mommy sucks at discipline."

Hailey freezes, and I instantly realize what I'd said. *Our own.* As in, our own kids. Well . . . wow. I can't believe my thoughts went there, but I honestly can't say I mind.

"You . . . want to have more kids?" she asks slowly.

I sit up too, making sure the bedsheets are covering my junk. This conversation suddenly got a whole lot more serious.

"Yeah, I do." I decide to up the honesty factor. "At least two more."

Her dark brows soar. "Two more."

"Yeah." Heat creeps up my neck. "I've always wanted, ah, four kids."

"Four kids."

"Yeah. Or five."

"Or five."

"Yeah." I pretend she's not staring at me as if I've grown a pimp mustache. "I was an only child," I explain quietly. "And growing up, all I ever wanted was a sibling. Most of my friends had a sibling or two, but this one buddy of mine—Cody—had two older brothers and two younger sisters. Every time I went over to his place for dinner, it was pure chaos." I can't help but grin. "I loved it. Always wanted that for myself. Kara and I . . ." I stop for a second, because it's awkward to bring up my ex when I'm in bed with another woman.

"We wanted more kids," I admit. "But we had a tough enough time conceiving the girls, and there were complications during the delivery, so the doc advised Kara not to have any more children. She got her tubes tied a year later."

"Oh." Hailey gasps softly. "I had no idea."

"That's probably one of the reasons she's so overprotective of them, because they're all she has, you know?"

"I get it." She pauses for so long I wonder if she's going to speak at all. But then she does, and the change of topic surprises me. "Did Kara apologize when I left you alone at the hospital?"

"Yeah, she did. She said I was right about her wanting out of the marriage. But that she'd never imagined herself getting a divorce."

"So she made it your fault."

I swipe a hand over my forehead, wondering why she took the discussion in this direction. "Yeah, honey. But it's okay. I'm in a good place."

"So good that you want two to three more kids," Hailey muses.

I nod, and search her gorgeous blue eyes. "Are you ducking this conversation? I thought you said you and Jackson were planning on having children eventually."

"We were." She slides closer and rests her head against my shoulder. Her silky hair brushes my bare skin, sending a shiver up my spine.

"Do you still want that?"

"With Jackson? No. We're divorced."

I reach over and tug on a strand of hair. "Smartass. You know what I meant."

She flashes a sassy smile before her expression grows serious. "Yes, I still want it." Her voice is soft and breathy. "But you're awfully close to suggesting we'll be doing that together."

"And that freaks you out?"

She blinks. "No, that makes me ridiculously happy. I just need to know if you're joking or not."

I grab her by the hips and pull her naked body onto mine. "Not joking, hottie. If it's something you can handle, I want a family with you."

She takes a deep breath, and it comes out shaky. "Two or three kids sounds pretty wonderful to me, Matt."

I can't explain the pure joy that floods my chest. Or the instant hard-on her words produce. I guess the idea of knocking her up turns me on. Hell, everything about this woman turns me on.

My mouth is on hers before she can say another word. She

STAY

squeaks in surprise, but my hottie knows how to rally—within seconds, her tongue is eagerly slicking over mine as if she wants to lick every inch of my mouth. The kiss is sizzling hot and groan-inducing and a few minutes later I'm rolling her over, my body covering hers while my hand slides between her legs.

"Matt," she gasps when I slide two fingers inside her.

"You like that?"

She arches against my probing fingers. "*Yes.*"

Christ, I love her responsiveness. And my dick throbs to convey its jealousy that my fingers are getting all the action. I quickly amend the situation by lifting her knee and thrusting deep.

We both moan happily the moment I sink home. I love being inside this woman. I love fucking her and I love kissing her and I—

"Love you," I choke out.

Hailey stills for one moment, her fingernails digging into my back. "You what?" she says breathlessly.

"Love you," I repeat. "I love you, Hailey Taylor." I leave out the *Emery*, because she's not married to Jackson anymore. She's Hailey Taylor, and she's all fucking mine.

"I . . ." Her breathing sounds shallow to my ears. The hammering of her heart against my chest matches the same frantic tempo of mine. "I love you, too."

EPILOGUE: RETURN TO THE DEATH NEEDLE

JULY, FIVE MONTHS LATER

Matt

"**Y**ou look amazing," I tell Hailey as she steps out of the bathroom wearing a sleek green dress. It's *our* bathroom now. She moved into my apartment last month when her lease was up.

"Thank you!" She smiles at me. "You don't look so bad yourself."

I smooth down the lapels of the jacket I'm wearing. It's a summer-weight blazer, and I'm not wearing a tie. But since I'm taking my girl out for a birthday dinner, and she always looks fabulous, I need to represent. I'm feeling a little fidgety about the dinner destination I chose. But, hey, it's a special occasion.

She grabs her bag and sashays past me toward the door. And I groan right on cue. It's a backless dress and she knows that makes me crazy. All evening I'll be catching glimpses of her ivy tattoo, and thinking dirty thoughts about peeling the dress off to see the rest of it.

"Come on, big guy. You can lick the tattoo later," she says, reading my mind.

STAY

I catch up to her at the door to our apartment. Rufus whines, but I just walked him fifteen minutes ago. "Sorry, pal. You're not invited." I grab the shopping bag from under the coat tree Hailey bought. There are more pictures on the walls now, too. A few. And one or two new rugs. My apartment looks homier than it used to, but I can't quite give credit to the things Hailey brought when she moved in.

It's *her*, really. Not our belongings.

Following her out the door, I step into the elevator she's holding for me.

"Where are we going, anyway?" she asks. "You wouldn't say before."

"360 at the CN tower."

She laughs. "Very funny."

"No," I say quietly. "That's really where we're going."

Her eyes widen. "That's a really strange choice, Matt. You hate heights."

"I know. And it's kind of a tourist trap. But I just had the urge to take you there. Is it okay?"

"Of course. I'd love to go there with you." She beams. "It's your funeral."

"That's not funny," I grumble and she laughs.

Ninety minutes later, our plates are cleared, leaving us to sip the exquisite wine I chose as we admire the sunset over Lake Ontario. "How about this view?" I say with forced nonchalance.

"It's perfection," she says, trapping my foot between hers. "Are you sure you're okay?"

"Perfectly," I say. "As long as I don't look down at the street."

"That's the point of coming here, though." She gives me a soft smile.

"No, see, as long as I look out toward the horizon, it's okay. Only straight down bothers me. When the cars look like little ants . . ." I shake my head, trying to clear the image. "That part isn't easy for me. But if I take the long view—" I point at the pink sky in the distance. "—it's gorgeous. And that's what you help me do."

"What?"

I meet her clear gaze. "Take the long view. I was really stuck last year worrying about my troubles. I forgot for a little while what happiness looks like. But you're good at reminding me."

"Thank you." Hailey blinks. "But I'm pretty sure we do the same thing for each other."

I'm pretty sure she's right. "All right. It's time to move on to the gift-giving portion of this birthday dinner."

Hailey looks over her shoulder, scanning the room. "You didn't ask the waitstaff to sing to me, did you? Should I be worried?"

"No!" That would have been a fun idea. Next year, then. "But I have presents." My stomach does another dip and roll. I'm terrified, but this time it's not because of the heights. Reaching into the shopping bag, I pull out two beautifully wrapped boxes, each one about eight inches long. Jenny at Fetch helped me with this project. I owe her big.

"Okay, these look identical. But this one is heavy . . ." I point at a box. "And this one is light. Which do you want to open first?" I meet Hailey's eyes, hoping she can't tell I'm nervous.

"Hmm!" Her eyes dance. "This one." She reaches for the lightweight box.

I quickly cover her hand with mine. "Nope, sorry. Open the heavy one first."

Hailey laughs. "You asked! Okay, fine." She slides the heavy box toward herself and pulls the ribbon. I smile as she lifts the top off to reveal . . .

"Omigod!" she squeaks, lifting the long-lost trophy from the box. "I thought this was lost forever!" She sets it on the table, stunned. "How did you find this! I called the cab company. They were so unhelpful . . ."

"Yeah," I admit with a sigh. "They were. Jenny tried again. She spent hours on it. But then I just called up the Toronto

Women's Business Association and asked if we could order you a new one. I sweet-talked them into it."

"That was so nice of you." Joy shines in her eyes. "It can go on my new desk."

"Exactly." Hailey is getting Jackson's office when he opens the Rosedale branch in November. She and Jackson timed their expansion to happen during the hockey season, so that she and I could spend a lot of the summer together before her life gets crazier during the opening. And Jenny is getting Hailey's office, along with a promotion to location manager. Jenny reminds me of this all the time, because she knows it makes me roll my eyes.

"By 'sweet talk,' I assume you had to donate to the foundation," Hailey guesses, laughing.

"Some money may have changed hands, yes."

She gets up and moves around our table to sit beside me, wrapping her arms around my neck. "Thank you, honey. That was a really thoughtful thing to do. I don't need the trophy, but . . ."

"It's kind of cool to have it," I finish.

"It sure is."

"This, uh, might be cool to have, too." I scoot the other box toward her.

"Hmm . . ." She lifts it and gives it a little shake. There's no sound at all. She tugs on the ribbon, and it releases into another heap of satin on the table. Hailey opens the box to find a rather sizable roll of tissue paper. She starts unwinding it to get to the gift at the center.

I stop breathing.

It's easy to tell when she spots the little satin pouch with the jeweler's insignia on it, because her whole body goes still. She picks it up with shaking fingers and widens the mouth of the tiny bag, sliding the diamond ring into her palm.

"Oh, *honey*," she says in a hushed tone.

"Do you like it? I mean . . ." I clear my throat. "Can we get married? Will you be my wife?"

When she turns to me, it's with tears in her eyes. "Any day

of the week," she declares.

"Yeah?" I crush her to me. "That is the best news ever. It's almost worth spinning around up here in the death needle."

She giggles into my shirt collar.

"I mean, restaurants aren't supposed to revolve." I'm babbling now, but I'm so happy I might not be able to stop.

"The ring is beautiful," she says, and I pull back to see it sitting in the center of her palm. She's staring at it with wonder on her sweet face. "I can hardly believe this is real."

"Oh, it's real. And if you try it on, then you have to marry me."

She smiles down at the ring, then slowly slips it onto her finger. "What kind of wedding do you want to have?" She searches my gaze. "I don't need it to be a big, fussy affair. For a second wedding that seems a little weird."

"It's not weird to celebrate when you're finally getting something right," I say.

"That's a good point."

"But we can still throw whatever kind of party you want." I pull her in for a kiss. And then a second kiss. And one more just for luck. "Hottie?" I smile against her lips.

"Mmh?"

"I don't even have to change your nickname."

"What?"

"You'll still be HTE after we're married. I have an E, too."

She giggles. "It was meant to be!"

It was, too. And I kiss her again just to tell her I agree.

THE END

Thank You!

CPSIA information can be obtained
at www.ICGtesting.com
Printed in the USA
LVHW020401120523
746824LV00002B/6